ASHLEY MACK

Everything is Alright

To my purely platonic neighbor boys: Travis and Eric.

Trav, if you'd told me when we met at 9 years old
that we'd become, let alone still be, friends,
I wouldn't have believed you.
But here we are, lifelong bros.
You're never getting rid of me now!

Eric, I'm still mad at you for that time in 8th grade when
I watched the Matrix for the first time and
you said it was okay if I didn't "get it."
I forgive you because you married my lobster, and make her happy.

I used to rely on self-medication
I guess I still do that from time to time
But I'm getting better at fighting the future
Someday you'll be fine
(Yes, I'll be just fine)

"Everything is Alright" - Motion City
Soundtrack

Sometimes perfection can be...it can
be perfect hell.
"Bruised" - Jack's Mannequin

Contents

1

Author's Note and Content Warning

This book takes place in 2008. A 2008 as I experienced and culturally knew it in Wisconsin. We've come a lot further than you think since then.

Our male main character, Logan, loses his father to suicide. That's triggering enough, but at that time in that place, suicide, mental health, and specifically male mental health were treated with more shame than sympathy. Logan and his mom are rejected, treated with shame, and removed from their religious community. The Catholic church is probably one of the villains in this story. This perspective comes from personal knowledge and experience. It might not be your experience or your perspective, for better or worse. Some of this plot line is working through my own trauma. If this reaction to suicide is going to be triggering for you, please read with caution or don't read at all. In the US, if you need help, please don't hesitate to call or text 988.

There's also both subtle and overt homophobia. Being out in the 2000s, especially in high school, was uncommon. I don't use any slurs, but these moments won't be missed. If that will be difficult for you, please don't read.

Our female main character, Sadie, is recovering from a physically and sexually abusive relationship. I do not describe the assaults in graphic detail. Sadie chooses not to report this assault, even when she finally discloses it to the people around her. As someone who works with survivors in my other life, there is no right way to respond to this happening to you. We want to believe that reporting to police means something will happen, but we are, tragically, incorrect. Sadie makes the choice that's best for her well-being. Please go into this with care for yourself and your well-being. If you need to talk, you can get help 24/7 by calling RAINN - 1-800-656-4673.

Other content warnings: sex and sexual situations, physical abuse by a parent, neglect by a parent, sexual assault, relationship violence, and trauma responses to sexual assault and abuse, forms of self harm, and definitely taking religious terminology in a spicy direction.

2

Sadie

I might be 17 and childless, but sometimes I think I can understand how tired new mothers are. I empathize with someone always needing something from me, demanding something from me, never having a moment to myself, constantly jolting awake from sleep that's never deep enough to offer any recovery. The panic that I might not hear a cry and respond.

Except the being I'm trying to keep alive is myself, and I am always on alert for me to make a mistake. I'm exhausted. I can't remember the last time I wasn't tired.

I can't remember the last time I was allowed to show it.

"You need to get that recommendation letter from Principal Stein." That's what I'm greeted with instead of a hello. Mom doesn't even look at me. She can sense when I enter the room, as if an aura of disappointment precedes me. Instead of laying eyes on her child, she continues prepping her lunch for the next day.

"He told me he'd have it done by tomorrow."

"The application is due at the end of the month."

Which is two weeks away. "I have plenty of letters from Coach Minski, Father Marchetti, Mr. Colbert, and Dana Achinde on City

Council."

Mom stiffens and I know I've said the wrong thing. I brace myself as she turns, predator-like, and finally looks at me. Her eyes drop down my frame, taking in my choice of clothing. Soft blue jeans and an over-sized Edgar's Bluff girl's soccer hoodie that goes halfway down my thighs. I'm wearing wool socks that went under my duck boots because it's February and freezing in Wisconsin for at least 8 more weeks because the groundhog saw his shadow. My hair is blown out straight, and I'm wearing mascara. That's as done up for school as I get, and it's what I wore today.

This morning she was already gone so couldn't make me change, and she was home late and missed dinner.

Her lip curls in distaste, and I can see the creases in her foundation from here. I'll get blamed for that later too. It's not worth it to argue with her that I'm a jock, and this is how we dress. Or that it's cold out, and this is cozy.

Nothing I do will be good enough. If I wore more makeup and dressed a little more feminine she'd accuse me of "showing off" and say everything except "being slutty." There's no winning with her, so I'd rather wear what makes me feel good. Feel safe.

"A letter from the principal will address your accomplishments in academia more thoroughly. Get the letter. I want to know the application is in the mail by Friday. Send it certified, I'll pay."

I nod. "I'll get it from him first thing."

"Dress nicer." As she snaps this at me, dad enters the kitchen. He pauses, mid-step, looking between the two of us.

"Okay." I promptly attempt to let the criticism go in one ear and out the other but it still feels like a hammer to my self-esteem.

"You look like a slob. No one is going to take you seriously if you look like this. If you never make an effort. Your appearance should reflect your ability, Sadie."

4

"She's at home," dad starts, but mom whips her gaze to him and he draws back, looking at the floor. He's so beaten down by her all it takes is a glance.

"I need some air and then I'm going to bed." I start moving through the kitchen toward the back door. Before I take the handful of steps toward the back landing, she barks out my name.

"Tomorrow, or there will be consequences."

I don't say anything. I grab my heavy Carhartt that I leave on the hook by the back door, slide into my boots, and step outside as I put on the coat. Like I can control the principal's schedule. The man who has to run our whole school and keep a few thousand hormonal teenage idiots in line and hopefully learning something.

The coat is cold as I slide my arms inside, and I inhale deeply. The frozen air burns my lungs and dries my throat but I don't care. I can't care. I'm too tired to care. If I care, I won't survive.

I lean against the house and keep breathing, letting the ice inside to freeze me and my emotions. My thoughts, my needs, as if I could destroy everything inside me with it. Feelings and emotions are weapons, and I won't hand any to her to use against me. It's gotten to the point I almost envy her coldness. If I had it, she wouldn't be able to hurt me.

A muffled "fuck" comes from my left, and I glance over at the neighbor's detached garage, where Logan keeps all his tools and works on fixing up the piece of junk he bought two years ago after he turned 16. Because he's actually very talented and has access to the right stuff, it runs now. Mostly. I never asked what kind of car, I only know it looks better than when he bought it and runs with a soft rumble that's oddly comforting.

I wander across our yards, my footsteps crunching in the stiff, old snow. He hears me coming, and he knows it's me. I can tell by the way he stills and then sighs. Logan puts whatever tool he's holding down

5

and grabs a cloth to clean off his hands.

We've known each other our entire lives, but we're not friends. We're not enemies either, but we're more than acquaintances. I don't know what Logan and I are, really. Symbiotes? Sometimes I bother him over here when I need a quiet place and he lets me exist without expectations until I stop caring about whatever the hell else is going on in my life. We're just quiet. No judgments.

Logan is different than I expected him to be. When compared to what he looked like as a kid, I mean, but I guess grief can physically alter a person's development. He's tall, with his mom's laser blue eyes, and a broad, muscular build that makes him appear threatening just by existing. His jawline is so sharp and so attractive that you want to cut yourself on it on purpose. When he clenches his jaw, the girls absolutely swoon. Logan vaguely notices it, but I've never seen him go around with anyone from school even if I believe he's far from untouched. He keeps his hair in a buzz cut because he has a tendency to rub his head when he's feeling any sort of emotion.

He's feeling something now because he rubs his rough, calloused hands over his fuzzy head, and then takes out a cigarette from the pack in his back pocket. My eyes never leave him as he lights up and takes a deep inhale.

"How's it going?" I ask, waving a hand toward the car.

"Almost done." He blows the smoke out right into my face as I step in front of him, but it doesn't get to me.

"You always say that."

"Mean it this time."

He cocks an eyebrow when I reach over and take the cigarette from him. I put my mouth around the filter and take a pull. It's damp from his saliva, and when I pull it away I lick my lips. The hint of his taste is there, and it amuses me when his eyes drop to my mouth. I exhale the smoke, enjoying the burn and the taste even though I know it's terrible for me.

"You a secret smoker, Brainiac?"

"No, just not as innocent as you think." My parents almost never let me go out, but there were a lot of sleepovers at Darcy's house that started out with going to parties at the houses of older members of the soccer team.

"Sure thing, Sadiebaby." Logan says it automatically and we both flinch, a burn behind my eyes I wasn't expecting. His dad used to call me that. I don't know the last time I heard it. The last time he was around to say it. I don't know why Logan says it now.

I keep the cigarette and start walking down the driveway.

"Where do you go?"

I stop and turn around to face him. I don't give Logan an answer, I wait for him to elaborate. It's a game we play when we talk. Sometimes I come over to the garage and hide out, sitting on a small stool in the back and watch him work. He never asks why or what I'm doing. We don't speak. He works and I hide. When he's feeling squirrelly he pokes at me, asking vague questions that I give vague answers.

"Around." I give him a shrug and take another drag of the cigarette. We stare at each other for a long second, and I know he wants to ask more.

I also know that he won't. After the moment stretches from a pause into silence, I turn around and continue walking.

Logan doesn't want, nor does he need, to hear that I walk around the neighborhood until I'm so cold that it hurts. I have familiar paths that I wander, and other night people like me who keep an eye out.

Mr. Bailey, two blocks down, who watches TV in his garage no matter how cold it is because he doesn't want to wake Mrs. Bailey.

Arnie Tucker, across from the refurbished firehouse, who watches everyone out his window all night and sleeps all day. Dad once told me he was in Vietnam and was never the same after he came back. I know he watches out of fear but he makes me feel safe.

Miss Serena, the retired dentist, who walks back and forth across her deck as her dementia gets worse, watching and waiting for a husband who died almost two decades ago. Her nurse, Nadia, watches from inside the door. She'll bring her in when it gets too cold or it's too much.

There's a guy who walks the neighborhood too, but I don't know his name and we've never spoken. He's older, scruff on his face that's salt and pepper. When we pass each other we nod. I'm tired, he's devastated, and those are two ships that can peaceably pass each other in the night. Sometimes I know he *sees me* because his brow creases with concern. Still, we don't speak.

I take these walks a few times a week.

My parents never stop me. Never ask where I've been.

Somehow, I have all the trust in the world without being granted any trust at all. I can walk alone at night for hours. I don't have a curfew or a bed time when this is what I'm doing. They know I won't get up to anything. Except when I want to do anything fun or social, spend time with other people, even other family, the suspicion is raised. My freedom is curtailed, and the rules are tight and have painful consequences.

As long as I'm alone it's okay.

Because when I'm alone, there's nobody to whisper my secrets to except myself.

3

Logan

Sadie Braverman is a goddamn mystery, and it drives me insane.

I spend enough energy telling myself not to think about her, and when that fails, I spend the rest of that energy trying to figure her the fuck out. When I think I know her, when I think I can fit her into a pattern and guess what she's going to do, she throws me for a loop.

Like walking over here and not only taking the cigarette that I was smoking, but taking a drag like she does it every damn day. Watching her cold, dark pink lips wrap around the filter where mine had been made my dick hard, and then the way she licked her lips before exhaling? Fuck off. That's going to be what I think about when I jerk off before going to sleep tonight.

Perfect Sadie Braverman taking a drag, licking her lips, and then exhaling. Surrounding herself in a cloud of smoke, obscuring everything but her glowing eyes. A shade of brown and gold, inherited from her mother, but warm where Jodi's were empty. As the smoke cleared she came into view - round cheeks, full, plush lips, wisps of brown hair around her face poking out from the hood of her Carhartt, and a fucking smirk she tries to smother.

I've gotta stay away from Sadie. She's not for me, I'm not for her, but I know there's things going on in both our houses that we can't talk about. Words that can't make their way out of our mouths even if we wanted to speak. So when Sadie walks over to my garage and hides with me, I can't stop her. I don't want to. There's a whole symphony of information shared in that silence and if I give her shelter, so fucking be it.

It also gives me a chance to antagonize her when the mood strikes, and get as good as I give when she's feeling it.

She's not my friend. She's a fellow inmate and we've got a deal going on for our mutual protection. Fuck if I know what she's protecting me from, but the time will come. No matter how much I turned away from her after my dad died, our ties to each other remain. Sometimes they're a bridge, and sometimes a noose.

I stay in the garage until I see Sadie wander back down the street and up her driveway. The lights are off in the garage and I don't think she can see me. She doesn't look this way anyway. Her heavy steps echo in the quiet night as she slips in her backdoor. The sound of the lock turning is loud because I'm listening for it. Sadie is safely locked away.

Now it's time for me to face my sentence.

There's a light on in the living room when I walk inside our house. I strip out of my boots and coat, then walk as quietly as possible through the house. My mom is sleeping on the couch, looking severe and blank even in her sleep. I make sure she's covered up and that her work phone is plugged in to charge.

If there's anything that will upset the delicate balance in our house it would be her not hearing her alarm and being late for work. She's important at work. It's the only reason we stay afloat without dad. Her income is more than enough, although most days it feels like we have nothing.

The stairs creak beneath my feet as I head up to the second floor.

The master bedroom door is closed like always. She sleeps in there maybe once a week. One day a week she lets herself be surrounded by the things we never got rid of, one day that she can handle it. The bathroom is the next door, then dad's office, then my room.

Sadie flits through my mind, and I go into dad's office instead of my room.

It still smells like him even though it's been years. Too many years.

For some reason I called her Sadiebaby tonight. It's a nickname I don't even let myself think, let alone breathe into reality. It hurt us both. I hate that.

His desk is exactly how he left it, his chair pushed in and ready for action. The small couch crammed inside and pressed against one wall is more used. I have a spare charger in here and a blanket he used for his "thinking naps." Without lingering on what drew me here, I lay down, plug in my phone, and pull the blanket over me.

Every night I sleep in a haunted house, and both of my parents - one living and one dead - are the ghosts that dwell here. It makes me feel like the last living soul in the world. As if I could look out the window and everything beyond would be empty, every house unoccupied, every voice long silenced.

I am a survivor on a lone island, and I can't wait to get out of here.

4

Sadie

First thing in the morning, I'm walking down the hall toward the office. I'll get that stupid letter and I'll send the scholarship application by Friday, and then maybe I'll get a weekend where mom leaves me alone. Maybe I can hang out with my friends or my brother without it turning into a battle.

It's the hope that kills you, but I still keep hoping anyway.

Maybe I'm more of a masochist than I thought.

Principal Stein is walking down the hall and lights up when he sees me. He's a very tall man with a very shiny bald head, glasses, and teeth that are crooked in an oddly comforting way. He's a huge dork but students actually kind of love him. He's fair, and that's the best that can be said for any administrator. Principal Stein doesn't believe in zero tolerance; he preaches unconditional positive regard and always hears people out.

"Sadie! Just who I was looking for." He steps toward me and reaches into inner pocket of his blazer, removing an envelope. "Your letter. It was the easiest I've ever written."

"Thank you, Principal Stein." I take the letter and give him my best fake smile. It's not that I'm fake happy, but I know that my ability to genuinely react to anything is low right now. I don't have the energy or the desire. It's easier to force myself into patterns and keep everyone happy.

"While I'm very proud and excited about your future, we'll miss you here. You do so much." He offers me his hand and I take it.

"Thank you, Principal Stein." He gives me a firm shake, pats my shoulder, and turns back toward the office.

"Thank you, Principal Stein," a male voice does a poor high-pitched imitation of me.

I turn on my heels and cock an eyebrow at Thor Brantner. He's a sophomore that runs with Logan and his crew, and his mouth writes a lot of checks that his ass can't cash. One stony look from me and he's stepping back.

"Aw, it's everyone's favorite goody two-shoes," Ethan Pisarski croons. "What rules are you going to follow today?"

The group of them lean against the lockers and try to look menacing. To be honest, if I hadn't known all of them their whole damn lives, I probably would be intimidated. They're tall, pierced and tattooed, rough and angry. They've all got hands warped and injured from working with machines, broken teeth and cracked knuckles from fighting, and outside of school grounds I would bet on any of them in a fight.

Except Thor. He's a kid trying to find his place, angling to take over when these guys graduate. Him, I could knock down in three hits and one good kick to the knee.

My eyes flick along them until they land on Logan. He's looking at me, waiting. Always looking and waiting and I never know for what. His friends love to pick at me, talk some shit, but he never says a word.

He doesn't stop them, but it matters that he doesn't join them.

Thor steps toward me, smirking back at them now that he believes Ethan has his back. He reaches out and flicks the letter in my hands.

"Love letters from the principal? Scandalous, Sadie. Or is it an excuse to get out of yet another class with us lowly idiots?"

I say nothing, just wait and let him talk himself out. For some reason I've been Thor's favorite target lately. Ethan always talks a lot of shit but he does that to everyone. He hates most people, so I don't take his low opinion of me personally. Thor, on the other hand, is not going to be allowed to use me to cut his teeth.

I look at Logan one more time, not sure why, and his cheeks are red. He's not looking at me this time, his gaze is fixed on Thor.

Thor leans close, barely taller than me. He smirks at the expression on my face. "Oh, are you going to start something, teacher's pet?"

I shift from an unimpressed glower to a smirk and he pulls back, confused. I talk quietly, pitching my voice high and innocent. "I could do anything I wanted to you. With my reputation, who would believe you?"

"Oh!" His boys crow behind him, laughing.

I step around Thor and head toward my locker.

"Bitch!" Thor shouts at my back, and I send him an insouciant wave of my middle finger over my shoulder.

Mentally, I'm already rearranging my errands after school to include putting the scholarship application in the mail. Between my summer jobs and all the tutoring I do, I have a really nice nest egg of college money. When I realized at 14 that a job was another time mom would let me leave the house without complaint, I found jobs. All of the jobs.

That doesn't mean the scholarship wouldn't be amazing. $25,000 that can be used for whatever I need - not only paying for classes, but also room and board, books, other living needs. I can stretch that money out, especially if I go to Madison like I want. It's a great school and I can save money with in-state tuition.

I haven't told mom that it's my top choice. I'm not ready to have that fight again.

Apparently, it's not prestigious enough to brag about at work. Her co-workers will have kids getting in to Madison too. Even though I've also been recruited to play D1 soccer there and that would come with additional funding.

Star pupil, star athlete, stellar reputation. She wants all of my blood, sweat, tears, and screams to be something that adds to her pedigree.

But it's not her life, it's mine. Madison is what I want.

Darcy and her girlfriend Amelia are waiting at my locker, whispering to each other. Sexy whispering. For a second, I feel a flash of envy. Then I remember that love isn't worth it for me, and I'm never going to let myself be vulnerable like that ever again.

People love to hurt me. It scratches some deep itch inside them to cause me harm, so I refuse to put myself in that position anymore. The people who are supposed to care the most are the ones who know how to cut the deepest.

Amelia pokes Darcy after she sees me, and Darcy turns with a coffee from our favorite local place, the Bronze Cabin, in her hand. She holds it out to me with a smile.

"You're the best person in the world."

"I know," Darcy agrees, completely serious. "I also know you went wandering again last night because I could pack for a gap year in Europe with the bags under your eyes. We have a quiz in Physics and I thought you'd need the boost."

I take a sip of the dark chocolate mocha that I would happily allow to replace every fluid in my body. Mom doesn't let me have coffee, but what she doesn't know might just kill her. Nothing will keep me from coffee. I'd say it was the only love I have that can't hurt me, but I've burned my tongue too many times when I'm eager for a taste for that to be true.

"What did I do to deserve you?"

"Kicked Ryan Kemp in the nuts when he teased me for getting my period in 7th grade." Darcy answers and Amelia laughs, and I join in. It was one of my finer moments of fury. It takes a long time for my temper to explode, but when it does there's nothing that can stop me. I keep a tight leash on it. It's not worth the consequences.

"I was talking to the coffee," I tell her.

Darcy leans against the locker and looks me over. Over winter break, she finally cut her chocolate brown hair into a pixie, and it's really working for her. She's got a narrow face and it makes her cheekbones look sharp and vaguely threatening. It's stunning on her. Amelia, her girlfriend of about a year, practically drools as Darcy goes into analyst mode.

"You're going to burn out if you keep doing this," her voice is quiet.

"What's past burn out? Because that's where I am. I'm trying though, I promise. I'm not working at the Cabana this semester, I cut back on my tutoring jobs, and I want to enjoy my last season of soccer. I swear. I'm trying."

Darcy nods. She's heard all of this before. "After graduation, you're taking three days to sleep."

"Deal." I link my arm with hers, and she links her other arm with Amelia, and we make our way toward the class we all share together first period: Calculus. The absolute worst.

Not because I don't like math, but I don't like math for math's sake. I like doing math for science. Otherwise it's like mental masturbation - what am I doing with this math? This math has no value outside of a practice problem. I'm not proving or solving anything.

I'm just mathing around.

Darcy distracts us both by talking about the latest place her mom is going to travel to, and which travel memoir she read that led to that decision. Sometimes it's like Darcy's dad only exists to fund the thing Darcy's mom wants to do. If they weren't so obviously, sickeningly in love with each other it would be sad. Instead it's cute. He goes wherever her finger lands on the map.

The countdown is on to getting away. In the meantime, I have my friends to keep me going and there is finally a light visible at the end of the tunnel. I will get out of here, and I refuse to let anyone break me any further. If I stick to the plan, I might make it.

5

Logan

The second Sadie turns the corner, I've got Thor by the throat.

I slam him up against the locker and lean over him, forcing him to extend his neck as far as it will go so he can look at me. Little fucker is great with his hands but he's getting strike after strike with me for running his mouth lately.

"You got a thing for Sadie?"

"N-n-no," he stutters out. "She's just-"

"She's just fucking nothing to you. You keep picking at her, like a little boy with a crush, pulling a girl's hair to get her attention. The fuck you doing?"

Thor shakes his head as vehemently as he can while my hand is holding his head in place, but he's pale and panicking. The kid couldn't take me if he had an extra set of arms.

"She's an easy target," he squeaks out.

"Not for you. We won't back you up when she really rips you a new one."

"Hey," Linc says and grabs my arm, pulling me off Thor. "He knows better now." I glance over at the redheaded asshole that I call my best friend. I'm tall but he's freakish, and ginger on top of everything else.

18

Girls absolutely swoon all over him. He's one of the only people who can calm me down.

The only one I've ever admitted to that I'm possessive over Sadie. That I'm trying hard not to be interested. To care. To want. The one who knows the things I won't say out loud.

"Don't fuck around, you will find out," Linc warns him.

"But Ethan," Thor starts.

"Is a dick to everyone," Ethan finishes the sentence. "So I don't count."

I take a step back from Thor and look at him. "Think about how you treat women. Now, while you're young and can still fix it. You go after a woman that way, you'll never be with one worth having. Got it?"

"Got it."

"Grow some respect, kid. If you don't do it on your own, Walker will set you straight." Linc adds to the conversation. Walker is his dad, but we're an odd group of lost boys and he might as well be father to all of us. God knows he's been my replacement parent since everything happened. The Andersons are my family.

Linc drags me away from glaring at Thor. Between his picking at Sadie and his constant flirting with Janet, Linc's younger sister, he's about to get the beating of his life if he fucks up anymore. He's got potential but that's not good enough.

"What was that?" Linc hisses. I follow him to the hallway where we both have the Senior Reading Seminar, which counts as our fourth year of English. Unfortunately, we're not in the same class.

"Sorry. Tense."

"When are you not?" Linc sighs. "Something happen last night?"

"Sadie."

He drags a hand down his face.

"I know. But she took my cigarette and..." I trail off, owning how fucking crazy I was about to sound. Linc likes Sadie as a person, but he doesn't get what has me wrapped up in her. Especially when she has no idea. Never has, and probably never will.

"How was your mom?" I haven't kept any secrets from him about what it's like in my house. About the neglect from my mom. Linc and his family were the ones to help me pick up the pieces of my life and figure out how to keep going.

Everyone abandoned me except them.

Sadie carries that failure, too, even if she doesn't realize it. Even if she was just a kid.

"We're almost there. Dad said we could move out early," Linc offers.

"I'm not moving in to the apartment yet. I need to finish this."

"Why? Why stay there? She wouldn't even notice if you left."

It hurts like a punch straight to the heart, but he isn't wrong. My mom acknowledges my existence maybe once a week. There's groceries in the kitchen, and money for anything I need, but it's not parenting. I'm no better than a pet in my own house. But even pets get attention.

"Yeah," I tell him, and he knows he went too far. There wasn't any malice in it, but there's still something in me that wants to protect my mom. Even if it's from people sharing a harsh truth. I can be disappointed and hurt, but I still love her. Even if I'm going to leave her.

We nod at each other and head into our separate classrooms.

Linc and I are moving into the apartment above Anderson's Garage and living there while we do our training and apprenticeships at the shop. It's his legacy, but it's going to be my home. We could probably do all of our testing and certifications now - I've been working in the garage since I was 12, and Linc since birth.

I'm going to work alongside my best friend and my chosen family, and find my place in Edgar's Bluff. There's no reason for me to leave, but I'm trying to find a reason to stay. To restore the home this place used to feel like, and erase the fallout from the bomb that was dropped when my dad died.

I'm ready to move on from this prison, and find what freedom looks like for me.

But I won't cut my mom off sooner than I have to, and not without trying to explain it to her. That I'm letting her go. I'm not the only one who needs to be set free.

6

Sadie

After mailing my scholarship application, I sent a text to mom and didn't hear back. I'm assuming that I am off her shit list for that duty. The house is blessedly quiet when I get home, and I take over the dining room table with my homework. Not that there's much to do because I either work ahead or get it done during my free periods.

The advantage to being smart is that I front-loaded everything that I could. Every requirement was done so I have two study hall periods during the day where I finish most things. However, I absolutely still lie to mom that I need to hide in my room and finish homework, or that I need to go to the library or Darcy's house to study. Since my grades never slip, she has no reason to doubt me.

The back door slams shut when James gets home. He's 13 and built like a Great Dane puppy - all feet and height he doesn't know what to do with yet. When he gets control of that, he's going to be such a heartbreaker. We look alike - same brown hair, same golden brown eyes, same big lips. My brother is one of my favorite people in the world.

He sighs when he sits down next to me and gets out his own homework. While he's smart, he lacks the focus that I seem to have innately. Mom doesn't push him the same way she's pushed me, and I think he takes it personally. Like she doesn't believe in him.

So I do.

"Got an A on my math test."

"Of course you did," I smile at him. "How are you feeling about your English essay?"

"Good. Other than some grammar stuff all the feedback on my draft was good. Even though the book was boring."

I roll my eyes at him. "Sure, that's why you spent an entire Saturday reading it and ignoring everyone."

James blushes. Despite his gangly nature, he's a good athlete. He plays club volleyball and basketball at school. Everyone expects that to be all he thinks about, all he wants to do, when secretly he's fairly bookish. Mom almost never agrees to let our friends come over, so none of his even know about his giant shelf stuffed full of books.

We fall into our comfortable after school homework silence, and then the back door shuts with force once again.

The change in both of us is immediate. My back straightens, our jaws clench, and James hunches, his shoulders heading toward his ears. Mom glides into the room, giving an approving nod when we're doing what's expected.

Usually, she turns the other way and heads to her bedroom to change. There are two bedrooms on the main floor, two upstairs, and a weird converted bedroom space in our basement. James is in the other bedroom on the first floor with our parents. He asked exactly once about moving into the other bedroom upstairs to be closer to me.

I don't know what was said but James came out of it pale and crying, and never asked again. That was two years ago.

Today, mom sits down at the table.

I didn't know it was possible for us to stiffen further, but we do.

"I have some bad news," she begins, and her voice is soft. My mind is overtaken by complete terror that dad died. We can't be alone with her. He's weak but he's still a barrier. He's better than nothing.

"Is dad okay?"

Mom frowns. "He's fine. It's Uncle Dave."

Dave is mom's older brother. He's...interesting. He's a licensed psychologist but no one needs one more than him. Dave is a manipulative, controlling wiener. The idea that Dave is dead doesn't make me sad at all.

"There was a fire at his house. Dave, Julia, and Cole are going to be staying with us for awhile."

James nods like this wasn't surprising information, and I feel like I'm going to throw up. Dave married Julia this past summer. Cole is Julia's son from her first marriage. He goes to the Catholic high school, Holy Angel, and is known the town over for being their star receiver - fast, good with his hands, recruited to play at Notre Dame after graduation.

He's also my ex-boyfriend.

And fucking psychotic.

"Now I want to give them some privacy, so Sadie I need you to move out of your room and into the basement. Cole can stay in your room, and Dave and Julia can have the guest room."

I'm frozen. Not only will I have to put up with Dave's bullshit, but Cole will be living in my house. He'll have invasive access to me. He's never even been in my bedroom before, and now he'll be sleeping in my bed. Every piece of me in that room will be another thing he can use as a weapon against me.

While I'm sleeping on a bed in a room without a door.

The fear that ripples through me is so strong tears spring to my eyes.

"Sadie, get moving, now," mom snaps at me.

I spring up from the table and pack my homework up. I leave my bag by the kitchen door, ready to be taken to the basement before rushing to the other side of the house and up the stairs. The good news, I guess, is that I'll have easy access to sneaking out the back of the house. The back door leads to a small landing with stairs down to the basement, or a smaller set up into the kitchen.

In my room, I pull out two empty totes from my closet and start throwing everything I can inside. Ripping every card, note, and photo off my mirror, sliding all my makeup and toiletries into the bin with no finesse or organization. Every trinket, trophy, ribbon, is off a shelf and into the bin. I make sure that all of my notebooks and journals make it in, too. He can keep the books for himself.

I pull all of my things out of the bathroom between the two rooms. Even the stuff I barely use. The cupboards and drawers are empty of everything except towels and spare toilet paper. I'm breathing hard from how fast I'm trying to do this. I run back into my room and try to look around and think what else I need to take besides my clothes.

What else I need to take to hide myself from Cole.

There's a knock at my door and James waddles in with two of the largest suitcases we own.

"Thought you might need these." He stares at me. James doesn't know the whole story of why Cole and I broke up, but he knows that it was bad. He saw the bruises. James doesn't know how to ask what I need, and I don't want him to because he's my little brother, and it's my job to protect him.

"Can you just grab bunches of my clothes from the closet and take them downstairs? Then the bins?" This is how he helps me. The last thing I want is for those assholes to get here and I get cornered in my room by Cole.

James starts making trips and I empty my drawers into the suitcases.

It's a little weird that pretty much my entire life fits in two suitcases, two bins, and a thick stack of hanging clothes. I stare around my disheveled and stripped room. This is what it's going to look like when I leave for college. Emptied of all the things that make it mine. That breathe my life into it.

I don't want to leave anything behind that would give either of my parents the impression that I intend to return. Once I'm gone, I will never be under her thumb again. The only reason I'll play nice at all is for James, and then I'll help him escape too. We won't look back unless we want to, and I doubt we will.

We get everything downstairs and James stays to help me, trying to get my clothes and things organized. Since there was a fire, it's likely this is a stay of months, not days or even weeks. Even if their insurance company would pay for other accommodations, mom would never let Dave stay anywhere else. No, no, she has to be there for her big brother and take care of him.

Barf.

I'm sure mom didn't offer and Dave didn't ask. I guarantee he called her and told her this is what was happening. The only person who can boss mom around is Dave, and everything he says becomes gospel in our house.

It's why we aren't allowed to have marshmallows anymore, because the gelatin could be made from pig hooves and that's depraved. Don't even get me started on Dave's rants about coffee which led to mom forbidding it. Now our whole house is going to smell like his favorite stinky tea. Yay.

James and I don't stop unpacking when we hear them arrive. The room downstairs has one small dresser and a wardrobe. I get most of my clothes arranged, but now I don't have a desk or anywhere to keep my books and notebooks. I decide not to even bother unpacking the bins. I'm choosing minimalism.

"Dinner!" dad calls down.

Before I can take a step toward the door, James mashes into me, and puts his arms around me. We might be 4 years apart in age but he's almost as tall as I am. He rests his chin on my shoulder and squeezes hard.

"It's going to be okay. If you need me, I'll sleep right next to you."

Tears burn my eyes, and my stomach twists. He's guessing more than I told him, more than I want him to know. It's like he read my mind how unsafe I feel. It wouldn't be so bad if this room had a door that closed and locked. There's just a large open doorway, and a small living room on the other side.

No one uses that living room anymore. When I was dating Cole that's where we were allowed to hang out because there was nowhere to hide. The couch faced the entrance to the staircase. It didn't matter though. We still made out and messed around because mom thought Cole was a good Catholic boy. Part of me wants to throw it in her face that the good Catholic boy deflowered her daughter on that couch while she was sitting in the kitchen up the stairs, but even the good memories with Cole are tainted forever.

Marred by a series of acts I would never have believed he was capable of doing, especially not to me. Love is a trap, and I fell into it.

I hug my brother in return.

When we pull apart he automatically checks my face to make sure it doesn't look like I've been crying. It's not the first time we've done this for each other and it won't be the last. Mom has no sympathy for tears. James nods, and we go upstairs.

Everyone is already at the dinner table, and I take my seat before looking up, letting my good girl mask fall into place.

Dave is sitting at the head of the table, in dad's place. Because of course he is. Julia is on his left, mom on his right. James sits next to mom, I sit next to James. Across the table, Cole is in between Julia and dad.

Dad gives me an encouraging, empty smile. James and I both got his fair skin and brown hair, and his desire to avoid confrontation.

I let my eyes slide over to Cole.

He's watching me with a soft smile, like he's trying to hide that he wants to full on grin at me. A lock of his dark blonde hair falls down across his eyes, a hazel green that I used to lose myself staring into, trying to pick apart each pigment ring and color. I would get lost stroking his soft hair away from his face, staring into his eyes as he watched my expressions. No one had ever looked at me the way Cole did.

Cole always told me I was perfect. I was everything. I was wonderful. Words I needed to hear.

Until the words became judgment.

I was perfect, so I didn't need to hang out with my less than perfect friends. I was such a talented soccer player that I didn't need to spend any time bonding with my team because I was a star. I was so smart that surely I could do my homework with him without being distracted. I was so beautiful how could he possibly stop himself from taking me when he wanted me? How could he be anything less than bewitched by me?

We were together for two years. Eighteen of those months were amazing. A dream. They were all undone by 6 months of hell.

Dave is talking as we all start eating. I try to think what to say that will appease mom the most.

"I'm so sorry about your house, Uncle Dave, what happened?"

"Electrical fire in the garage. The house is mostly smoke damage. We were very blessed." Dave stares at me, and I can't hold his gaze. Where James, mom, and me have more brown than gold, Dave's eyes are just enough on the gold side to be disconcerting. I have no idea how any of his patients can bring themselves to talk to him.

"It sounds like it. I'm glad everyone is safe."

"Yes," Dave agrees, and reaches out to take Julia's hand. Like her son, her hair is dark blonde, but everything else about her is pale. Pale blue

28

eyes, pale skin, pale lips. Even a pale smile when she looks into Dave's eyes. Despite dating her son for years and spending time at her house, I barely know her.

"I think this is the Lord giving us an opportunity," Dave continues. He still attends church regularly at the Holy Angel Chapel.It's the one thing mom never bent to his will over - we still go to St. Stan's every Sunday. I'm even on the church choir.

They never told me why or what happened, I just know that I'd been expecting to go to Holy Angel for high school and instead was enrolled at EBHS. Mom said it was because it was more academically rigorous, which is true, but it still felt...weird. I learned not to ask too many questions early, so I didn't push it.

I was relieved, actually.

It's kind of a big deal to be Catholic in this town, and a lot is determined by your congregation. My life would be so small if I'd gone to Holy Angel.

"I agree," mom chimes in. "A good chance for Cole and Sadie to clear the air and reconnect."

"I'm so grateful you're letting us stay," Cole smiles at mom. That fucking wolf smile that no one seems to see for what it is but me. How does it not scream predator to the rest of them?

Mom beams at him. "But the house rules are still in effect - no being alone in the bedroom spaces."

Cole raises his hands in surrender. "Of course."

I'm not sure what happens to me in this moment, but I think my brain overheats and then breaks. All I can think about is that the adults in this house are actively conspiring to get Cole and I back together, and I cannot handle that. Part of me wants to stand up and scream at them what he did to me, what he did to me for months without any of them seeing, but I know they won't listen to me.

So instead, I say the next best thing I can think of, with an odd, hysterical laugh: "Oh, I wouldn't do that anyway. I have a boyfriend."

The table falls silent. No one eating, drinking, I'm not even sure any of us are breathing, as I sit there with a rictus grin, all teeth. James is looking at me with his mouth and eyes wide open because he knows I don't have a boyfriend.

Cole looks furious, and I get an ounce of joy out of that. The best part about not going to the same school, and that I have a mom I want to hide everything from, means he has no means or information to contradict me.

"What?" mom hisses.

"Yeah, I have a boyfriend, so, haha, just cousins now, Cole." For some reason that statement increases my nausea, and I stand up abruptly. "I need a moment."

Then I book it out the back door before anyone can stop me.

7

Logan

The Firebird is pissing me off tonight. I can't seem to get anything to do what I want, and I'm having trouble sourcing some parts to get her running more smoothly. I'm so fucking close to being done with the internal shit and working toward fixing up the body and the interior. Stuff I can't do in my garage at home.

I'm about to throw in the towel, literally, when I hear a door slam.

My head perks up automatically, checking the Braverman's back door.

Sadie is rushing across the lawn toward me, and I take in a lot of information very quickly. First, she's not wearing a coat or shoes. She's stomping across the snow in fuzzy wool socks. Second, she looks fucking terrified.

Without thinking, I rush over to meet her before she gets too far, pushing her back onto her cleared driveway rather than standing in the wet snow.

"I need you to be my boyfriend until May," she says, her hands clinging to the sleeves of my jacket. There's panic on her face, and her eyes keep darting between mine, trying to give me some desperate message I can't quite make out.

"Starting right now," she begs.

My brain stalls out.

"What the fuck, Sadie?"

I've had a lot of fantasies of Sadie Braverman telling me she wants me, that she wants to be my girl, but not a single one of them went down like this.

I'll take what I can get.

"Remember creepy Uncle Dave?"

I nod, recalling Sadie's psychologist uncle who asks super invasive questions and gives weird advice. Haven't seen him or spoken to him since I was a kid though, when he tried to therapize me after dad died.

"There was a fire at his house so him and his wife and her son are staying with us, but the thing is, his stepson is my ex-boyfriend and they're trying to get us back together and in a panic I lied and said I had a boyfriend and I need you to pretend it's you."

"So you want to use me to make him jealous?" Well, that fucking sucks. Without my consent, my heart twists.

"No! I would never do that to you," she says it so softly it makes everything inside me smooth out. "I don't want him. I want to make it really, really clear I don't want him." Sadie bites her lip and the panic fades a little. "Plus, it'll really piss off my mom if it's you."

I huff out a laugh. She has no idea.

"I will owe you. Anything you want. Please, please, please?" Sadie shakes me, and I know that in another context, I'm going to make her beg for me like that again. There's not going to be anything pretend about me and Sadie, and I'm not even going to fake that. I'm going to make sure she understands her own intentions, and then I'm going to turn the inch Sadie is giving me into a mile.

"Why me?"

Sadie's face gets serious. "Because I trust you." Her eyes fall and she looks away as she keeps speaking. "Things did not end well. I need

Cole to stay away from me."

Rage threatens to tear me away from her, because there's so much implied in that statement that makes me want to find the fucker and rip him to pieces. Then something she said gets through to me. There's no Cole at our high school. I didn't even know she'd been dating anybody. Which is probably a good thing because I would've lost my shit and found a way to break them up. It means she dated someone from another school, and there's only one guy it would be.

"Cole? Cole Edwards?" Please no. Anyone but him.

"Yeah," she blushes, but it's not cute embarrassment, it's shame. She's ashamed of the fact that she dated him. That helps a little.

"Like the Cole that used to be my best friend?"

Sadie's mouth drops open in a cute little O and I want to bite into her bottom lip and suck. It's distracting enough to stop me from being angry.

"I'd...forgotten that."

I would never forget that fucker. Friends are supposed to be there when you need them the most, and Cole disappeared without looking back. I haven't heard from him in years, although being a golden boy football player I've heard plenty about him. Jealousy floods my system because I can see how perfect he and Sadie must've been together. All preppy and beautiful, accomplished, the kind of people everyone assumes good things about.

No one assumes good things about me. I'm trouble all around, and most of that reputation has been earned.

Then again, Cole disappointed her. Hurt her. This is my chance to show the girl of my goddamn dreams that no one will ever be as good for her as me. She's the only one I'll be good for. No one will ever love her like I can. She's already given me her trust. That's one important step toward giving me her heart.

"I'll do it, but I need you to understand something." I step closer to her, and pull her body into mine with one arm wrapped around her waist. Sadie gasps but she doesn't fight me. "You're my girl now, Braverman," I whisper and lean closer, her lips so damn close to mine. "I'm not going to waste time being *fake* anything when we could be having a *real* good time."

Sadie gulps.

"So that's the deal. I'll keep you safe and...satisfied." Sadie's eyes drop shut and her lashes flutter. I'm getting to her. Good. "And you'll be my girl. Deal?"

"Logan, I don't-" Sadie starts to protest, and I'm sure I've got her all off kilter with an answer that she didn't expect. It's delicious to make her unsteady when she's normally so controlled or contained. I want to see Sadie out of control. I want to make her lose her mind. She's been an angel for so damn long she's forgotten what it's like to face off with the devil.

Not only am I going to capture her heart, but I'm going to corrupt her soul. Sadie needs it, and I'm going to give it to her. I'll drag my angel into the dark, give her a taste of another side of life, and when the time comes...I'll let her go.

I want Sadie, but I'm not meant to be her forever. She needs me to be her saving grace right the fuck now, and I can do that. I can live on this piece of her for the rest of my life. I'll always know that I got Sadie Braverman's love, if only for a little while. That's what I want out of this deal. For Sadie to admit that she loves me.

The sound of someone coming down the back stairs of her house spurs me into action. I tug Sadie the last inch closer, and our lips connect.

Immediately, the taste and feel of her untether me from sanity and I groan into her as I part her lips with my tongue. Her mouth is hot compared to the cold air, and she surprises me by not fighting back for a single second.

Sadie's body melts into mine, her hands sliding under the denim of my jacket and along my hoodie until they're linked together over the small of my back. I've got her sweet face in my hands, and I'm devouring her.

I open my eyes to look at her. To watch her lashes flutter and her eyebrows relax as she lets me have my way. My eyes drift shut, focusing on the feel of her. In my arms, mouths connected, tongues entwining, right where we both belong.

A throat clearing snaps us apart.

8

Sadie

To say that I have never imagined kissing Logan Kurowski would be a lie. To say that I've never thought about doing more than kissing with Logan Kurowski would also be a lie. I'm not saying he's the most consistent player in my spank bank, but he spends very little time on the bench. He's so damn good looking, with that hint of danger.

So I thought that my imagination had done a great job of conjuring what kissing Logan would feel like.

Actually kissing Logan puts my imagination to shame.

I'm still processing that he wants me to be his girl, but I'm too busy kissing him to think about that right now.

We fit together perfectly, like our bodies were built to line up with each other. He only has to tilt his head down a little, and I only have to tilt mine up a little, the perfect amount that nothing would ever get sore if we did this for hours. I fit inside his arms, and the feel of him in mine is intoxicating. His body is so warm that I want to sink against him and stay there. Logan holds my face like it's precious and the size of his hands makes me feel tiny.

This is the most perfect kiss in existence and I didn't expect it at all.

Every sense is open, absorbing him, feeling pleasure from everything about him.

The feel and taste of his mouth. The way he smells like motor oil and fabric softener. How damn soft the denim of his jacket is, and the even softer texture of his hoodie.

I could live in this space, in this moment, forever.

I want to die here.

That's the weirdest thought I've ever had because for the first time I mean it in a good way. Not as an escape but as a resting place.

One kiss from the most unexpected person and I think my world-view has reoriented.

A throat clears and I step back, breaking the connection of our mouths but keeping my hands on his waist. Logan stares at me for a second before dropping his hands from my face to my hips, and we both turn to find my dad watching us.

He looks amused, which fills me with relief.

"Wrap it up and come back in the house, okay kids?" he laughs as he turns to go inside. When I turn back to Logan, there's a dark look on his face, but by the time he's focused on me again it's gone.

"Why do you want me to be your girlfriend?" I ask, puzzled.

"You too good to be my girl?" he cocks an eyebrow and on impulse I reach up and run my finger over it, causing him to drop both the brow and his eyelids.

"I'm too boring for you."

Logan's eyes snap open and he gives me a devilish grin. I don't understand what's happening right now. We went from casually wasting time with each other to somehow discussing entering a relationship. It feels like we missed a step in the middle somewhere.

"I have my reasons," he says, cryptic as ever.

I stare, trying to read him. "I won't fall in love with you." It comes out as a whisper, and his face falls before he pulls it back into something harder, more guarded. "I'm never giving someone that kind of power over me ever again."

Logan's hands clench on my waist, and I think he understands me. His cheeks turn red so I know he's upset, but he doesn't challenge or press me. I can practically see him holding back his questions in the way he's moving his lips.

"Maybe I just want to see you rebel a little, Sadiebaby." This time, neither of us flinches. It's like we were both waiting for him to say it. For him to reclaim the nickname. "You got it in you?"

I laugh and throw my head back. "Fine, corrupt me." My head tips forward, and his eyes are dark and focused on my mouth. The most intimate, inner muscles on my body clench at the lust in his look. I feel it, too.

"Oh, I will." Logan captures my mouth again, his tongue gliding against mine in a filthy way that makes me imagine it somewhere else, and now I'm starting to get wet.

I push him away. "I have to go." I need to breathe.

"You have to go with me to Ronny Ingram's party this weekend."

"Okay." We'll see how I convince, cajole, or lie to my mom to make that happen.

Logan lets me go and takes a few steps back, sliding his hands into his pockets. He flicks his head, directing me to go in the house. I step inside and turn to lock the door. He doesn't walk away until he hears it click.

What in the hell just happened? And why do I feel so safe?

9

Sadie

The dining room is still silent when I come back, and everyone except James and dad look like they ate lemons. Mom looks especially sour. I sit back down and resume eating, not giving anything away until I'm asked to do so. I don't think dad told them what he saw, but the annoyance that I have a boyfriend is still palpable.

"Who are you seeing?" mom finally snaps out. "Who is this boy?"

"What if it was a girl?" Shit. I shouldn't have said that. We're barely recovering from Darcy coming out as it is. Mom's gaze drags to me, and it's good to know her homophobia is alive and well. I roll my eyes, then clear my throat and focus on my food. "Actually, it's Logan."

"Kurowski?!" she screeches. "Since when?"

"We've been talking for a few weeks. We made it official recently." This entire sentence is a lie and a truth. We've been talking for years, and she's been unaware of it. Logan has been a safe place I didn't know I needed, even if there wasn't actually much talking going on. And we made it official 3 minutes ago.

"This is another blessing," Dave cuts mom off. "Logan is in need of a good influence." To say I'm shocked would be an understatement. Then again, Dave knows that the second they try and make him forbidden, it'll make him all the more enticing. Well played, Dave.

He has no idea how much I'm intrigued by Logan's desire to be a bad influence on me. How badly I want to give into that opportunity. What else can life possibly do to me? Aren't I due for some fun? Damn the consequences.

I talk a big game but I doubt I'm capable of damning the consequences. I've been too brainwashed into behaving. Fear trained me to behave without thinking about it.

I tune out the rest of the dinner chatter until mom says my name.

"Help Cole get his things upstairs." That sounds like a contradiction of the no bedrooms rule, and I start sweating in fear. I'm fine. It's fine. James is here, and all I need to do is scream for my brother to have my back.

I don't look at Cole as I leave the table, but I feel him following me. Their bags are the bottom of the stairs and I can't stop the pang of sympathy that hits me as the smell of smoke emanates from them. Cole grabs the things that are his and then steps back, waiting for me to lead the way.

Like he doesn't know how stairs work or where they go.

I walk like an inmate heading to the death chamber. It's not that different. Something is going to happen. Cole can't help himself. I'm bracing for impact.

The look on Logan's face when he realized that something bad had happened with Cole, his fury, comforts me. Worst case scenario, I have somewhere to run now. Someone who would love any excuse to pummel his ex-friend. How had I forgotten they were friends?

Since pre-K, Logan and I had gone through the Edgar's Bluff Catholic school system. Through 8th grade at St. Stan's for me, but Logan moved to the local public middle school at the end of 6th, after his dad died. Cole had been in school with us too, and they'd been pretty much inseparable. Smartasses but sweethearts. I wasn't around

40

the two of them together all that much, so it never really registered with me that they weren't friends anymore.

The public and Catholic schools were always in competition, and very few people crossed the lines for friendships or relationships. The rivalry was indirect and ugly. EBHS was bigger, had a more robust academic curriculum, and because we had a more competitive conference, our student athletes got more scholarships, recognition, and awards.

Holy Angel had funding. The teachers were better paid but had less to work with, and the athletic teams basically would take what they could get. It's why Cole was such a big deal. He could turn a team into success even if he only had a mediocre quarterback.

I hadn't seen Cole since the end of 8th grade when I changed schools, and hadn't thought about him.

So much had happened and changed for me in my first year in public school; the year things got more intense in terms of expectations and rules. When the punishments started.

Then the summer before sophomore year the Holy Angel football coach asked my soccer coach to work with their kicker and punter, and Coach Minski asked me to help out. I think he knows more about my home life than he lets on, and he could pay me. A job got me out of the house, so of course I said yes.

Cole and I locked eyes one day when I was on the field. That night he messaged me on AIM and we talked for hours. I was immediately smitten. We started talking, flirting, and suddenly he was my boyfriend. Every second that wasn't school or soccer was somehow spent with him.

Nothing made me happier. Nothing was more of an escape. Even though we were pretty physical with each other, it also felt like he was my friend. Cole listened and reassured me, he talked about our successful futures with certainty, and not in a way that added extra

41

expectations. Although he was nice to my mom to her face, he always talked shit with me when I needed it, always validated that she was too controlling.

Spring semester of junior year, things changed.

I still don't know why.

Even when I escaped the relationship, I couldn't escape him. Dave met Julia because we were dating. We'd been thrown back together at their wedding.

A night I wish I could burn from my brain.

At the top of the stairs, I point. "That's the guest room, the bathroom is here - I emptied everything so you can unpack your stuff." I step over to my bedroom door but don't enter the room. "You're here. The closet's empty."

Cole frowns at me and doesn't enter the room. "You packed up everything?"

"Yes."

He steps closer, not touching me, but making a hostile, intimate bubble between us. "Afraid that if you have to come in for anything, you'll be tempted?" Cole tries to reach up to brush my hair back from my face but I flinch away.

"Do you need anything else?" I huff.

Cole's face falls. "You. I need you, Sadie." He presses into me and panic spirals, causing me to freeze. I can't move. "Don't you miss me? Miss us?" Cole lifts my chin and leans in, and the fact that he's going to kiss me jolts me out of petrification.

I step to the side. "No, Cole. I don't."

Before he can say anything else, I dodge around him and race down the stairs. Luckily, he doesn't follow. He knows he's got all the time in the world to get me now. Logan might have put up a barrier but he's not in my house.

The dining table is cleared when I walk through, and I can hear mom and Julia in the kitchen. I keep moving fast, through the kitchen and race down the basement. I stop in the living room, staring at the open walkway, my heart racing and my breathing erratic.

Not safe.

I am not safe.

But I also know Cole, and he won't try anything tonight. He has to lull everyone into the false sense of family, of safety. I guarantee tonight mom will stay up late to make sure he doesn't try and sneak down to the basement. She might even do it for a few nights, just to be sure, and then when she thinks she can trust him I will be out of luck.

I turn on the lamp beside the bed and crawl into it, pulling out my phone.

"Hey babe," Darcy greets me. "What's up?"

"There was a fire at Dave's house. They moved in with us."

Darcy's silence blankets me. "When you say they, you mean Cole."

I do. Cole has no relationship with his dad. Not only because his dad doesn't really want it, but I have been subject to many a rant about divorce being a sin and that his dad abandoned and betrayed Julia. His dad walked away and didn't look back. In any other divorce situation, that's where Cole would go when his primary home was not livable. But it's not an option, and given the access he now has to me, he would've found a way to be here anyway.

"Yeah. Mom put him in my room."

"So where are you?"

"The basement," I whisper, trying to stop my voice from shaking. It doesn't work, and the tears I've been holding in start to fall, and a strangled sob escapes.

"No. No. This is unacceptable. Come stay at my house. I'll come get you."

"She won't let me leave," I cry openly, knowing that Darcy understands how heavy this is for me. That I need my best friend to share the burden of my pain and fear with me. I've done the same for her. Not a lot of people would be brave enough to come out as a teenager in this town, and the team stood by her, no questions. It's what we do.

"We won't be asking."

I laugh. "It would almost be worth it to see you fight her."

There's a loaded pause. "What if you told her?"

"They wouldn't believe me." I sigh. "Julia will side with Cole, so Dave will side with Julia, and mom will side with Dave. They'll think I'm being hysterical and overreacting. Plus, to them, the wedding looked like I went off and rekindled the flame."

"That's bullshit."

"I know." I take a deep breath. "I'll figure it out. I always do."

"I'm here. In a second. I will come get you. In a blizzard. A tornado. And if not me, Amelia."

That just makes me cry again, because I know it. Her parents wouldn't even bat an eye, they'd just make sure there were enough clean towels and that they knew what kind of breakfast cereal I preferred.

It wouldn't be the first time I hid out over there until mom dragged me back home.

"That's not even the weirdest thing that happened tonight."

"The fuck," Darcy exhaled. "What else could be weirder than your evil ex living in your bedroom?"

I tell her about my panic at the dinner table and my declaration that I had a boyfriend.

"So we have to find someone to pretend to be your boyfriend," I could hear Darcy shrugging over the phone. "That's going to be way easier than you think."

"Uh…"

"What did you do?"

"I asked Logan to be my fake boyfriend."

"KUROWSKI?! Like the super hot neighbor that you said in a game of truth or dare in 7th grade you would choose to lose your virginity to?" In this moment, I really hate that Darcy remembers pretty much everything ever. I got teased about my answer to that question for weeks. She has never let it go.

"And he said he was going to be my real boyfriend."

"That tracks."

"What?"

"I've always thought he had a thing for you. You've never seen the way he looks at you. Watches you."

I shiver, surprised how much I like the idea of that. "We'll see, I guess."

"Does Logan know about...Cole?" Darcy asks hesitantly.

"He knows he's my ex and it ended bad, and that's why I need a boyfriend, but he doesn't need to know more. I could barely tell you. There's no way..." I trailed off thinking about when I told Darcy. Still in my dress from the wedding, sobbing so hard I was puking, huddled against the cool porcelain of her bathroom toilet as I recounted not only that night, but everything before.

She'd tolerated Cole, but after everything she knows the only person who might hate him as much as I do is her. Someday I'll leave this place and I will leave my anger behind, but right now it's what keeps me safe. I can't soften. I can't give in. No forgiveness. No moving on. Not yet.

"You have me, but I think you need to accept that now you have Logan too. And he's right next door. You can go crawl into his bed and beg him to keep you safe with his dick. Or bend you over that car he's always working on to make sure everyone knows who owns you."

"That's kind of gross, Darcy." It's not. Not even a little bit. Everything she said became a vivid image in my head and I want exactly that. For Logan to fuck the fear out of me. That's dangerous. He's dangerous.

But isn't that why I agreed to be with him? I want danger. I want

45

edge. I want corruption. Someone Cole will think twice about messing with. But also someone who takes care of what belongs to him.

"I might only be into women, but that does not mean I don't want all the sexy details when you give in. You're repressed."

I sigh again, and laugh. She's not wrong. I haven't had sex I enjoyed in over a year. Proximity to Logan is going to be devastating for my libido. If he keeps touching me and kissing me the way he did, I'm going to be way too horny to keep him at a distance. Logan might demand that it's real, but I still have to draw lines and boundaries between us.

Eventually, I know I'll give in to our bodies, but I have to make sure before I do that he has no chance at my heart.

Darcy and I wrap up our call, and she tells me I need to update the rest of our friends. They don't know everything that Darcy does, but they know enough that they'll freak out about Cole being in my house. Our chat is Darcy, Amelia, and my other closest teammates, Chloe and Layla. I sign on to the computer in the living room and pull it up.

Me: There was a fire at my uncle's house and now Cole is living with me.

Layla: the fuck.

Amelia: you can live with me

Chloe: are you sharing a room

Me: No. I'm in the basement.

Layla: ew.

Chloe: are you okay

Me: don't know yet

Darcy: tell them the good part

Me: Logan and I are a thing

Layla: called it.

Chloe: about time you get down and dirty yet

46

Me: no. kissed.
Layla: yum.
Darcy: we'll talk about it tomorrow
Amelia: are you okay
Me: okay enough
Amelia: seriously come stay with me
Me: I'm good. Going to sleep. Someone bring me coffee.
Amelia: i got it

I was not going to be sleeping any time soon, and I loved Amelia for offering her house too. Mom tolerated Darcy because we'd been friends our entire lives and her mom was the city attorney and that association was important enough to tolerate. But Amelia, no way. Despite the fact that she was the exact brand of sweet and polite mom loves, and the kind of put together that mom always wanted out of me, her lesbian status was a no go.

Mom never stopped me from having them over, and I loved the way Amelia was always a perfect angel to my mom, leaving her disgruntled and frustrated. Mom is horrible to me and James, but to the rest of the world she's not generally hateful. It's a struggle for her to be mean to other people because it was so ingrained in her to be good, to be polite, to wear the good girl mask she's also forcing on me. I get a twisted sort of joy to see her beliefs at war. It's impossible not to think well of Amelia. Even for her.

I start a CD of my favorite band, put the volume low, and turn off the lamp. I sit up against the headboard, surround myself with pillows, and stare at the doorway until I can't stay awake anymore.

10

Logan

I slept in dad's study again. If mom came home last night, I didn't hear it. I'm not sure where she goes on those nights. Sometimes I think she stays at work and sleeps on the couch in her office. The few times I've been there in the last 6 years, there was a blanket on the couch and a pillow in her file drawer.

The thing is, I look like her, not him. She shouldn't look at me and see dad. All the sharp angles of my face, the coloring of my hair and eyes, those are all the spitting image of her. The masculine mirror image. The only thing I got from dad is my height.

And my skill with my hands. He could fix anything.

Except himself.

By the time Henry picks me up for school with Ethan smoking in his backseat, I'm tired and in a jittery mood. Sadie threw me for a loop last night. Not only finding out that she kept an entire relationship secret, but that she was scared enough of my ex-best friend and current golden boy that she had to find a shield.

When Sadie said that she came to me because she trusted me, it meant more than I will ever be smart enough to have the words to describe. Not a lot of talking went on in the garage when she would come hide out with me. It was a habit she started at the beginning of high school. Somehow, despite our differences, we could exist peacefully in the same space. Not only because we didn't try and get in each other's business, but because we didn't need to.

That's the machine her mother made her.

I'm going to let out her soul.

"What the fuck are you grinning about?" Ethan grumbles.

"You'll see."

We're doing our usual thing, wasting time by Linc's locker, when I get a text.

Sadie: is this...still happening?

I grin. I didn't even know she had my number. I got hers when she wrote it down for someone else during a study hall we shared sophomore year. It helps to have perfect vision.

Me: come and find out.

My stomach is having a fucking riot waiting to see her. Waiting to see what she'll do. Sadie is an all-in kind of person. When she commits to something, she throws all she's got into making it work, making it happen, making it great. It's going to be entertaining to find out what that looks like when it comes to me. I need to know she's not holding back.

We might be neighbors, but socially, we're from opposite sides of the tracks. I wear metal t-shirts and have been accused of worshiping the devil, and she sings in the church choir. I'm a troublemaker headed toward blue collar manual labor, and she's college bound. A leader. The future. The dichotomy is amusing. One of my favorite words I picked up in senior seminar.

Sadie comes around the corner like she does almost every morning, but this morning her eyes seek out mine. The second they meet, she breaks into a smile like I haven't seen on her face in a long time. I notice that her shoulders drop, and she takes a deep breath, like she'd been wound tight until I came into view.

"What's got teacher's pet all happy?" Thor grumbles. Still hasn't learned his lesson, but damn he's about to and I'm going to laugh my ass off.

"Taking a walk on the dark side, Sadie?" Ethan snarls. Sadie shakes her head at him. He opens his mouth to say something, but then she steps past him and into the middle of our group. I open my arms for her, testing, and she steps right into them.

Sadie wraps her arms around my waist like she did last night and presses our bodies together. I tilt my head down to look at her. The smile hasn't dimmed a bit on her, and it's genuine. No matter what else is going on, Sadie is happy to see me. Genuinely, brightly happy.

I don't know the last time I felt that kind of emotion aimed at me.

Sure, my friends like me, and we have a good time, but I've never caused them joy.

"Hi," she smiles.

"Hey, Sadiebaby." I wait, seeing again what she'll do. In my periphery I can see that my friends have gone still, I can see Thor's mouth hanging open. They're all watching us.

Sadie presses up on her toes, brushing her nose with mine. It's all the invitation I need before kissing her. I expected her to try and keep it chaste since we're in school. To push back when I try and take it deeper, but she doesn't. When I slide my tongue along the seam of her lips she opens for me, kissing me back like no one is watching. Fuck.

I should've gone for her a long time ago.

I could've saved her from hurt.

I could've saved myself from a fuckton of it too.

How can anything hurt when she kisses me like we've been doing it forever. Like it's the most natural, familiar thing in the world. I feel like I've spent my life knowing her kiss, as if me and her exist outside normal time. We've always been together, we were just waiting for this reality to catch up.

That sounds insane.

That's how she makes me.

Sadie breaks the kiss but doesn't move away from me. Looking down into her face, this close, I can see how tired she is and how hard she's trying to hide it. There are dark circles under her eyes and some redness that makes me think she's been crying. I'll find out why. She needs me, and I'm determined to be or do whatever that entails. I touch my nose to hers.

I might have a reputation as a tough guy, and being unafraid to be affectionate only reinforces that in my opinion. It's a dare for anyone to say anything, and find out what happens. This is my girl and I'm going to make sure everyone knows it.

I've known Sadie our whole lives. Yes, we're neighbors, but our parents got houses next to each other on purpose. Her dad, Chris, and my dad, Brian, grew up together. Grew up best friends. Until the summer I was 11, our parents were a foursome. They did everything together.

They never forced Sadie and I to be friends, but we still spent plenty of holidays, birthdays, and celebrations knowing each other's business. Her parents were as much of an authority over me as my own. They were people I went to for help or comfort as easily as my own parents.

Sadie felt the same. Dad was an engineer and he helped identify at a young age how agile her brain was. They would do puzzles together and he would teach her advanced math, going over concepts with her that sounded like another language to me. I was never jealous because he taught me as much if not more, it was just different. He saw us as the individuals we are, and encouraged accordingly.

We were a large extended family.

Then we weren't.

Dad was gone, and her house changed. A lot of people dropped out of our lives after dad, I just never expected it from the people right next door. Mom wasn't in a place to try and maintain relationships, let alone ask for help, and I was too young to know what to do. They left us in the cold, and we've been surviving in the tundra ever since.

I never held it against Sadie, even when I tried. At that age, we're the victims of our parents as much as we are in their care. I've always suspected that a lot was kept from her. Maybe even the truth. Plus, I knew what her mom was becoming, how she was treating Sadie, and I didn't have the strength at the time to help her fight that battle.

Some people are forged in fire, but me? I found a way to take strength from the ice. I found another family, one that stayed, one that healed me and pushed me. Without anyone's opinion, I made decisions about my future and what I wanted from my life. I spent two years regularly seeing the school psychologist. I sought her out. I asked for help. It didn't take me long to realize no one was going to step up and do it for me.

While I was finding a way to exist alongside everyone else, Sadie was being crushed into a box. The door wasn't open for me to help, but it is now.

"I'll see you after school," I say quietly. "Garage time."

Her eyes are dilated. "Yeah." My little brainiac sounds dazed, and I love it.

As she leaves the safety of my arms, I want to stop her, but I let go. Sadie doesn't look at any of my friends as she walks further down the hall to where her friends are waiting. Darcy gives her a cup of coffee and as she drinks it they all go "Ohh" and tease her. I like that.

My smile falls and I look back at my friends who are all staring at me in varying degrees of shock. Except Ethan, he's watching after Sadie and her friends.

When he turns back to me, he gives me an amused nod. "Nice work. She's alright."

That might be the nicest thing I've ever heard him say about anyone. "What the hell?" Linc hisses.

"Is that why you were a dick yesterday?" Thor asks. Janet elbows him in the stomach and I know she does it hard because he bends forward, hand flying to the spot she hit. No one messes with Janet. The fact that Linc or I would kill them helps, but she's fierce all on her own, living up to her namesake, Janet Guthrie - the first woman to qualify and compete in the Indy 500. All the Anderson kids are named after something to do with cars. Lincoln is literally the car brand because his great-grandfather worked in the factory. His older sister Tori is actually Victoria because, as their parents love to remind them, she was conceived in the back of a Crown Vic.

The warning bell rings before I can say anything and everyone leaves for their classes except Linc and Janet.

"When did that happen?" Janet asks, amused but also concerned. She's a sophomore and the sister of my heart. She's also a giant worrier who trusts no one, and is a punch first in a panic and maybe ask questions later kind of person.

"Last night."

"How did that happen is the better question?" Linc presses.

"We talked." I cock an eyebrow, letting him know I'll tell him more when Janet isn't around. I already know he's going be concerned about this, especially once he finds out that Cole plays a role in the whole thing.

"Well I guess I'm glad you got your head out of your ass," Janet sighs out as she claps a hand on my shoulder. She's almost a foot shorter than I am so her attempt to be patronizing is amusing. "She's had your balls for years."

"You do not ever discuss my balls," I warn her. "But thank you. Now I just have to worry about Sadie's ass."

"Ew. Bye." Janet walks away and when I look at Linc I can tell he's considering wringing my neck.

On the way up to class, I tell him how everything went down last night, including some of the context of creepy Uncle Dave, and that I demanded she really be my girlfriend because I wasn't going to fake shit. I did tell him that we kissed but without all the sappy details and what that did to my feelings.

"Why can't you be her fake boyfriend? This is going to fuck you up."

"She needs me, man."

Linc stops and stares at me. "You're delusional."

I shake my head. "I'm not. I know this has an end date, and I'm prepared for that. But this is my chance, and I'm not going to miss out on her."

He throws his head back and glares at the ceiling. "Fuck. Fine."

"That means you look out for her like she's your girl. No one fucks with her, or they will answer to us."

Linc nods. "Fucking right they will." He punches me in the shoulder. "Whatever you're hoping to get from this..." Instead of finishing his thought, he shakes his head and walks into his classroom.

It's going to be fine.

Better than fine. It's going to be fucking great.

11

Logan

The ride to Anderson's Garage after school is quiet. Linc is chewing on his words, his mouth twisting as he tries to keep it inside. It's amusing, even if it's going to be annoying to hear his completely valid points about why this is a bad idea. How it's disrupting our plans and I'm destined to get hurt.

But I have the full-proof answer: I don't fucking care.

I don't care if it hurts. I want it to hurt. I want to feel it.

Janet is staring at the two of us from the backseat, her eyes darting back and forth, probably guessing more than we'll ever admit to her. I worry about what things will be like for her when we're gone. Idiots like Thor won't protect her. Growing up surrounded by her big brother's friends kept her more isolated than we ever intended. Girls used her, or only stayed friends with her for as long as they were in our circle. It made her feel used, and it made it really hard for a girl to gain her trust.

So far, no one has earned it. She's going to be by herself soon, and it scares me. I wouldn't have survived without my friends. I would've gotten into a fight I couldn't win or ignored the brakes in a race, I would be 6 feet under. As dead by my own hand as dad. Janet needs people.

When we pull up in our spot next to the garage, Janet rolls her eyes at us and leaves.

I wait, because now is Linc's moment.

"What the fuck?" he sounds more flabbergasted than anything. "Why?"

"She needs me."

Linc shifts in his seat to look at me. "Yeah, but you don't need this."

"Her ex is Cole."

"Ah," Linc's face relaxes, like it all makes sense, even if it has very little to do with it in the end. I kept that bit of information to myself this morning because I knew he'd give it more power than it deserves for my choice.

"He hurt her."

Linc stiffens, brow lowering, face clouding. For being a bright ass ginger, I know he can go dark. I know that if I was on the receiving end of that expression I would be well and truly screwed.

"We can take care of that without her being your girlfriend."

"Where's the fun in that?"

Linc shakes his head and a half amused smile takes over his face. "I'm still gonna be worried. For both of you."

"And I appreciate that, but I know what I'm doing."

"She doesn't."

I grin at him, pure menace. "She will."

"Fuck," he grumbles.

"Sadie is so damn repressed. I've never seen anyone more in need of a release."

"And your dick is the magic trick?"

I snort. "Obviously. But I don't just mean that...I want to bring her out. I know there's more below the surface and I want to see it." I stare off into the distance, certainty gripping my chest. "I'm going to corrupt her, and she's going to like it."

"Do I need to organize an exorcism?" Linc sighs. "Fine. And I'll be here to clean up the mess, whatever that might be."

I slap him on the shoulder, and then move to get out of the car. We don't say much as we change into our coveralls and check the sheets for what Walker wants us to work on. He's got the other guys on oil changes and tune-ups, but we got put on detailing duty.

It's tedious, but I kind of like it. Cleaning up the car, making everything shiny and smell good again.

Plus, once we aren't vacuuming, we can talk shit.

"Yeah, whatever, you're going to sleep on the floor in a sleeping bag. Dirty ass clothes as your mattress," Linc snorts as he washes the windows. "You'll give in the first time you want to bring a girl home."

There won't be any girls, I think but manage not to say out loud. It feels like that now but once Sadie leaves me, it's not like I'm going to be a monk.

"It's not like you've got a mattress either. Planning to take your cute little twin?" Linc still has bunk beds that we outgrew a few years ago. When I crash at his house I sleep on the floor because both of us are afraid the top bunk will collapse beneath our weight.

"It's worth spending the money."

The fucked up thing is that I'm going to have plenty of money. Despite the manner of death, some of Dad's insurance money still paid out, and Mom signed over my college fund to me on my 18th birthday. It was robust, and she had continued to diligently add money even after he died. I can live comfortably during my apprenticeship.

I could buy everything for our apartment to be stocked like adults and still have the money I needed to live off.

Linc suspects, but he doesn't ask.

I talked to Walker about it and he told me to keep it as a safety net, and go into all of this on equal footing. Linc wants to put up his half, and I need to let that happen. It's a struggle because I want to give back to them all, but I also know that it would make Lincoln feel like he owes me.

It's always going to be me that owes him.

"Don't worry, mom is already clearance buying and stocking up. She's got boxes of crap we're expected to take with us. There were a lot of dish towels."

"She's seen the mess you make in the kitchen."

"That's why you're gonna be the cook, Lo."

The plan is falling into place.

It's full dark by the time I get dropped off at home, and I can't fucking wait for the roads to be clear enough for me to get my bike out. Maybe this weekend.

I hate needing a ride from people. I hate depending on anyone for a means of escape. My cheap junk car needed new breaks, but I'll have it back by the end of the week. Then I won't need to rely on anyone else, especially with the weather getting warmer.

Someday I'll have the Firebird to get me to where I need to be, or as a way out. It's why I've never given up on that stupid car - I want to run on my terms, and that car is part of it. Something I did entirely on my own, just for myself.

I'm almost to my back door when I hear voices.

It's too easy for me to recognize that one of them is Sadie.

I walk around the edge of their shed, staying out of view, spying. I don't regret it. I've watched her more than she'll ever know. I'm a damn expert at Sadie watching. Sadie listening. Soon enough I'll be an expert at Sadie tasting too.

The thought makes my dick twitch, so I tune back into my eavesdropping.

"Sadie," a male voice sounds condescending and perturbed.

"No. Stop it." There's the sound of scuffling, and it makes me see red.

I come around the shed and start stalking across her yard, my heart racing and adrenaline sliding through my veins as I prepare for a fight.

The fucker has his hand wrapped around her wrist and even over her hoodie it's got to hurt. He's looking at her, but she's looking at me.

"Logan." Sadie tries to hide the relief, but I don't miss it. She yanks her arm back again and Cole lets go, holding his hands up like he didn't just have one on her. Like it makes him innocent.

I move to her side and pull her into me, sheltering her under my arm. I turn to the fucker with a smile that is nothing less than threatening. I want him to look at my teeth and know that I'm prepared to rip out of his goddamn throat with them.

"Cole, long time no see, huh?" It cracks like a whip between us, and Cole has the gall to look ashamed. Sadie leans into me, and her arm comes up to wrap around my waist.

"Logan, hey man. It's good to see you." My smile widens because he doesn't mean it, and I get great peevish joy from that. "I was just talking to Sadie."

"I think Sadie was done talking to you. I mean, you're already invading her house and taking her space, the least you could do was listen to her when she tells you to go."

Cole's face clouds with anger but I watch as he smooths it out, as if it never happened. He's as controlled as Sadie but Cole is hiding. Sadie is surviving. He looks away from me as if I hadn't spoken.

"We'll continue this another time."

Sadie doesn't say anything. Instead, she turns into me, burying her face in my chest. Cole watches and looks vaguely stricken. Like it never occurred to him that not only would she get over him, but that she'd also move on. His eyes lift to meet mine, furious. With a sharp nod he moves around us and into the house. I wait to hear the door shut before saying anything.

"Sadie," I start, but she shakes her head, her nose burrowing into my chest.

"No."

"Baby, are you safe?"

The question makes her stiffen, and I feel how much effort it takes for her to take a deep breath. I knew things were bad but the absolute defeat I can feel inside her scares me down to my core.

"Yeah, I'm safe." She takes another deep breath and then lifts her head to meet my eyes. The mask is back in place. Sadie lied, and she thinks she can hide the truth from me. Thinks I don't know her voice and expressions and can feel the truths from the lies.

I sigh now, telling myself not to push it. She's not ready, and while she trusts me on one level, she doesn't trust me with this. Yet.

I keep my arms around her, and lean down so my forehead touches hers. When Sadie's eyes close in relief, I know I did the right thing. There's so much thinking involved in trying to take care of her, and I'm doing my damn best. I've been waiting for the chance to be the one for her, but I'm going to blow it all if I can't learn some patience. She'll see. I know she will.

"If you tell me that you're alright, I'm going to believe you, Sadie." I kiss the tip of her nose. "You don't have to be alright for my benefit. You don't have to be perfect with me. I like you messy. I want you messy."

"Sure," she gives me a sad smile.

I don't let that sit. One of my hands drops down to her ass and I squeeze. Sadie gasps and I feel her soft breath on my face and smirk when her eyes blast open to meet mine.

"That's how I corrupt you. By giving you permission."

Her cheeks turn pink. "Permission for what?"

"Anything you want."

She stares at me skeptically, and I stare back. Outlasting her.

"One more time, Sadiebaby. Are you alright?"

"Everything is alright."

Alright enough, I think, and let it go. Whatever was going on, I've soothed her.

"Okay. Now fucking kiss me."

Sadie leans in close, her eyes locked on mine. I can feel the heat of her lips as our bodies press even closer. It wouldn't surprise me if she could feel my dick pressing into her stomach. That asshole has wanted her for years and he knows his chance is coming. My brain has to stay in control of this situation.

At the last second, Sadie dodges to the side and brushes her lips across my cheek. She darts to her back door before I can turn and pull her back to me.

"Goodnight," she sings over her shoulder. When she's safely behind the storm door she sticks out her tongue at me. I stick mine out in return, and revel in her smile before she closes the main door. We watch each other through the window as I listen for the turn of the lock. I nod at her and walk away when I hear it thunk closed.

It's dark inside my house. On instinct, I know it's empty.

I turn on the light in the kitchen, and I'm surprised to find a note on the counter. I lift it up and there's $100 underneath it.

On work trip, gone 5 days.

That's it. It's not signed. No "love, mom," no information about where she's going or where she's staying, zero ability to contact her in case of an emergency. Her cell phone is unreliable at the best of times and who knows what kind of coverage it has wherever she is. Then again, she actually remembered to leave a note this time.

Last summer she was gone for four days and it took two of them

61

before she answered the phone and told me where she was.

The note crumples satisfactorily in my hand and I toss it in the trash.

I don't second guess going upstairs, stripping down, and sleeping in dad's office.

This is a bad habit that I need to stop.

But not tonight.

12

Sadie

It took everything in me to behave myself over the next few days. To not run screaming next door and ask Logan if he'll help me run away from my life.

But I can't do that to James. I can't burn the bridge, no matter how much I want to take napalm to it. I might want to turn my back on them but I don't think he'll ever be there.

Saturday morning I'm forced into "family time" watching a movie together. My parents, Dave and Julia, Cole, James, and me. I can't even tell you what the movie is.

Because they make me sit next to Cole.

I don't see anything. I have to focus on keeping it together.

At least we're surrounded by our parents, and James is on my other side. I sit close and lean against him, feeling safer even if only 6 inches are between my body and Cole's. The tension running through me hurts, and I know that if I let go for even a second I'm going to start shaking.

Cole reaches his arm up and lets it drop across the back of the couch. I jump at the move, now perched on the edge of the cushion.

He laughs, entertained by the way he gets to me. The impact he still has on me.

I feel like throwing up on his lap.

When the movie is over, Dave makes a show of stretching. "What are your plans for tonight kids?"

"I'm going to a meadow party with Darcy." I figure if I tell rather than ask maybe my chances of going with permission will improve.

"Like hell," mom snaps before she can catch herself. She doesn't usually talk like that in front of her precious, judgmental big brother.

Dave frowns but focuses on me. "What's a meadow party?"

"The degenerates go have a bonfire in a field," Cole drawls. "I didn't know you went to that kind of thing Sade." There's condescension in his voice that I want to smack right out of his mouth. But I'm worried that if I lose control and hit him, I won't stop until he's dead.

I never thought I was capable of murder until Cole. Until I spent months dreaming about it, waking up smothering a scream and soaking my sheets in sweat. Feeling like even death wouldn't be enough to keep him away from me.

There's a divide between the EBHS kids and the Holy Angels. Occasionally a girl from Holy Angel will date an EBHS guy but we don't go to each other's parties. The only reason I was ever accepted going to Holy Angel parties was because I'd gone to school with most of them until high school, and because no one would say no to Cole. No one would ever question his decision to bring me around.

When we were together, other than soccer team events, I didn't go to EBHS parties. It was made very clear early on that he didn't want me to, and he wouldn't go with me. I should've seen that for the controlling behavior that it was. I swear Cole thought he was saving me from the heathens by bringing me to the Holy Angel social scene.

"The team is going," I feign nonchalance and shrug. "I want to be with my friends."

"Is Logan going to be there?" mom glares in suspicion.

"I don't know," I lie, "he doesn't control what I do." Cole's eyes narrow at that because he knows I'm talking about him. "I want to be with my friends."

"I think that's alright," Dave answers like he's my parent. I swallow thickly, trying not to roll my eyes at him since he's on my side about this.

"It's not alright. You know what these things are like," mom pleads with Dave. "Drinking, drugs, bad behavior. That's not who Sadie is, I don't think it's a good idea." She turns on me, glaring. "It's too close to the end for her to ruin it all now. It just takes one bad choice, Sadie."

"Why don't you go with her, Cole?" Dave asks, grinning like it's a brilliant idea.

"Uh..." Cole panics and it delights me. He wouldn't be caught dead at an EBHS meadow party, and especially not one at Ronny Ingram's house. It's one thing for someone to be a heathen, it's a whole other thing for them to be the EBHS star wide receiver - the same position Cole plays. He'd get his ass kicked and he knows it.

"No," Julia speaks up, and I'm surprised she entered the conversation. "Cole doesn't need to go." Her voice is soft but final.

Mom glares at me. "Fine, but be home by midnight." She won't disagree with Dave.

"Fine." That shouldn't be a problem, and I know she'll listen for me to come home.

Logan is waiting for me at the end of his driveway when I finally leave my house. I told dad I was leaving because I didn't want to go around with mom again. The expression on his face was guilty because he's knows that's why. He knows he has no power in this house. Accepting my goodbye is him agreeing to stand between me and her when she gets pissed that I left without saying anything to her.

I slow to a stop when I see that Logan is on his bike. He grins at me and holds out a helmet as he looks me up and down.

I'm wearing my favorite dark blue flared jeans, and layers so that all I need is a hoodie rather than a jacket. It's comfortable but also cute, and I even made some effort with my hair. It's gotten around school that we're a thing, but this will be our coming out of sorts. I know that it'll get back to Cole once it's fully public. I know it will eat him alive.

Logan is in his usual hoodie and a jean jacket, a chain hanging down and running from his belt into his pocket. He's got gloves on, and a black beanie. It looks so good it's annoying.

"There's only one helmet," I stutter out.

"Your brain is more important than mine." He lifts the helmet at me again and I take it, sliding it over my head. When I struggle with the strap, Logan slides a finger through my belt loop and pulls me closer to him. It shocks me how gentle he is when brushes my hands away and works the straps himself. The tips of his fingers graze my neck and I shiver, my nipples getting hard.

I like that my body is so physically responsive to him, but it's also really annoying.

"You good?"

"Good," I nod, voice muffled by the helmet. After a second of hesitation, I climb on behind him. My body notches perfectly against his, and I slide my hands around his torso under the jean jacket.

"Never had a backpack before," he laughs.

"A backpack?"

Logan looks over his shoulder at me, raising an eyebrow, and it connects for me. I'm wrapped around him like a backpack for his ride.

"Well, keep in mind that I'm precious cargo."

Logan laughs again and starts the bike, my body moving with his as he lifts up to slam his foot down. One gloved hand reaches down and he squeezes my thigh.

"You have no idea, Sadiebaby."

Then we're off, and nothing has ever felt so incredible. The wind against our bodies, the leaning of the bike, the freedom of movement, the high speed with nothing around us for protection. I'm so glad there's been a clearing in the weather for a time so that I can do this with him. Logan's going to get me addicted to this feeling.

I squeeze him tight, and he lifts one of his hands to place it over mine, squeezing back.

Where has this boy been for the last six years?

He's not the Logan I knew when his dad was alive, but he's not the guy that's iced me and everyone else out afterward. That moved away from everything he had been part of to find a new group of friends. I can't say Logan was happy, but he fit where he ended up.

For the last two years, I've sat in his garage and we talked about nothing if we talked at all. Now I'm wondering what I was missing out on.

We get to the meadow fast. He parks his bike next to another one, and near Lincoln's car. Logan's friends are around a ratty old couch and some lawn chairs on one side of the bonfire. My friends are on the other.

I walk over with him but stop before we get close. "I'm going to see my friends." Not a question or a request.

"Okay. Find me when you need me," Logan leans in and whispers it in my ear, and I can almost hear his smile when I shiver. I turn to look at him, reading his face for any sign of anger or annoyance that I'm not going to be his arm candy.

Logan's face is beautiful, relaxed and open, one eyebrow slightly cocked. He takes my chin between his fingers and pulls me the rest of the way to him. Our lips slide together, and he holds me there, lingering.

It takes me a second to realize that he's stepped back, and the knowing look in his eyes annoys me. I frown at him before walking away. Logan's laugh follows me.

"Holy shit!" Darcy yells when I come around the fire and she sees me. "The fuhrer let you out of the house?!" I can tell from the tone of her voice that she's already had a few drinks, but I accept her back cracking hug. The other girls cheer and I join them, falling easily into conversation.

Layla sidles up next to me.

"How are you?" Her hair is in two french braids. She's the braider on our team, and they're so tight it makes your scalp hurt, but it means hair doesn't get in your eyes during a game. I don't know how she does it to herself with the same ruthless efficiency.

"I'm fine," not sure why she's asking.

"You and Logan kind of came out of nowhere," she hedges. "Don't get me wrong, I love it, but..."

"But what?" Layla had seen my bruises and knew they weren't from the season or my club team. She never said anything but I don't blame her - what do you say when you're 17 and know your friend is being hurt? Especially because I made it clear I didn't want anyone to do or say anything.

"You swore off relationships after..." she trails off. "And you've talked a lot of shit about love. I don't want you setting yourself, or him, up to be hurt."

Layla has a point. I nod, and look across the fire to where Logan sits with his friends, talking and laughing. There's girls near him, mooning at him, and a flash of annoyance goes through me.

"We've been really honest with each other," I answer her, not looking away. "No one is going to get hurt."

"Except maybe those girls sniffing around your man," she laughs.

I shouldn't care. Even if Logan says this is real I know that it's not. It can't be. This is a relationship of convenience. He's helping me out. There's no reason for me to be jealous or feel even remotely possessive of other girls flirting with him, or paying attention to him. It shouldn't be obvious anger on my face.

Except it needs to appear real, and Logan told me that it was.

Real in-a-relationship-Sadie would not put up with this. Real Sadie would stake her claim. So that's what I need to do.

Without another word, I walk toward Logan.

He's sitting on the back of the couch, his feet resting on the seat. The girls keep trying to talk to him and he gives them a cursory amount of attention before turning back to Lincoln. This is how he's always been at the parties I've been at though - they flirt and he brushes it off. I know he hooks up, there's been enough rumors about him, but he never makes it obvious.

I wonder if I'll be able to ask him why that is, and if he'll tell me the truth.

As I get closer, Logan notices. Our eyes meet and hold, a challenge in his. He's waiting to see what I'm going to do. I have to figure out how aggressive to play this.

Logan slides down off the back of the couch until he's sitting on the cushion, and he rests his hands on his thighs. It's a clear invitation, and I'm going to take it.

I weave past one of the girls, not even paying attention to who it is even though I probably know her, and invade Logan's space. I drop down onto his lap and wrap my arm around his neck, my other hand coming to rest on his chest. He wraps his arms around me and tugs me closer. My ass rests firmly over his crotch, and I give a little wiggle.

"Hey," I tell him, and reach up to pull off his beanie. My hands slide over his soft, shorn hair, and I pull him forward. Instead of kissing him, I suck his bottom lip between mine and then tug it with my teeth.

I watch in fascination as Logan's eyes flutter shut and he groans softly. His hips move just a bit underneath me. I let his lip go and pull back.

"You'll pay for that later," he grumbles at me. I laugh and settle in to my new seat, and put on his beanie. Neither of us looks at the girls that were around him as they move away. No hard feelings, I can't really blame them for paying attention to him. And nothing publicly claims a guy like taking his hat.

I rest against Logan and let my mind drift while they talk about cars. It's familiar in a weird way, and it reminds me of his dad. Brian could talk about machines for hours, and taught me so much about science. It's what's inspired me to pursue physics in college. I want to understand how everything works, and make it work better.

"You in, teacher's pet?" Ethan's voice snaps me back into the present. He's holding out a smoldering joint, the look on his face telling me he thinks I'll say no.

I reach out and take it, putting the soft paper between my lips.

Out of the corner of my eye I can see Logan grinning again.

I keep eye contact with Ethan as I take a deep inhale, feeling the smoke fill my lungs. Ethan takes the joint back from me, watching with increasing amusement as I don't exhale. He takes the joint back and waits.

I turn to Logan and hook a finger under his chin to pull him closer. Our mouths seal together and I exhale. Logan inhales, the action incredibly intimate. I've never done this before, and it's heady. We're sharing breath, sharing smoke, and he's open and taking it from me. Letting me own him in front of everyone.

Some smoke escapes and whirls around us.

I pull back and exhale the rest.

That's when I realize his friends are hooting and cheering, and that Ethan is even clapping for me, the joint perched in his mouth.

"Damn, pet, I did not see that coming." Ethan shakes his head.

"I have excellent lung capacity. I go for 80 minutes, ya know."

Ethan looks past me to where my teammates are hanging out. "I think I might want you to introduce me to your friends."

We laugh, and I let the pot slide into my system and relax me.

"That was hot," Logan grumbles against the top of my head. "You corrupt so easily."

"I guess I've been waiting for the right devil," I murmur.

13

Sadie

The ride home from the meadow was even better. I felt like I melted into Logan, our bodies merging and moving together with each turn and shift of the bike beneath us. The streetlights blurred, the traffic lights blinked, turned off this late at night. It was still almost an hour before I needed to be home.

I wanted to beg him to keep going. Keep going on this road out of this town until we ran out of gas. Then we'd walk. Then we'd crawl. Anything to get away.

He hadn't said it, but I got the feeling he wanted to escape as badly as I did.

Maybe not Edgar's Bluff, since all his plans revolved around staying here, but from our houses. From the remaining ropes of our childhoods, tethering us somewhere we didn't want to be anymore. Tethering us to people we hadn't been in a long time.

Logan pulled into his driveway and stopped. I didn't move.

His big hand and his strong arm reached back, and before I could really comprehend what was happening he had pulled me around his body. My legs straddled his hips and our chests pressed together.

I stayed still, dazed and relaxed, as he unclipped the helmet and pulled it off. My hair crackled with static and I shook it and laughed, throwing my head back to look up at the dark blue sky. Even here, there were so many stars visible.

My laugh turned into a moan when Logan pressed his lips to my throat. The heat of them seared through my cold skin, and my hands flew to his shoulders. I let one slide up along his scalp, pressing him closer. Telling him with my actions that I liked this. That I want it.

"Kiss me," he murmurs into my pulse, and I tip my head down to oblige him. In this position, I'm higher up. I have control of the kiss. I press hard into him, sliding my tongue along his lips and unable to hold back a smirk when he opens for me. We go on like that, tasting each other with filthy depth, until I have to break away and take a breath.

His lips are kiss bruised and I'm sure mine are the same.

"Why are you doing this?"

Logan blinks. "What do you mean?"

"Entertaining my need for a fake boyfriend. Helping me."

His face splits into a grin, something decidedly mischievous. I see the younger version of him in the expression.

"Does this feel fake to you?" He grabs my hips and shifts them, grinding his erection into my core. My inner muscles squeeze, suddenly bereft at being empty. I shudder.

"No," I admit.

"It's not fake for you either, Sadie. I've seen the way you look at me. I always have."

"So just physical attraction then."

Logan laughs darkly. "No." I wait but he doesn't say anything else.

"Why are you doing this?" I ask again.

"It turns me on to watch the good girl go bad. To corrupt you like the devil I am." Logan leans in and runs his teeth down my chin, speaking into my neck. "I want to steal pieces of your soul, one sin at a time, until all of you is mine."

I moan softly. "Church really fucked you up, didn't it?"

Logan stiffens slightly and then huffs. "Something like that."

It shouldn't be so hot that he thinks about me like that - like someone he wants to darken, tarnish, to reveal the bad that hides in between the good. It shouldn't turn me on to think about what he means by corrupting me. It shouldn't thrill me to think about all the things he could probably get me to do.

"I don't know if I should take you seriously." I draw back from him and put some needed space between us. I've been so bound up for so long that I'm diving into this more quickly than is healthy. I'm being reckless for the first time, and since I have no idea what I'm doing or what my limits are, I have to stop letting him hypnotize me.

I have to stop thinking that I know Logan because I so clearly don't. On the surface I do, but who he really is, the guy underneath, he's a mystery. He's a danger. I can't forget that. I can't get swept up in emotions because that's when I get hurt. That's when I give him the opportunity to hurt me.

Corrupting me is fine. Breaking me is not.

"You should take me very seriously." Logan sighs and shifts me like I weigh nothing, moving me off the bike and holding onto me until I'm steady on my own feet. It's hard not to marvel at the grace in his movements when he gets off himself, and I smile a little dreamily when he leans over me.

"When I'm done with you, you won't be able to deny that this is real."

That scares me more than anything else he's said today, and I take an instinctive step back. Away from his warmth and temptation. His face falls slightly, but he covers it up with amusement.

"Sweet dreams, Sadiebaby." Logan crosses his arms and waits.

I look back as I walk across my backyard, and again when I reach the back door. I know that he'll stay there until I get inside and he hears the door lock. If only he knew that I'd be safer outside than trapped in this house.

As I turn the lock, I watch him. I wait for him to move toward his door before letting myself settle.

The light in the kitchen is on, and I know that mom will be sitting at the small table we keep there. Waiting. Chewing her cheek and fine-tuning her lecture. I take a deep breath and head up the three stairs from the back door landing.

Mom looks so calm on the surface. She's in her nightgown, wearing her quilted pink bathrobe. Her hair is down around her face, and both her hands resting on the table, woven together. A typical mom waiting up for her child to come home.

It's the coldness in her eyes that betrays her.

There's no relief in seeing that I got home in one piece, with 45 minutes until curfew. No pride that I didn't get in trouble and I didn't even try to break the rules.

"What are you doing?" she hisses. Keeping quiet so she doesn't wake dad, or alert anyone else in the house to this late night dressing down.

"Coming home and going to bed," I answer, voice flat.

"I mean with *that boy*," she says it like a curse word. "You are wasting your potential, and you're almost to the end, Sadie. What is wrong with you?"

I say nothing. There's no response that she will hear or understand.

"Your grades are perfect, your community service and extracurriculars are going to open any door you want, and you could even keep playing your sport." Soccer is another curse word in our house. She wanted me to play something more "dignified" like tennis or golf, even volleyball, but nope. I play a sport that turns me into a muddy mess, gives me thick strong legs, and gave me a team of supports that she hasn't succeeded in isolating me from.

"What does that have to do with Logan?"

"He's going nowhere. He's not even going to college."

"Because he already has a job. He'll make more in the next four years than I will."

Mom shakes her head in disgust. "It's manual labor."

"It's essential work that makes great money. It's respectable. And it takes talent and knowledge. How dare you look down on him that way," I'm getting angry and can't quite draw it back in. Her face is getting redder with every word out of my mouth. Maybe it's the pot but I can't stop. "You can't do what he can."

Mom gets up from the table and gets in my face, her finger harsh and accusing and right in my face.

"It's below you."

"You're below me," I snarl.

The smack comes so fast I can't even register it until my face is already turned at the force of the blow. Heat crashes across my cheek and I inhale sharply.

"I won't stop you from seeing him, but I want to remind you that actions and choices have consequences."

I don't press my cold hand to my cheek even though I want to soothe the ache. Instead, I stand up straight and look her in the eye.

"You're right, actions do have consequences." The contained anger in my voice gives her pause, but I doubt it's ever occurred to her that it's her actions that she'll pay for someday. That I'd let her burn alive in this house rather than coming in to save her. Part of me wonders if she could ever change. I don't even know what that would look like.

"Don't fuck this up, Sadie."

Mom turns around and leaves the kitchen, the door to the dining room swinging silently in her wake.

I was tired before, but now I'm wired.

I go back down the stairs to the back door, and instead of turning to head into the basement I unlock the door and head back into the cold.

I take my Carhartt with me. I need to go for a walk. I turn toward the driveway to take my usual route.

And nearly jump out of my skin when I see Logan leaning against the house.

14

Logan

It took every ounce of control I have not to break open her backdoor and go into the kitchen when I heard what I knew to be a slap.

I'm not sure what compelled me to go over to the Braverman's and listen. Maybe it was seeing the kitchen light on and curiosity about what kind of lecture Sadie would get. Then I stayed because hearing her defend me to her snob-ass mom filled me with pride I've never felt before.

Being a mechanic is useful, but I would never think to describe it as essential.

Sadie doesn't look down on me. Not for my wild friends or my small dreams. I like that. It doesn't surprise me either. She's always been good at seeing things clearly.

But then the blind rage that I had to beat back when I heard the smack of skin meeting skin, biting down so hard I drew blood from my own mouth. I think I prefer the ghost of my mother to the monster of hers. Not something I ever thought I would think. That I'd feel almost grateful to be invisible to her.

Without thinking it through, I lean against the house and wait.

Knowing Sadie, she'll either come outside, or I'll stop her before she can go downstairs. I'm not letting her sit with all this alone. I'm not going to actively make things worse for her either. As much as I want her, I'd rather protect her.

That's the only thing that kept me away from her for so damn long.

I was keeping her safe from me, and from the truth.

Now I wonder if that mattered at all.

Patience settles over me when I hear the lock turn and I don't move back when she moves to step out the door. I let Sadie smack into the solid wall of me. Stopping her in her tracks, stopping her from running, and forcing her to be in my space and acknowledge what I just heard.

"What the hell was that?" I sound far angrier than I mean to, but I am still angry. Not at her, though.

"Nothing."

I wrap my hands around her biceps, keeping her in place. Sadie says nothing and keeps looking down. We wait each other out. I lose.

"I thought you needed me because of Cole."

Sadie's head snaps up. "I do."

"Then what's going on with your mom?"

"They want us to get back together. Me and Cole. Apparently, they're where he learned not to take no as a final answer." Sadie speaks through gritted teeth, and I clench my own. Trying to hold in my fury because it shouldn't be directed at her.

"Does your mom know?"

"No," Sadie says hollowly. "I don't think she'd believe me. Or care."

There's so much emptiness in her words that I react rather than think.

I wrap my arms around her shoulders and pull her into my chest. Sadie takes my hug, unable to return it. It doesn't matter. I hold her to me, I rock her softly from side to side. When she shudders, I feel it in my own lungs. Inch by inch, she relaxes. Her shoulders drop, her cheek gets heavier against my chest, and then slowly she raises her arms to rest them on my hips. Holding me back with all the energy she has right now.

To lighten the mood, I tease her a little. "You really mean what you said about me?"

Sadie lifts her head and gives me an impression of her usual smirk. Not quite back to okay yet. "Are you surprised I think well of you Logan Jeremiah Kurowski?"

Oof, full-naming me. I'd kind of forgotten she's one of the few people who knows my middle name. Who knew me when I went by "LJ" for a few short, embarrassing years. I'm not an LJ.

"Sometimes," I admit to her, and her smile gets a little more real. "Come on, we're not done hugging yet." I raise my hand and press her head back into my chest.

"Is that what we're doing? Because it feels like slow dancing."

"It can be both." We stay like that for a few minutes longer, holding and rocking. It's more intimate than anything I've ever done with her. Probably than I've ever done with anyone. Sadie softens me.

"When you need me, I've got you," I whisper to the top of her head in the cold dark.

"Okay."

"I mean it."

"Okay." This time it sounds more certain.

I pull back and look down into her face. "Everything alright?"

"Everything is alright now."

I stroke my thumb over the red mark on her cheek. Only a faint hint of it will be visible tomorrow, but it makes me angry all over again to see it.

"Goodnight, Sadie." I kiss her forehead, and walk away. I don't want to ruin that moment by making it romantic or sexual because it wasn't. It was something else. Something I don't have a word for, or maybe I do, but I don't want to say it. As I walk across our backyards I hear Sadie's backdoor close and the lock click into place.

Hours ago we were flirting in front of half the school and she was giving me a secondary high with smoke from her lips. Now, I feel like we've lived a whole other night, one that was brief and dark, but bonded us together in a new way.

I still want to corrupt Sadie and see how far I can push her, but now I want to save her, too.

15

Logan

Even though we finally connected on a real level, Sadie keeps me at a distance. Her schedule makes that easy for her. She'd always been teased for being a goody two shoes and involved in everything, first to work or volunteer, but I never really understood what that meant.

Before hearing her argument with her mom, I never understood why.

Sadie says yes to anything that will get her out of her house.

She's in school clubs, does tutoring for free and for pay, volunteers every other weekend to do garbage pick up in the parks and along the highway now that the snow has melted, helps train a kids soccer team, plus all of her training and preparation for her last season of high school soccer. Then there's all her homework, the random walks she takes at night, the time she spends with James, the limited time she's allowed to see her friends, and I'm still trying to demand that she spends time with me.

I'll be the greatest escape she can find. Nothing will set her free like I will.

Other than seeing each other in the hall, and a few times when she's come over to sit in the garage while I work, I haven't gotten quality time with my girl. Can't corrupt her thoroughly if I don't put in the time.

It's been a wet, muddy March so far, and she's going for her late night wandering walks in a raincoat these days.

Late on a Friday, I can't take it anymore.

I wait up until she comes back, and smirk when she comes around the corner of the house and jumps when she finds me leaning against the door.

"Hey Sadiebaby."

"Hey," she sighs, her body relaxing immediately when she realizes its me. On the one hand, I like that, but on the other, it makes me worried that Cole is fucking with her in the house. For that kind of fear and vigilance, it's not just the past, it's the present that's messing with her too.

"What are you doing tomorrow afternoon?" I crowd her and reverse our positions so I'm leaning over her and she's pressed against the house. "You know what? It doesn't matter. You're hanging out with me and the guys. Paintball."

Sadie cocks an eyebrow, and I love that expression. "Am I?"

"Yes." I lean closer, faking her out that I'm going to kiss her. Instead I tilt my head up slightly and gently nip the tip of her nose. I've never done anything like that before in my life but it makes her smile so it must've been the right instinct to follow.

"Your friends can come too."

Sadie laughs harder. "Your boys might regret that."

"Bring it on, Braverman."

She pushes me away and I relent, stepping back and waiting as she goes into the house. Sadie looks back, holding the storm door open. "You're going to eat paint, Kurowski."

I stay as she closes the storm door, locks the inside door, and I still don't move as she walks straight down the stairs into the basement. I stay in the moist, cold, midnight air until I see the lights down there turn off. It kills me that she feels vulnerable in her house and there's not a damn thing I can do about it.

I may have made a mistake.

I'm sitting behind a tree, ignoring the throbbing in my thigh from a hit that was far too close to my balls for comfort, and I know that I'm a sitting duck.

This isn't a battle, it's a massacre.

The guys and I play paintball on the Anderson's land all the time. We've got our own field set up in the woods with different places to hide, obstacles, and in some cases secret stashes of extra paint. I've been hit plenty of times, nursed the bruises that form, and I've even lost spectacularly enough to have to run the gauntlet. When we play it's an every man for himself kind of game, ten hits and you're out, the last man standing wins. I thought I knew what it meant to be ruthless and competitive.

I didn't know shit.

Sadie and her friends, all of whom are on the soccer team with her, thought it would be fun to play boys versus girls because we had even numbers. The guys and I thought this would be a cakewalk, since most of the girls had never played paintball before and we had to gear them up and provide them guns. We had even joked about going easy on them.

But we didn't know how to play as a collective, and that's all they know how to do.

Their attacks have been tightly coordinated, each member playing their part and absolutely decimating us. Getting one of us alone so we have no defense against all of them. They hunt in a pack, like wolves.

They won the first game easily, and once we knew what we were in for, we demanded another. We'd been playing for years, we knew these woods with our eyes closed. It had to be a fluke, beginner's luck, or us holding back because they'd never played before.

I've never been so turned on to be wrong. Their viciousness is hot as fuck.

It's down to me and Lincoln, but I have no idea where he is. He could be out already and I would have no idea.

I have no idea where they are, either.

It's almost funny the way my heart races as I strain to hear the sound of a person moving closer to me, but there's nothing. I can only hear my breathing, the background noise of the woods, and one of the Anderson dogs barking up near the house.

I've got to be safe to move, and I have to find Lincoln so we can watch each other's backs. Losing is inevitable, but I want to at least put up a good fight.

I start crouch running through the trees when I hear the telltale airy thump of a gun firing. I try to dodge behind a tree, but I'm not fast enough.

Then my ass is on fire as the pellet of paint dives into my vulnerable right butt cheek, pain spreading across it and down my thigh.

"FUCK!" I shout and drop to my knees, then try to crouch further and roll into a more defensive position. That was hit number nine. One more and I'm out.

Giggling haunts me in my hiding spot. I recognize the sound of Sadie in that giggle so I'm sure it was her shot, but I doubt she's alone.

"That wasn't funny," I shout.

"Yes it was," Sadie shouts back. Damn. Despite the pain, her skill and sass make my dick wake up and pay attention. Her voice comes from somewhere to my left, but when I scan through the trees I can't see her.

"I'll make you kiss it better," I grumble.

"You wish," Sadie says, so close it makes me jump. I turn my head to see her standing a few feet away from me to my right, gun aimed for my chest where I wear a vest.

She grins as she pulls the trigger, and I'm dead from shot ten.

I thump back against the tree.

"Lincoln?"

"Dead."

"I regret this." I frown up at her but from the twinkle in her eye she knows that I'm full of it. I loved this. I loved seeing how in sync her and her friends are, the way that they understand each other and can accomplish a singular goal. It makes something inside me go soft to see how much she's known and loved. That when I couldn't do or be what she needed, Sadie wasn't entirely alone.

I've never gone to any of her games, even though it crossed my mind. My crew isn't exactly big on school spirit and if I was there it would be conspicuous. There would've been questions I didn't want to answer.

After today, I'm looking forward to being able to openly come and watch Sadie and her friends play. To yell to anyone that will listen that's my fucking girlfriend being a beast on the field.

I smirk up at her.

"What?" she looks suspicious.

"Next time, we're on the same team."

Sadie flushes. "Okay." She blows it off but I know it touched her. It's the kind of praise she likes. I take her hand when she reaches out, and stand up. Instead of letting go, I drop my gun and yank her close. Sadie doesn't fight when I take her gun and toss it away.

"What are you doing?"

I don't answer her, just lean in and suck her bottom lip into my mouth. My eyes never leave hers, and I get up close and personal with the way they dilate. I let her lip slide through mine, but don't move away.

"What do you want from me, Logan?" Sadie's voice is low and

breathy.

"Everything. You're mine, Sadie. My girl. Body, soul, past, present," I trail off and don't say future, because I know that's not in the cards for us. "I want your time, attention, thoughts, breaths," I feel hers huff out with each word. "I want to write myself into your DNA, Sadie. Intrinsically a part of you." *The way you're a part of me*, I almost say but catch myself.

"That's a lot, Logan." Her voice trembles.

"You can take it," I tease, letting the innuendo break the tension.

Having her alone like this is so intoxicating. Sadie's hands are on my chest and I feel a sense of victory when she slides them up around my neck, resting on my nape.

"Still trying to corrupt me?"

I pull her hips closer to me so she can feel my hardening dick press against her stomach. Sadie tries to suppress a shiver and fails.

"Succeeding." I tilt my head to kiss her neck, and she sighs, turning her head so I can reach more of her. It takes all my self control not to bite and suck so I leave a mark on her soft, unblemished skin. She lets out a slight moan and tries to hide it.

"You sing so sweet for me, Sadie. My little sinner." I pull back and look down at her flushed cheeks and sparkling eyes. Sadie is as turned on as I am. "Should I make you perform for me, right here, where we could get caught?"

Sadie's mouth drops open, then closes, then opens again.

"There's a rumor your dick is curved," Sadie blurts, a blush darkening her cheeks further.

I've heard that one. I suddenly don't love that Sadie's heard rumors about me having sex, it makes me feel oddly slutty, but it's amusing that's where her brain went when she started to get flustered. I'm getting to her, and she can't fight how much she wants me for much longer. I'll let her know I'm interested, but every step further is in her hands. I want her desperate, begging, and certain that she wants me to give her what I'm offering.

I roll my hips against her again. "Want to find out?" It's bold, but it's also a test. Where is she at in recognizing how she feels. In chasing after her wants and needs. No one else lets her do that, but I'm determined to satisfy both.

Sadie squeezes her eyes shut for a second and then opens them, heated eyes meeting mine. "Yeah, I think I do."

I can't even smirk I'm so turned on. We move together, mouths smashing violently as we start kissing. Even though our hands cling, we can't get under the protective gear we're wearing, and it's not enough. I need more. Even if I could make her cum right now, I don't want to - not this first time she lets me have her. That's only for me, and I won't risk anyone hearing it.

If she's got a thing for getting off in sneaky situations, we'll explore it another time.

This one is just mine.

I take her hand and start guiding her through the woods, back to the Anderson house where the cars are parked. I drove me and Sadie here, so thank fuck I don't need to worry about giving anybody else a ride. They'll find a way home.

As we both rush inside, I send a text to Lincoln letting him know that I needed to go and it was urgent. I'm sure he'll read between the lines and make sure Sadie and her friends get home.

Or try again and get their asses handed to them for a third time.

16

Sadie

We don't talk or touch on the drive home. My phone buzzes from text messages, and so does Logan's, but we don't look. We don't answer them. It's like bringing our friends into this would burst the bubble we're in.

The sexual tension is like nothing I've ever felt before.

As if this is going to change everything. Even if I'm not sure I want that, let alone that I'm ready for it, I can't deny that I want Logan Kurowski in the most sinful way. There were definitely times in life where I grappled with guilt over having premarital sex, but I get the feeling that sinning with Logan is going to feel like paradise.

He wants me.

I can't entirely believe it, but I felt him against my stomach. The look in his eyes was raw and the desire easy to interpret. There have been guys in the past who acted like they wanted me because sullying the goody two shoes is like climbing Everest, and I can tell the difference in what they wanted versus what Logan wants.

Logan wants to corrupt me because I'm good, that's true, but it's not for him - it's for me. He wants to bring out another side of myself instead of taking some kind of credit for dirtying me up. He's trying to show me what I already have inside me but refuse to acknowledge or let out. Logan has the sinner in me on her knees and I am done fighting her. I want her to come out, too.

I laugh when he whips into his driveway, the car crooked, and we both open our doors at the same time. Logan comes around to take my hand and pull me toward his house, and I yank back, tugging him to me.

Logan turns, intensity still burning, but I'm so damn giddy I can't help but smile.

He steps to me, pulling my body into his and looking straight down into my grin.

"I'm going to fuck that smile right off your face," he whispers, and a shiver shoots through my body that has nothing to do with the slight chill in the early evening air. The smile drops, desire overtaking me.

"Remember all that art of saints in religious ecstasy?" He leans his head and whispers in my ear. "That blend of pleasure and pain? Uncontrollable divine euphoria. That's what I'm going to give you, Sadiebaby."

It's profane. Irreverent.

It makes me more turned on than I have ever been in my life. I think I blackout for a second as all the blood rushes out of my head.

I haven't been with anyone in any remotely sexual capacity since the last time Cole hurt me. I didn't want to. I was afraid I couldn't really feel that way again, or that it would be a long time and a lot of trust before I did. Maybe that's why I can feel like this with Logan - I trust him. With every aspect of myself. He would never hurt me on purpose, never take something I wasn't willing to give.

Eve's biggest sin when it came to the apple wasn't the bite itself, it was making the choice to bite it.

Logan will always let me make the choice.

There aren't really words for how healing that is for me.

I push up on my toes to kiss him..

"Sadie!" Mom's voice snaps across the yards and right into my ears, freezing me mid-kiss. I drop down and take a deep breath, bumping my head against Logan's chest in an advanced apology. His warm hands squeeze my hips in solidarity.

I turn toward one of the monsters I live with and find her with her public smile on her face. There's hatred in her eyes, but the smile remains as fixed and polite as ever. The mask she wears that somehow no one sees through.

"Logan." She barely contains her snarl, but it makes me feel better when there's a huff of laughter blocked by my head. Only Logan would be amused by my mom's fury and dislike. He's not afraid of her at all, and it makes me feel stronger.

"Mrs. Braverman," Logan answers, his amusement not hidden at all.

Mom's lip curls but she looks away from him and back to me. "You're just in time for dinner."

Crap.

"That would be great," Logan answers and pushes me forward toward my house, inviting himself along. Mom gives a tight smile in response, not expecting his response, turns on her heel, and marches back toward the house. I'm sure she'll grumble to herself as she sets an extra place at the table.

"What are you thinking?" I whirl around and punch him in the chest. Logan puts a hand over it and fakes a pout. It's highly unlikely I actually hurt him, but I immediately feel bad and put my hand over his nonetheless. "Sorry."

"I want to get a read on things. Catch up with Cole and his mom. Say hi to Uncle Dave."

I shake my head. "You're insane."

"Yes." Logan nips my nose and then moves around me, grabbing my hand as he goes. It says a lot that I allow this man to drag me into hell

91

and I actually don't feel desolate. I can handle mom if I've got Logan.

My steps stutter at the thought. At how much that means to me, and how dangerous that is. I can't rely on anyone but myself, especially when it comes to my family. If Logan starts to feel like armor, then I'm in trouble. I'm in deep, deep danger of getting hurt.

Logan looks back to check on me and I give him a tight smile, pushing the thoughts and feelings down. Putting on the armor that I've built for myself and letting the mask that protects me inside my house drop into place.

We head straight to the dining room, no hesitation, because Logan used to have dinner here all the time. His whole family did.

I don't know if Logan's even been here since his dad died. I can't remember.

One day his parents were my parent's best friends and then it was as if we never knew them at all. We were less than neighbors. I never questioned it, and I wish I could remember more from around that time that would explain it. Why did my parents cut Logan and his mom off? The way we left them alone to grieve makes less and less sense the more I think about it.

Logan takes the seat he always occupied before - the one between me and James. He offers James a fist, which I am happy to see my brother bump. I can't believe I'm offering up Logan Kurowski as a positive male role model, but here we are.

He looks so out of place at the table. Shaved head, baggy clothes and rock band t-shirt with a skeleton on it, scarred hands permanently grease stained, his relaxed expression still containing some level of threat and his eyes still burning when they meet mine.

I can't look away from him, and when he reaches under the table to take my hand I automatically flip it palm up and let him weave his fingers through mine.

This is not good.

"What are you doing here?"

I don't look away from Logan, and I know he doesn't miss the way I try to smother my flinch at the sound of Cole's voice. Logan's brows drop even lower.

"Having dinner with my girlfriend's family," Logan says without looking at Cole. He gives me a sinister smile before turning toward my ex-boyfriend turned step-cousin.

Cole glowers at both of us, but his focus is on where Logan's arm is angled toward me under the table. Logan's fingers pulse against my hand three times before he lets go.

Cole opens his mouth to speak but for once we're saved by Uncle Dave. He comes into the room and starts talking as if we were all mid-conversation, or really, listening to him monologue with our complete attention.

Dave finally stops and looks around, checking that everyone is there so we can say grace. He rears back when his eyes land on our guest.

"Logan?" Something between shame and horror dances in his voice and it makes more questions float through my head. The idea that I'm missing something big when it comes to our fallout with the Kurowskis gets more certain every time I see an adult in my life interact with Logan.

"Hey," he gives a lift of his chin and then returns to his pissing contest with Cole. I can't even hold it against him. It distracts Cole from trying to talk to me, and is also very amusing.

Dave looks shaken, but we all join hands as he leads a prayer, one that I don't close my eyes or bow my head for. When I turn to see what Logan is doing our eyes catch and we both have to smother our reactions. On the other side of him, James opens one eye to look at us and shakes his head.

I look past Logan to my mom, and she's staring at both of us with hatred in her eyes.

Crap.

I'll pay for this, but oh well.

Automatically, I murmur "Amen" when the prayer is over, and shift in my seat. I wait for everyone else to start eating before I do. Mom does the same. I don't know how that habit started but I've struggled to break it.

"So, Logan, what's your plan after graduation?" Uncle Dave starts while piling his plate with food. "Cole is going to Notre Dame."

"He's going to be a mechanic," Cole answers, barely keeping the sneer out of his voice. *Like he even knows how to change a tire*, I think, and have to contain an eye roll.

"Didn't know you kept tabs on me, Edwards. Sweet of you." Logan keeps a perfectly pleasant expression on his face as he takes a bite of beef, chews, and swallows. Then he faces Dave. "I'm working at Anderson Auto Repair."

"The world always needs mechanics," Dave laughs, and mom forces a titter. Dad stares as his plate and eats and I want to shake him. This is his best friend's son. His dead best friend's son. He knows most of the people at this table are vultures as well as I do, and yet he hasn't even looked at Logan.

"You'll have to tune up Sadie's car before she leaves for...Madison." Mom can barely get it out. Hearing her say it out loud, to acknowledge my choice, is oddly satisfying though. It's like her inability to deny it makes it more real.

"Do you play any sports?" Dave continues his interrogation.

"Nope." Logan grins.

Uncle Dave's mouth opens and closes a few times. He doesn't know what to do with that. All of Cole's friends are like him, bound for college and filling their time with sports and clubs. He has no idea what else could fill up someone's life. It's so privileged it's kind of gross.

"Sadie is quite the soccer star," Dave finally gets out. "I'm sure you'll be too busy to come to her games this season but we'll all be there."

Logan clears his throat, the grin getting bigger. "Oh, no, I plan to be at every single one."

That's news to me and I turn to blink at him in question.

In front of my whole damn family Logan leans over and kisses my nose. "I've always got her back."

Is it possible to melt? I mean, I know it's not, but I just did.

"Behave at the table," mom snaps.

I pull away from him, a heated blush washing over my face. When I look up, I don't miss the look of fury on Cole's face. He'll probably find a way to punish me for this too, but for some reason I'm not as afraid of it as I was before. I can take him. I've survived before. It's evidence that I can survive it again.

The rest of dinner we stay quiet, letting Uncle Dave lecture the table about the value of drinking water on mental health and that there are too many chemicals and hormones in our food and it's going to ruin us all. It takes everything I have to ask him for evidence, studies, articles, from reliable, respected sources for this nonsense.

When we're done, I stand up to start clearing the table. James will do the dishes.

Logan joins me. "Let me help you, Sadiebaby."

Both my parents flinch. Hard enough that it rattles mom's silverware and when I look over her face is pale. I can't decipher her expression but it isn't one I've ever really seen before. She looks from Logan to me and then away. If I didn't know any better, I'd think she was holding a sob from the way her shoulders tense.

We keep clearing the table, taking trips from the dining room to the kitchen. Neither of us says anything but there's a charged tension between us as we both process their reaction to Logan calling me by my childhood nickname.

Without talking about it, we go outside and say goodbye.

Logan slides his fingers into my hair, cradling my head, massaging away the tightness at the base of my skull. I whimper slightly and let my head fall back, putting the weight of it in his hands.

"Don't make those noises," he groans, and kisses the tip of my chin.

"I'm sorry you got dragged to dinner instead of…you know…" I trail off and close my eyes.

"We're not in a rush, Sadie. It'll happen." Logan pulls me close and guides my head to rest on his chest. He speaks quietly into my ear. "For now, you'll have to fantasize about my curved dick some more and all the things I'm going to do to you. The devil is going to take you to heaven."

Abruptly, he pulls back, presses a lightning fast kiss to my lips, and then saunters away.

Whistling, toying with the chain that connects his wallet to his jeans.

It's so sexy and I don't understand why.

"Asshole," I mutter.

"I know," he tosses over his shoulder.

I watch him go, and I know he knows it. Logan might feel like we have time, but I don't. I'm leaving, and with soccer season starting I'm only going to get busier. This wasn't something I knew I wanted, let alone needed, and now it's as if time is slipping away from me like water through my fingers.

17

Sadie

The best day in March is here which is saying a lot since this month also includes my 18th birthday. It's Bluebird opening day.

Bluebird is an ice cream place that's been around since the 50's, and their recipes probably haven't changed much since then, including locally sourcing the ingredients for the ice cream. They're only open from spring to late fall, usually March to October. It's within walking distance of our house, and since I was 14 I've taken James on opening day.

For a few years we didn't go because before that...well, it was Brian taking us. Logan, me, and James. Rounding up the kids and getting them ice cream at 7:00 in the morning. It was a giggly, sleepy day and it was one of those things we did over and over and all the memories of it blur together until the memories stopped.

Then it was time for me to make the memories. To make them for James - an escape that we needed. It seems so silly but at the same time sometimes silly is the biggest release you can imagine. The thing that you need even if you're embarrassed to need it.

I sneak through the house in the dark and toward his room. Everyone should be sleeping. Mom doesn't keep track of the Bluebird opening to get in the way and stop us, and I know where to step in the house so she doesn't wake up. It's actually easier sneaking from the basement rather than my room upstairs.

It's odd but I'm starting to not think of it as my room anymore.

When they move out, I don't know if I'll be able to go back in there. Knowing that Cole slept in the bed that I used to call mine. That his essence lived in my space, invaded it, infected it. I'll never be able to lay down in it again and not think about the fact that his body rested there, too. Nope.

Given the fact that Uncle Dave and Julia don't seem to be in any rush to get out of our space, I'll probably be able to swing staying in the basement through to graduation, maybe even until I leave for camp in July.

What Mom doesn't know, only James does, is that I've tentatively accepted a place in pre-training camp over the summer. Players from a bunch of different schools converge to train before they're expected to report to their colleges and universities. It's a collective with a bunch of coaches to create more opportunities for women's sports. This year, it's being hosted in Madison. So I won't have to go far and I'll be in the place that I want to be. Everything I've worked for is finally falling into place.

I have to wait to sign the paperwork until I'm 18. Then Mom can't stop me.

When I walk into his room James throws off his blankets, already dressed and ready to go. I smother a laugh. We tiptoe out and through the dining room and kitchen to the backdoor. I've already got our outergear and shoes waiting. It's still freezing in the morning and we've got a two hour wait.

At least it's only a 10 minute walk.

James holds open the storm door while I very, very slowly close the main door until I hear it click shut. We move the storm door just as gently.

We don't talk as we walk down the block, make the turn, and keep going up the street that will take us right to Bluebird. We could probably walk there with our eyes shut.

It's the opposite direction of where I go on my walks, so it keeps the experience of this walk fresh even if it's a lifetime of familiar.

James keeps his head up, looking around, watching for every bird sound, eyes flicking to the windows that already have their lights on, starting the day. He's almost taller than me now - so close that it'll happen officially any day now. It doesn't matter how tall he is though, he's still my little brother and he still needs me to protect him.

It's sad how much of a release this is. How much we had to do to keep it a secret so that no one would stop us. It's one of the most innocent things I can think of, and yet we had to act like spies in our own house. We didn't leave, we escaped.

The line has already formed when Bluebird is in sight, and we end up taking a seat on the sidewalk - we'll probably be the 20th people served this morning. The lights are already on inside, the opening day workers moving around and getting everything ready. The people at the front have been here since the night before, ready to get their picture on the First Serve of the Year wall. I'll do that someday.

I lay down and put my head on James's leg. He doesn't care.

He starts telling me all the stats of his volleyball team, everything about the other players, and what he's hoping for next year during his first high school season. Anyone who doesn't think boys have complex internal lives and know just as much gossip about each other as girls is in denial. James knows everything about every guy on the team. I think he's also just one of those people that people tell things - he's got a face and a presence that makes him feel trustworthy.

"But then Brett started dating Kyle's ex-girlfriend Katie and he spiked a ball right in his face and it was like hey I made you bleed because you're dating the girl that broke my heart and now we're cool."

"Did Katie really break his heart though? Kyle doesn't seem bothered."

James snorts. "That's because his mom hated her because no one is good enough for her baby boy."

"Mmm," I answer, the sky starting to get lighter, the line longer. My stomach grumbling with hunger. "Why'd they break up?"

James laughs. "She told him he smelled. Frequently. He takes a shower like the water is out to get him so I'm kind of not surprised."

"Can I say I'm glad you're only a semi-disgusting teenage boy?"

"You have no idea how disgusting I am."

I sit up and push him, and he cackles and falls over.

"What's so funny?"

I flinch, and turn to see Cole walking toward us. He's got major bedhead, dark jeans, a Holy Angel Football hoodie, and his winter jacket. Cole looks like the high school god he thinks he is, and he's got a smile on his face with the kind of confidence that he thinks I think so too. I want to kick him in the balls from this angle. I'd get a lot of power behind that kick.

"Nothing," James answers, sitting up abruptly and moving so that he's between Cole and I. My perfect, precious little brother.

"Sure, kid." I grit my teeth at Cole's answer because I've told him before that neither James or I appreciate that nickname. It's like he thinks James being younger than us means he doesn't matter. Cole never cared about the things that mattered to me if they didn't benefit him in some way and it took me a really long time to see it.

Cole ignores our body language and silence and sits down next to us. There's some grumblings about line skipping but since Cole is acting like we were waiting for him, they stop quickly.

"I didn't even check if you were home, I knew you'd be out for Bluebird day." He grins at me, and shifts slightly closer.

"It's kind of a me and James thing so…"

"We're all family now, right cuz?" Cole turns the grin at James and gives him a light punch in the shoulder. "I should be part of a family tradition."

"It's not our family," James mumbles, all the energy crackling out of him as fury at Cole. "It's the Kurowskis. We do this for Brian."

Cole blanches and I have to admit seeing the guilty expression on his face is almost worth his presence. Though it is shocking he's capable of feeling guilty at all.

"I didn't know that."

"Brian used to take us. Every year. Since before I was even born. It was just Sadie and Logan at first." James is glaring at Cole now, and it's brilliant to watch. "And when I came along and got older they didn't leave me out. Think about that though, right cuz? That Sadie and Logan go back their whole lives. No wonder the guy next door is perfect for her." James ends his little rant with a fake, polite smile as he sees Cole try not to frown.

Before anyone can say anything else, a foghorn blows to wake the crowd. It's opening time. James and Cole both offer me their hands to help me stand up, but of course I take my brother's. I want to take Cole's and pull some kind of fancy wrestling move where I throw him over my shoulder but I don't know how. Briefly it crosses my mind that Logan probably does and he could teach me.

Except then I think about another kind of wrestling I could do with Logan and a quick shiver goes through me.

Cole puts his arm around me. "You cold, baby?"

"Ew, we're family, I'm your cousin," I say loud and exaggerated, stepping out from under his arm. I hook elbows with James and we turn, putting Cole at our backs until we get to the front of the surprisingly speedy line.

Behind us, Cole starts holding court. Greeting other Holy Angel students and their parents, teachers, even alums who act as boosters for the sports teams. The only slight sympathy I have for Cole is the way everyone acts as if they are responsible for his success. Like he owes them something for getting into Notre Dame.

It's the same way mom thinks that I owe her; only I'm not repaying her in the way that she wants.

The pressure gets to Cole. Not that it's any excuse for what an absolute dick he is.

James and I keep walking forward and Cole keeps "accidentally" bumping into me, brushing his body or his arm against me. Part of me wishes that I'd thought to ask Logan, but I need to learn to assert myself with Cole.

And it could be painful for Logan and I don't want that.

We get to the window and one of the owners is working the register. Jeanie has been working here since she was a kid and now her own kids work here too. She smiles at me, recognition but not quite knowing, a semi-familiar face in a swarm of semi-familiar faces. Everyone comes here.

"Two small flavor of the day cones, please," James orders for us. The opening flavor is always dreamsicle and always delicious. The flavor is exactly the same every year. There's value and comfort in that kind of consistency. When you make a thing well, make it like that over and over again. Don't mess with perfect.

We pay and wait.

I'm trying to figure out how to ditch Cole when he makes it easy for me. After he orders, he's called over by people further back in line and goes over to talk to them.

When our order is up I run to the window before they can call it. A guy I kind of know looks surprised as I rush up to him and grab our cones.

"Have a nice day?"

"Thanks, Jesse," I give him a tight smile.

We might've ordered smalls, but a small at Bluebird is a swirl of soft-serve five inches above the rim of the cone. James takes his and reads my mind as we hustle around the corner of the tiny shop and take the long way home. Cole won't see us and won't think to go that way.

His order of a root beer float is shouted out behind us and we walk faster. When we turn the next corner we both slow down to a mosey and eat our ice cream.

"You okay?" James asks. He knows I won't elaborate on anything, but wants to check in. Someday when he's older, we'll talk about it all. Right now we're both white knuckling it through living in our house. He'll be alone next year. It breaks my heart to think about, but he's strong enough to handle it.

"Yeah. More annoyed than anything."

We walk as slow as possible. We don't want to go home. For all we know everyone is still sleeping since it's barely 7:30 AM. Still, the feeling of our house is so heavy that the closer we get the more we feel it.

The quality of our silence changes. Instead of comfort and companionship it's fear of being overheard. Of being caught smiling or laughing and being interrogated about what was so funny, what was that for, why are you feeling emotions. It's psychologically exhausting.

We finish our ice cream just as we reach the back door. I can hear mom moving around, but beckon James down to my room. We leave our coats and stuff on the floor and lay down next to each other in my bed and try to get some more sleep. Maybe she'll think we stayed like this and won't realize we went to Bluebird. Maybe...

"Sadie Braverman get up here right now! And bring your brother!" Mom's intense and furious shout shocks James and I out of sleep, both of us jumping up like a fire alarm went off.

Crap.

"Don't," I warn James. "Just go into your room while she's yelling at me."

"But-"

"No. This is on me, she's only mad at me. Don't get pulled into this."

"Sadie." He gets up and stands, crossing his arms like he thinks he can stop me. He might be taller but I've got years of maneuvering on him.

Mom screams my name again, getting more shrill.

I don't say anything else to James, I turn and walk through the downstairs. I expect to see mom waiting for me, but she isn't. I glance behind me before heading up, and I'm relieved to see that James didn't follow me. My heart aches at the thought that I won't be able to protect him next year, and that she'll have no choice but to make him the center of her attention and ire. I don't know how to protect him from her when I'm not literally here to do it.

I walk up the stairs, ready for my verbal execution.

It's only mom standing in the dining room. Her cheeks are red and her eyes are narrowed, and I know I'm really in for it. She's standing extra still like if she didn't force it, she would fly apart. The skin on my cheek pulses with the memory of the last time she slapped me and I have a feeling I'm in for that again.

"Sadie, did you go to the opening of Bluebird this morning?"

"Yes."

"Was Cole there?"

I frown because that's not where I thought this line of questioning was going, and her glare deepens in response.

"Yes?"

"Is that an answer?"

"Yes, he was there."

"And you left without him?"

Now I'm even more confused. "He didn't come with us and he was talking to his friends."

"So you left him there? Sadie," she admonishes, so good at making my name sound like a curse.

"What? I don't get what the big deal is. He's 18 years old, it's not like I needed to hold his hand to walk him home like a kid. It's something I do with James. He wasn't invited."

Mom swells up and I know I said the wrong thing. "Cole is a guest in our house and you will invite him to everything. You will make him feel welcome and comfortable. What you did was rude, Sadie." She takes steps closer and gets up in my face. "You're being petty and childish. Cole is family and you will treat him that way."

"No."

We're both shocked when I say it.

"He might be family by marriage," I continue, my voice shaking, "but that doesn't mean he gets to invade my life. He's done enough of that already."

Mom's eyes widen at the venom in my voice, and there's a question in her eyes that I know she won't ask. She never asked why we broke up, only expressed her disappointment. There was no way she didn't notice the bruises. Or the blood. She's choosing ignorance, and it's almost enough to make me want to throw it all in her face.

Except then I'm giving her a weapon to use against me, so I push it all back down and away. It's not worth it to tell her the truth.

"It's a tradition that's just me and James." I take a few steps back from her. "I wouldn't invite you to go, either." It's probably the mouthiest thing I've ever said to her, and before she can answer I turn on my heel and start walking back toward the basement.

"Sadie. Sadie!" Mom calls my name but I ignore her and she doesn't come after me. For once I stood my ground, and I know that's an inevitable punishment, but in this moment it feels like a huge relief.

I said more than I should have, but nothing that revealed any of the truths I'm hiding so carefully. Mom worked hard to get me back together with Cole, especially when he was calling the house and kissing her ass, sending me flowers, and I refused to talk to or about him. What was I going to do, show her the bruises on my stomach and my wrists? She wouldn't have believed me even with the evidence right in front of her face.

Or she would've taken the church-wife stance that he's sorry and he won't do it again. That forgiveness is a virtue and I should try to practice it. Next thing I knew I would've been talking to a priest about my sex life, and probably told that I deserved it for not waiting until marriage.

It got worse after Dave and Julia's wedding. When Cole did it again and I was too frozen to fight back or try to stop him. When all the parents saw was a couple they wanted back together sneaking off for alone time. They were too far to see how hard he was holding onto me, or the way I tried to pull back before giving up. They didn't see his hands digging into my neck while he forced my face to his, and smashed his lips so hard against mine that my teeth cut into the flesh and I was raped with the taste of my own blood in my mouth.

Then I had to listen for weeks as mom smiled and teased that Cole and I were getting back together. All I gave her in return was silence. The smiling and teasing stopped, the harsh questioning started, and all I said was that we weren't getting back together. She made it clear that was my fault.

James is sitting on the bed when I get back downstairs, and he reads the hollow look on my face. I'm sure he snuck up and listened, so he knows what she's mad about.

He stands and pulls back my covers, and then tucks me in like he's the older sibling.

"I'm gonna watch TV. I'm right out there. You're safe."

I nod at him and he walks out. I don't move, barely breathe, until I hear the subtle sounds of some sitcom from the TV in the next room. My eyes close, everything heavy. It's the first time in weeks I feel free enough to sleep.

18

Logan

The shop is on the slower side today, so Linc and I have been trusted with replacing the timing belt on an ancient Toyota. This thing will run until the body falls apart if the maintenance is good, and the owner takes good care of it. We're both elbows deep in car hood, carefully removing the worn out belt.

Tori, the eldest Anderson, is sitting in an old lawn chair flipping through a magazine. When she came in this morning, she turned down the music and took a seat. That was over an hour ago and she hasn't said a word. It's made Linc and I quiet too, because Tori is clearly building up to something.

"Your mom home this week?" Tori throws out the question without moving, still casually flipping one page at a time as if she never said anything at all.

"No." I exchange a what-is-this look with Linc, and he shrugs. Liar.

"Where is she?"

"Dunno."

Tori slaps her magazine closed and leans forward. "That's fucked up, Logan."

"Okay." I turn away and blow her off, getting back to work.

Tori stands up and walks over, reaching up. "So help me God I will slam this hood on both your heads."

"You're an atheist, he wouldn't help you," Linc says with complete sincerity. Tori glares at him.

"Stop," she snaps.

I do what she says and pull out from under the hood, standing up to my full height and looking down at her. I've got about six inches on her but that doesn't phase Tori at all. She has never hesitated to speak her mind, or verbally whip us within an inch of our lives. This time though, I don't care. I don't want to hear it. I am not taking her opinion into account regarding decisions I've already made.

"I finished the apartment this week."

I rear back because that's not what I was expecting her to say. Tori graduated two years ago and got certified in bookkeeping so she can help her dad with the shop. In her spare time, she was the one who cleaned up the apartment above the shop and was getting it to the point of being inhabitable for Linc and I, but that wasn't supposed to happen until the end of June.

"I called in a favor and got everything installed. New floor, new carpet. The fridge gets delivered next week and then all we have to do is switch the utilities into your names."

The smile on her face is all gloat and pride, and I almost feel bad to wipe it off her.

"No."

I take a step back and she grabs my arm.

"You should be with your family. You shouldn't keep letting her get away with treating you so badly."

"She doesn't treat me badly," I defend automatically. "She doesn't treat me like anything. I need to see this through, Tori."

"Why? You could move out and it would probably take her weeks to notice."

I throw down the tool I was using on a bench and walk farther away. I need space for this conversation. I do love the Andersons, and Walker and Maggie encourage me to make my own choices, but when any one of them surrounds you it's kind of hard to say no to whatever it is they're suggesting.

"Because I finish what I started. Her obligation to me ends when I graduate high school. I have to...I just have to."

"But why?"

"Fuck off, T," Linc steps in. "It's his choice and you're being a shitty friend pushing him when he's not comfortable."

"No, that's me being a good friend." She flips her brother off and focuses on me again. "Not to mention, Sadie Braverman? What the hell?"

I whirl on Linc. "Did you tell her?"

"Yeah, of course I did."

"Because I'm his actual best friend," Tori snipes and sticks out her tongue at me. It's a jibe we've been making at each other since the first time Lincoln brought me home like a lost puppy.

"The hell, man? I trusted you."

"You trust me, too." Tori throws her hands up in the air. I do trust Tori, but I don't trust her to keep her opinion to herself. That might be something she's incapable of doing.

The car catches me when I lean back, and I cross my arms over my chest. "Have at it. Lecture me. Tell me I'm wrong."

Tori opens and closes her mouth a few times, caught off guard that I'm just going to take it, but also angry that I'm already blowing off whatever it is she's going to say. Sometimes we get along because we're similar in the fact that we're going to do what we think is right, regardless of how other people see it. That doesn't work out well when we're on opposite sides of the action.

Tori sighs and then drops her arms in defeat. "Her dad abandoned you, what makes you think she won't?"

It takes all I have not to flinch. My teeth are clenched when I answer her. "Sadie is not her father. Just like I am not my father."

It's Tori's turn to flinch but she continues.

"How can she ask for something from you, knowing what her family did to yours? How can she take more from you?"

Before I answer, I take a deep breath. I'm about to say something out loud I've barely let myself think, and it is a factor that impacts all of this for me. "I don't think she knows."

"What?" Linc is the one who stands up in shock. "About...anything?"

"No. Her parents have always been overprotective and there are... similarities between her and my dad. I think they were afraid if she knew too much it would give her ideas."

"What the fuck," Linc whispers.

Tori nods, digesting that. "I don't want another person to hurt you or...leave...you." Tori blushes with embarrassment that she's pointing this out to me. Pointing out the inevitable end of me and Sadie. Despite the fact that she's got the red hair and pale skin of the rest of her family, Tori doesn't blush. Not like Janet and Lincoln do.

To her confusion, I laugh.

"It's part of the plan." Because it is. I'm getting what I can right now, taking in all of Sadie that she'll give, feeding that empty place inside me only she touches. I won't keep her longer than she needs, and I would never do anything to interfere with her dreams. Sadie's going to go and it's going to be bittersweet, but utterly worth it.

Tori still looks confused so I continue.

"I know she's going to leave. It's okay. I never thought I'd even get this chance...I never thought she saw me." It's my turn to blush and look away because more came out than I intended. Still, it's true that I never understood that Sadie trusted me. Hearing her say it was as surprising as it was humbling. Seeing the darkness inside her, the hint of her sexual nature I got the other day, seeing her corrupt her good rules and good behavior to do things with me...it was more fulfilling than I have words to describe. Sadie lets go of the constraints with me.

"You know we're always there for you," Tori says quietly. That's as close as she's going to come to saying she was wrong, now that she has more perspective on the thing with me and Sadie. Tori is a secret romantic, single most of the time not because she isn't interested but because her standards are high. The fact that I'm willingly hurting myself for love appeals to her.

"I know," I nod. "Right now, I've got to be there for her."

Linc frowns. "What's going on?" He knows me too well, heard the thing in my voice that I'm trying to keep down.

I shake my head. "That's her business. My dad..." I swallow thickly. I don't talk about him often. Not because I'm angry or ashamed, but protective. My memories are mine and sometimes sharing them feels like giving them away. "He always told me to do good and trust my gut. My gut is telling me that she needs me. And I need her."

"Ugh, fine." Tori throws up her hands. It tells me she's not going to give me anymore shit about me and Sadie, which is good, because if anything weird happens I'm going to need her advise.

Before any of us can say anything else, Walker comes into the shop. "Am I paying you all to stand around?"

"I'm not on the clock," Tori sings, and then goes back to her lawn chair.

Walker tries to smother his smile. "Get back to work, I need that belt changed by the end of the day."

"We got it," I confirm.

Linc and I duck back under the hood. He looks sideways at his sister who is fully absorbed back in her magazine, or at least appearing to do a good job of making us believe it.

"You good?"

"I'm good."

"Do we need to fuck with her?" Linc loves nothing more than pranking Tori, despite the fact that they are friends in addition to siblings. She overreacts and it makes it extra hilarious.

"I mean, yeah, but not for this."

"Got it." We get back to work.

19

Sadie

I'm tired.

I thought I knew what tired was, but I don't.

The night Bluebird opened, Cole came down to my room after I got ready for bed. He kept trying to talk to me, apologize for "siccing my mom on me" about ditching him, kept trying to hug me. I stayed silent and pushed him back every time he tried to come close. Eventually, he left, but I spent most of the night sitting up in bed, drifting off and then jolting awake in panic, my heart racing.

It's been like that almost every night since. They've been living with us for over a month but that was the first time Cole came down to my bedroom. He's settled in and getting comfortable now, which means it's more dangerous. Now he knows the house better, knows what he can and can't get away with. Knows when I'm vulnerable.

I haven't gotten really good sleep since before they moved in, but it's been three days now since I felt like I got any real rest at all.

To make matters worse, it's my birthday. The fact that it's on a Tuesday is kind of nice because it means I won't get dragged out to anything because it's a school day. I'll be forced to be with my family for a minimal period of time.

When I finally drag myself upstairs, there's a giant plate of pancakes on the dining table. A short stack is in front of my usual chair with whip cream and 1 and 8 candles on top. Julia comes forward and lights them. Everyone else is already sitting and waiting for me. There's a stack of presents, too.

"Happy Birthday!" Dad gives me a big smile. Mom's is much tighter.

"Make a wish and let's eat, don't want you to be late for school," Mom says. No actual happy birthday from her despite the fact that she did all the work to make this happen. It's for appearances, ultimately, and I don't think she would've done it if Dave wasn't here. For someone reason she loves looking like super mom around him.

I sit down and stare at the lit candles, the white wax melting down the numbers. Eighteen is so arbitrary, and not much will change for me until I graduate high school, but it should feel more significant than it does right now.

"Come on, Sadie," Mom prods, somehow speaking through that strained smile.

"First thing that comes to mind," Uncle Dave prompts.

What my wishes should be: that I escape my mom, that James is okay, that what Cole did to me could be erased from time.

What flashes through my head as I lean forward and blow out the candles: *I wish I could keep Logan.*

The thought stuns me and I sit silently for a second, absorbing, before I snap into action and remove the candles. I mechanically eat my pancakes, not really tasting them, lost in thought.

Mom takes my plate away before I'm finished and shoves the pile of presents at me.

By chance I open Dave and Julia's first, and it's actually really thoughtful - they got me a new Edgar's Bluff gym bag for the upcoming soccer season. It surprises me how much I mean it when I say thank you, and that Julia's returning smile is just as genuine. It makes me wonder again what she knows about her son.

James got me a book I'd asked for, and mom frowns at the illustrated cover with elves and trees. There's a ton of books in this series and I love every silly dramatic cover with brave heroes inside who try and save their world. It's a nice escape.

Mom and Dad give me an unsurprisingly generic card and a gift card to the local sporting goods store. More ways to stock myself up for the season without them having to be overly involved. Dad probably didn't even know what they were getting me until I opened it right now.

There's one gift left and dread pools in my stomach when I see that it's from Cole. I assumed it was from my parents since the card was sitting on top of it but when I glance at the label, I see his name below mine. He's grinning at me from across the table and there's a hint of something sinister there.

It's wrapped in red metallic paper, and it's soft and squishy. When I tear it away, because there's no way in hell I could reject his gift in front of my mother, the paper releases the scent of him right into my face. My hands move on their own as my body starts to panic and freeze, tearing the paper away as if I'm moving in slow motion.

It's a black Holy Angel football hoodie.

It was my favorite. I stole it from him all the time. When I was at his house, I was wearing that hoodie. Sometimes only that hoodie. I even took it home a few times and slept in it or snuggling it. Back when it felt like being apart from him was painful, when I had the innocent thoughts of what it would be like to sleep beside him all night, curled into his side, cozy and warm.

I was wearing it the first time he touched me even though I'd said no.

I wore it home that night to cover the bruises he left on me.

Cole's smile gets bigger and darker.

"I know it was your favorite."

Abruptly, I stand and leave the dining room. Mom and Dad both call after me, the tones of their voices polar opposites. Mom is angry, Dad is concerned, and I hear her stop James from coming after me.

At the backdoor I grab my coat and backpack and leave. It's a long walk to school but I need to move. I need to walk. I should get there right before the first bell rings and won't be late for class.

It's like I'm looking at myself outside of my own body. Knocked out of it by having to relive the first time I was assaulted in front of not only the person who did but also my entire family. I had one ally in that room and that wasn't enough to save me.

With each step, I take a deep breath, inhaling cold air. I make myself feel the cold in my chest. The cold on the tips of my uncovered fingers. The pressure of my backpack straps on my shoulders. I make myself listen to the thump of my shoes on the sidewalk. Listen for the hiss and grumble of cars driving past me. I smell the sidewalk, the perpetual damp of spring, the dirt and the petrichor. I taste the last remnants of maple syrup in my mouth.

"Sadie!" A familiar voice stops me in my tracks, and I look to see a car pulled over next to me. Logan looks out the passenger window, concern on his face. Ethan is at the wheel, their friend Henry in the backseat of the shiny two door. The car looks fast, but I don't know enough to know what kind it is.

"You want a ride?"

I can only nod.

Logan steps out of the car and pulls the seat up, waving Henry out. He climbs in the back and reaches out for me. Mechanically, I move, and instead of sitting behind the passenger seat I slide to the middle and press myself up against him. I'm so relieved when Logan responds by putting his arm around me and keeping me close.

Once Henry is back in the car, Ethan looks at us in the rear view mirror, characteristic snarl on his face.

"No fucking in my backseat."

"A general rule or because you're saving the first time for yourself?" I mutter.

Logan snickers and Ethan raises an eyebrow before he shifts and drives off.

"I've fucked back there," he mutters, defensive.

"Your hand doesn't count." I squeeze Logan's thigh, distracting myself from my spiral by messing with his friend. Logan's jaw flexes as he tries not to laugh.

Ethan glowers the rest of the drive, but when we get out of the car he gives me a nod. Ethan might talk a lot of shit and kind of hate everyone, but he respects people who hold their own and don't take him seriously. We had a few classes together and I know he's smart, he's just perpetually angry. It's tempting to ask Logan why, but at the end of the day it's not my business.

Logan stays with me as I walk toward my locker, and I'm here a little earlier than usual.

"You good?" He stops me with a tug on my hand, and pulls me to the side of the hall to make me look at him. "Everything alright?"

"Everything is alright...now." Now that I'm with him.

"On that note then, happy birthday Sadiebaby." Logan leans forward and kisses my nose. "Got a present for you and everything."

"Taking this boyfriend role seriously," I try to brush it off, thinking of my wish.

"Dead serious," Logan answers, and his expression matches his words. I never know what to do with him, and it's the kind of scary that feels good.

I roll my eyes and move back into the stream of people in the hallway, tugging him with me. The amount of looks we get - two very opposite people also clearly dating - is kind of amusing. I never knew people would pay attention to who I dated.

Or maybe I did and it's why I was so secretive about me and Cole.

Everyone wants to know if the good girl puts out. It's a weird, sexist fascination, but when I have a reputation of being uptight I can see why it's interesting to see me cut loose. It must be especially titillating for them because it's Logan, who has his own reputation. His is a lot sexier than mine, though.

We turn the corner and there are my friends - Darcy, Amelia, Layla, and Chloe are all decorating my locker. There's a poster that says "Happy 18th!" and they taped balloons and streamers to the door and wall above it. It's exactly what I wanted, and exactly what I did for them on their birthdays. I'm the youngest of our friends and the last one to turn 18 - I didn't think they'd do this for me.

I should be smiling, but instead, I burst into tears.

Darcy starts toward me, but Logan pulls me away. "I got her."

He does. He really, really does.

I can't see through my tears but he pulls me into a room and closes the door. When I lift my head I see it's one of the small study halls for honor students. No one is there.

Logan pulls me into his chest and holds me there, running his fingers through my hair as I try and pull it back together.

"What's the matter baby girl?" he whispers and then kisses the top of my head. "What do you need?"

"I don't know." I sniff and tilt my head back to look at him. Logan lets me go but before I can move away he's reaching up and using the sleeves of his sweatshirt to wipe the tears off my cheeks. It's soft and tender and I can watch his face while he works, the concentration and restraint making his jawline even sharper.

"I can't talk about it or I won't make it through school."

Logan stops wiping my face and meets my eyes. "Fuck school. You want to go? I'll get Ethan's keys and we'll fuck off for the day."

"No. It's not worth…the consequences. As nice as it would be."

Logan nods. "You change your mind, you find me. Promise?"

"Promise." It slips through my lips so easily, and I mean it, because I know he means it too.

Before I can say anything else, Logan cradles my face and slides his mouth over mine. I lean back into the wall, my backpack in the way, but I'm steady enough that I can lean my head back and let him ravish me. Even at his most desperate, even at the peak of me wanting him, Cole's kisses never felt like this.

With Logan, I feel connected. I part my lips and slide my tongue along his, and it's as if we meld into one being. Pleasure slides back and forth between us, and I pull him harder into me. Close but not close enough. My mind whirls and I slide my hands under his clothes until I reach skin, and we both moan into each other's mouths. Him reacting to my touch, me reacting to the warmth of his smooth skin.

Logan breaks the kiss and he's breathing hard. I drive him wild in a way that still feels safe. Logan won't take.

"I want to touch you."

I nod, breathing just as hard.

"I'm going to make you cum for me, and I'm going to spend the rest of the day with my fingers smelling like your pussy."

"Okay," is all I can manage to say. I start unbuttoning my jeans and Logan's grin is pure devil.

He wraps his hand around my hair and tilts my head back again. His warm, rough hand slides along my stomach before dropping low, straight beneath my underwear. Logan groans when he slides along my trimmed hair and down to my core. I can feel my pulse beating in my clit.

"I want you to spend the rest of the day uncomfortable in your soaked panties. Every time you squirm in your seat, you'll think of me."

"I think of you anyway," I blurt out as his skilled fingers part my lips and slide over my clit. It's as if he's watched me touch myself, the way he puts a finger on either side and pinches slightly, moving up and down. The pressure of him touching me, the reality that Logan Kurowski, bad boy neighbor, is the one touching me, basically makes my brain melt. I'm just nerves and feelings right now.

"Fucking right you do." He leans down and sucks my bottom lip into his mouth, his teeth grazing the sensitive inner flesh. I whimper into his mouth and cling to him, my hips rolling with the pace he's setting.

"You're mine Sadie. Say it."

"I'm yours, Logan."

His eyes flutter closed in ecstasy when I say his name with raw desire clear in my voice. When he opens them and looks at me, I'm stunned at the fire in his.

"Perfect Sadie, secretly dirty," he whispers as his movements get rougher, getting me closer to the edge. "You ever orgasm at school before?" I shake my head no. I've never even kissed anyone at school until him. "I'm going to make you cum right here, right now, one step closer to being my fallen angel, Sadiebaby."

He leans closer so his breath hits my neck as he whispers into my ear. "You going to let me fuck you at school, Sadie? Cum on my cock while I smother your screams so I don't ruin your good girl reputation?"

I moan, and turn my head to bite into his neck.

Logan groans, low and loud, and I can feel my body pulsing.

"Mark me, Sadiebaby. Mark me with your orgasm."

I cum, moaning into the skin of his neck, biting and sucking so that I stay quiet. My hips roll against his hand, and he keeps going and going. I don't know how his fingers aren't aching from holding the same position for so long.

I unlatch myself from his neck and slump against the wall. When I look at him, there's a darkening mark on his throat. From me.

Everyone knows we're dating, and everyone is going to see that. They're going to know I did it.

Logan slides his hand out of my jeans, his other still buried in my hair. He controls my head so I look at him as he takes a deep breath with his fingers on his lips. I'm mesmerized when I watch him lick them.

"I gave you a hickey."

"I know," he grins. "I love it."

"Everyone's going to know."

The grin gets bigger. "I know. They'll know sweet Sadie likes to bite." He kisses the tip of my nose and straightens me up, buttoning and zipping my jeans, running his fingers through my hair so it's less disheveled.

"I told you I'd corrupt you. Now everyone else knows it too."

Logan takes my hand and leads me out of the study room. He lets me go and flicks his head toward my waiting friends. Before I turn away, he blows me a kiss, using the hand that was just down my pants.

I'm in daze the rest of the day, and I don't regret it at all.

20

Sadie

At the end of the day, Darcy catches me by my locker before we head home. She hands me a gift bag with a huge green bow on top.

"Happy Birthday," she smiles, but it doesn't stay. Darcy is worried, and there's not a lot I can do to fix it right now. It makes me feel guilty regardless.

I paw through the bag and there's a travel mug for the Bronze Cabin and a $20 gift card. I don't know when I'll get to use it since I don't have a car and mom is hardcore about not letting me have coffee but it's nice all the same. Then again, mom doesn't know about all the coffee I drink now and won't be able to stop me once I leave.

It's sad that one of my current dreams is to drink as much coffee as I want when I want. To not have everything I do questioned, criticized, controlled.

Logan might think he's corrupting me but my real descent into hell is going to be paved with coffee cups.

"Thanks," I force my own smile and hug her.

She squeezes hard. "What's going on, Sadie?"

I sigh and lean against her. "Cole sucks and Logan is awesome. And I'm not sleeping. I'm so tired."

"Seriously, stay at my place this weekend. Please."

We pull back from our hug and she looks into my face, her eyes lingering on the dark rings beneath my eyes and the map of red veins in the whites.

"I don't know. I don't want to start another fight with my mom."

"Okay," she nods sadly, then gets a sly grin on her face. "So Logan is awesome?"

I bury my face in my shoulder because I can't meet her eyes. "We messed around in an empty study hall this morning."

Darcy laughs so loud people look at us. "Good. Your bad girl needs to come out."

"That's what he says. That he's going to corrupt me."

"Excellent." Darcy rubs her hands together.

"It is kinda hot."

"In Sadie speak that's extremely hot." Darcy hooks her arm through mine and we start walking to her car. She's giving me a ride home, and I hope Logan realizes that he doesn't need to wait for me.

When Darcy parks in my driveway, she locks the doors again before I can get out.

"I will drive off into the sunset right now if you need me to," she offers. "You don't have to go home, Sadie."

"Yeah, I do. But you're the best for offering."

She nods but I can tell she doesn't want to listen.

We've been friends a long time, and close enough that she saw my mom's descent into being more and more controlling. The better I did in school, the more motivated I was to be in activities and sports, the more she demanded of me. The more I had to perform to her ever-increasing standards.

It was like once she realized that people thought more of her when I was successful, it was addictive. The more credit they gave her for my achievements, the more she needed to feel good about herself.

It's not like mom wasn't accomplished on her own, but then again with a brother like Dave I can imagine he downplayed all of her successes just like he does with mine. The jerk would be so offended to be accused of being sexist and a misogynist, but I see the way he's brushed off my mom, and the way he always counters anything I've done with "well Cole" and that's not even his kid. He's only known Cole for a few years, and not long enough to have influenced his accomplishments.

But Cole is male, and therefore has more value.

It took a few years before I broke down crying in front of Darcy when we were studying for a science test together in 8th grade and I had so much anxiety about not getting a perfect grade that I snapped. I was sobbing on the floor of her bedroom so loudly that her parents came to check on me.

I didn't tell them much, but enough that they exchanged concerned glances and wanted to call my dad.

It took a lot of begging to stop them. I'm still not sure how I did, but it was after that Darcy told me any day, any time, any reason, her parents would come get me and I could stay over. It's not that I didn't have other extended family but things were weird with them sometimes. Darcy and her parents were my family in ways that mattered - like knowing that I'd be cared for and respected. Why was it everyone but my own family that looked after me?

"I know we don't say this a lot but like, I love you." Darcy stares me down until I nod that I believe her and say it back.

"I love you, too."

She waits until I turn the corner of the house before backing out and driving away. At the door, I pause and look over at Logan's house. His mom's car is there, but there's no sign that he's around. I'm not sure what I'd do even if he was, but it would make me feel better to know I could reach him easily if I needed. He's probably working at the garage right now.

I don't say anything when I get inside, and head straight down to the basement. James has volleyball practice so he isn't home, and I don't care to know who else is in the house or let them know that I'm here either.

I put on the radio, get out my homework, and focus on what's in front of me.

I'm so deep into my calculus that I don't realize anyone came into the room until I feel a tap on my shoulder and let out a scream.

"Whoa!" Cole steps back and holds up his hands. "Sorry. Your mom sent me to get you for dinner."

"Great. I'll be there in a minute." I turn away from him and pretend that I'm finishing the problem I was working on, but I can feel that he hasn't moved away. "Did you need something else?"

"Why'd you freak out when you opened your present?"

I keep pretending to work and force my voice to stay blase. "I don't know what you're talking about."

"Sure," he huffs. "What's your problem, Sadie? What did I ever do to you?"

The rage that blurs my vision is breathtaking, and an uncontrollable gasp bursts out of me like his words physically struck me.

"Leave." It's the only thing I can say that won't become threats of murder, or allegations that I don't want my family to hear. That I don't want them to pick apart and interrogate. Keeping my secrets keeps me safe, not only from Cole, but from them, too. The damage they could do if they don't believe me might be worse than what originally happened.

I can survive Cole. I am surviving Cole. Partially because I know there's an escape coming and that I control what's happened to me and how I respond to it.

Once they know, my control is gone. My ability to feel whatever

I want to feel will be compromised by them shoving their thoughts and opinions down my throat. The way I know mom will hold me hostage to make peace with Cole and forgive him for something he doesn't deserve my forgiveness for.

The priest we used to have at St. Stan's after Father Magnus left, Father Francis, he once gave a homily on forgiveness and emphasized that it's not permission for someone to hurt you again, but permission for you to stop blaming yourself for being hurt. He said that forgiveness is more about the forgiver - what are you willing to let go of, and does letting go of it serve your purpose for the Lord?

I'm not in a place where forgiving Cole will serve me, and it definitely won't serve any deity that I'm no longer sure I believe in, even though I sit and stand and respond every single Sunday like I do. Even when I sing praises to a God who doesn't seem to be listening to me anymore.

Father Francis got some shit for that sermon, but it's one of the best I've ever heard, and I've been dragged to a lot of mass in my time.

"Sadie."

I grip my mechanical pencil so hard that the plastic crushes in my palm and I can feel a piece of it dig into my skin. "Get. Out."

"I just tried to give you my sweatshirt," he grumbles, but he's moving away so I don't say anything else. When I hear his footsteps on the stairs, I open my hand. There's multiple pieces of plastic mixed in with the skinny broken pencil lead, and a piece of plastic is sticking out of my skin.

I pull it out and the blood wells quickly.

I'm alive.

I'm alive and I'm breathing and I'm trying.

Cole hasn't broken me, or stopped me. He's not going to break me. I'm going to be fine.

I wash my hand in the bathroom and band-aid a wad of tissue onto the gouge in my palm since the band-aid by itself wouldn't stay. Now that the adrenaline is leaving my system, my stomach hurts and my hand is throbbing because I can feel the pain now.

Everyone is already at the table, their plates full and ready to eat, by the time I get upstairs.

"Nice of you to join us," Dave says, giving me a reprimanding look.

"I cut my hand." I hold it up as my excuse.

"Hmm," with a frown is his response. "Sit down, we need to say grace."

I do what I'm told and bow my head as he prays over our meal. It's my favorite pork chops and mashed potatoes. A birthday dinner that doesn't feel like a birthday dinner at all because it's not really for me.

Dave finishes and everyone starts eating, the adults talking, but I'm staring at my blank plate thinking about how much I don't want to be here. In this moment even staying for James isn't enough.

"Aren't you going to eat? It's your favorite," Dad's voice breaks in.

"I'm not hungry."

"Eat, Sadie," Mom directs me like I'm a dog.

"No, thank you, I'm good." I move to stand up and go downstairs to finish my homework. Except Mom stands when I do, her face stiff with fury.

"Sit down and eat, young lady."

"I'm not hungry."

"I don't care."

"It's my birthday, can't I do what I want?" I snap back, my voice heavy with sarcasm.

"Sadie," she snarls, and starts to move toward me. Dave stands and holds up a hand to stop her. Because of course he has all the control even though this isn't his house.

"Sit down, Sadie."

"No. You're not my father, and I don't have to listen to you."

Mom really loses her shit now, but Dave tries to calm her down. In the melee of their power struggle, I leave. I leave because if I don't I'm going to scream, or throw things, break stuff, or hurt myself. I don't even know. I need to breathe and I can't do it here, now.

I have to stop a minute to get my shoes on but then I'm out the door and moving. I don't go down the driveway, I cut through our back neighbor's yard and onto their street, then cross, and then run through two more yards. I don't care if people see me or try to stop me. I need to go where they won't look for me. Where they won't expect.

Not that my parents know the routes of my walks, but I'm sure they know the general direction I head in.

All I can think is get out get out get out.

I make it to one of the main streets through Edgar's Bluff and start walking without no purpose. Every foot I get away from that house feels like a pound of pressure off my soul.

21

Logan

My hands are black and smell like grease after a long shift of oil changes at the shop. I don't try as hard as I should to wash my hands because it comforts me to catch a whiff of motor oil. To know what my hands are capable of and that I can be productive. I might not have had the brain power of my dad when it came to the science, but my innate understanding of machines comes from him.

My ability to suffer in silence clearly comes from my mom but I face my emotions better than she ever will even if I rarely talk about them. I don't deny my feelings.

As if I conjured her, I see Sadie walking down the street.

It's dark, getting cold, and she's only wearing a long-sleeved shirt. Her hair is a wispy mess around her face and when I pull the car over next to her, she doesn't even register me. I scramble out, rushing to get to her, and nearly trip over my feet and eat pavement.

"Sadie." No reaction. "Sadie." Nothing. "Sadiebaby."

She stills. Finally. I rush forward and around to see her face. It's blank. Blank like I've never seen before. Her eyes are red and puffy like she's been crying, but when they lift to meet mine they're empty. I've never seen her broken but this comes fucking close.

It makes something rip inside me that I thought couldn't tear any further. I hurt for her in a way that feels a lot like the grief I still carry for my dad. The same way his loss ripped me open. Nothing should ever hurt my girl like this.

I wrap my arms around her and pull her into the shelter of my body. Her face is so cold I can feel the ice of it through my shirt and it makes me hold her harder. Giving her all the warmth I can.

"What happened?"

"I couldn't breathe," she whispers, her voice raw. "I had to get out."

I know the feeling. So I'm going to take her where I go when I feel the same.

"Come on. I got you." Sadie lets me lead her to the car without another word. It's the beater I drive around until the Firebird is done. It runs decent enough and gets me to and from work and occasionally school. The door opens quietly because I take care of my things even when they're beat to shit, and I help her inside. Sadie doesn't move, so I lean inside and buckle the seat belt for her.

When I move to back out, her hands come up and she clings to my jacket. When our eyes meet, hers are finally full of a spark. Sadie tugs me closer until her head rests against mine.

"Where did you come from?" she whispers.

"What?"

"Always doing and saying the right thing. There when I need you like magic. Where did you come from?"

I can't stop my smirk. "I've been right next door all along, baby."

Sadie gives a hint of a smile back and I know that every minute with me is going to bring her back to herself. I tilt my head in question, and she answers by pressing her lips to mine. They might be cold to the touch but they raise the heat inside me.

"Thank you," she says against my lips and a shiver runs down my spine.

I don't say anything, but extricate myself from her grip and get back in the driver's seat. Without paying much attention to anyone else on the road or traffic laws, I flip a bitch and head back toward the shop.

Sadie reaches over and puts her hand on my thigh which is distracting when I'm trying to shift gears. The car is old enough to have a bench seat and I don't stop her when she unbuckles and slides across it so she can lean against me.

"You got a cigarette?"

At this point, I'm not even going to ask questions. I'll give her anything she asks for. I reach into my jacket pocket and pull the pack out, popping one up and taking it with my mouth. I swap that out for the lighter, and get it started for her. She takes it from me and I roll down the window. It's hard not to watch her as she takes a long, slow drag.

To think that I literally once jerked off to the fact that our mouths touched the same place on a cigarette and now this morning I got to lick the taste of her pussy off my fingers. We've come a long way.

I pull back into the shop lot. The lights are all off, everything is locked up for the night, but I have keys so it doesn't really matter. I'm not taking her into the shop, I'm going to show her a hint of my future.

She follows, her hand in mine, as I lead her up the steps attached to the back of the building.

"Tori fixed this place up - Linc and I are moving in after graduation."

"That's great, Logan." Warmth is back in her voice, even if her expression is still hesitant.

"We got a couple months to get stuff, start turning it into something livable."

"A big couch, two plates, two forks, and mattresses on the floor of your bedrooms?" She teases.

"You forgot the big screen TV," I tease, and unlock the door. The funny part is that the only thing we have so far is a big couch and two mattresses that are on the floor of our respective bedrooms. Those were a surprise gift from Tori since she was also concerned Linc would take the twin mattress from his bed at home.

I hold the door open and Sadie steps past me and into the living room. The kitchen is to the left, and straight ahead is a hallway with two bedrooms and the bathroom. It isn't much, but it's new and clean and it'll be the space I make feel like home.

"Tori did a good job." Sadie slides off her shoes, she isn't even wearing socks, and scrunches her toes in the thick carpet. It's adorable, but also makes me wonder how long she was outside wearing so little.

"I'll let her know you approve." I close the door and follow suit by removing my shoes, and then tossing my jacket on the floor. "We can stay here as long as you need."

Sadie turns around to face me, and she's so much more relaxed. Her shoulders loosen, the frown lines on her forehead are gone, and the corners of her lips are turned up. The little resting smile she seems to only have when she's with me. There's no lights on so everything is in shadow - I can see her by the light of the huge streetlamp outside.

She walks closer and puts her arms around my neck. "Forever? Forget anything outside of this place exists?"

"Angel, you think I wouldn't gladly keep you here with me? My prisoner, the soul that I own until eternity ends?" I keep my voice low like I know she likes, and she presses her body into mine. "I'm bringing you down to my level, Sadiebaby."

"You might think you're a demon, Logan, but you seem to be the person that's always pulling me out of hell." One of her hands slides down my chest and toys with my belt. It makes me instantly hard.

"Let's find heaven, then."

Sadie nods, fists my t-shirt, and drags my mouth to hers. I take over fast, using the height I have on her to gain control. She squeaks into my mouth when I bend down and pick her up, gripping her thighs and wrapping them around my waist. I want to take her to my bed but the couch is closer and I want more. Now.

I collapse back onto the couch and she breaks the kiss to lift her shirt over her head, and reaches behind her to undo her bra. I reach out and stop her.

"Let me, I want to enjoy you."

Sadie nods and brings her hands to my shoulders, making space for me. I kiss and lick along her neck, the curve of her breasts. I tease one strap down, my mouth following my fingers. Her breathing increases, and she gasps when I flick the clasp of her bra.

I run my teeth over her skin until I hook the top of the cup, and I pull it away from her with my mouth. Sadie looks down and grins, then takes it from me and tosses it over her shoulder.

I can't look away from her smile, even though she's topless in front of me and I've never seen her naked before. Thought about it thousands, maybe even millions, of times, but fuck it doesn't compare with making her smile. Especially when I know just minutes ago she was in a dark place.

I pull her into the light. Into the fire.

I thought I was bringing her down with me, bringing out the sinner, but now I wonder if this is redemption for both of us.

Since I'm caught dumb staring it takes me a second to realize she's pulling at my shirt, and I oblige her by reaching behind me and pulling my shirt over my head.

"Mmm," she makes an appreciative noise, wasting no time looking at me. I finally let my eyes drop as her hands start exploring my chest. She's got soft pink nipples that are hard and standing at attention for me. I lean forward and take one into my mouth.

Sadie moans and arches her back, pressing herself further into my mouth.

"I need you. I need you now, Logan, please."

She pushes away from me and stands up, unbuttoning and pushing her bottoms down.

Sadie Braverman is naked in front of me and I nearly pinch myself just to confirm this isn't a dream. I must be moving too slow for her when it comes to taking my pants off because she shoves my hands away and does it for me, pulling the fly down, then yanking everything straight off my hips.

If I had any concerns she wasn't into this, wasn't ready, that action made it fly out the window. Sadie's eyes drop and she grins.

"So there is a curve."

"Let me show you how good it feels." I reach my arms out for her and she crawls back into my lap. Then I still. "Fuck. Condom."

"Uh, I'm on birth control."

"Wait - we - with nothing?" My brain is scrambling but my dick is getting even harder at the thought of being raw inside Sadie. Fucking and cumming inside her pretty pussy, taking that with me forever.

"This time." She wiggles in my lap and starts kissing me again, emptying my brain of everything except the feeling of her body. Her wet pussy slides up and down my dick, soaking me in her need. Sadie wants it, and she wants it bad.

"I want to feel you," she whispers into my mouth before reaching down and wrapping her hand around me, lifting up until I'm right up against her. "It's okay."

"Okay," I agree, every thought except how she feels leaving my brain. She pushes down onto me. "Fuuuuuck," I groan as her tight heat wraps around me, the best it's ever felt. My head falls back and I look up at her.

Sadie's forehead is crinkled in concentration but her mouth is open and slack, her eyes focused on me. She lets out a sharp noise when I'm all the way inside her. She starts to lift, but I stop her.

"Grind, baby. Trust me." I wrap my hands around her hips and start rocking her back and forth. The curve rubs against the front wall of her cunt, hitting that secret intense spot most girls don't even know they have yet. It also presses her clit into my pelvic bone, giving her direct pleasure in two places.

Sadie keeps her eyes on me, and I get to watch as she gets closer and closer to releasing everything that's so pent up inside her. Her hands don't stop moving and it drives me crazy, my neck, my chest, my face, her nails dragging along my scalp and teasing the short hair.

I can feel her tightening around me, and it takes everything I have to hold off until she tips over the edge.

"Logan," she pants, her hips moving hard, her breath stalling in her chest.

"Louder baby, there's no one around to hear you sin for me."

Sadie's fingers dig into my skin, her nails marking me, and she screams my name. It sounds better than it ever did in my imagination, and I watch as pleasure washes over her face. The way she tightens around me, the breathy sounds she's making, it's too much.

Sadie's eyes open and meet mine. "Please," she begs.

I wrap one hand around the nape of her neck, pulling her down to me, while the other digs into her hip, moving her the way that's going to finish me off. Our eyes are centimeters away, gazes locked, desperation and pleasure swirling between us.

Everything disappears except her eyes as I cum inside her.

"Sadie," I breathe, because she's the only thing that matters. The only thing that has truly existed for me in the last 7 years. Sadie is all that's kept me alive when I was on the edge of dying, even if she didn't know it.

We stay that way, breathing deep and recovering from our orgasms.

Watching her come undone that way was like being let in on a secret. Seeing the uptight good girl experiencing carnal pleasure, embracing the feeling and riding it, was incredible. I'm going to do that to her as often as she'll let me until she leaves. It was beautiful.

"Happy birthday?" I throw out.

Sadie laughs and I groan, my dick sensitive and her laughter is more than it can handle from the inside.

"Was this my present?"

"No," I shake my head. "That's in my garage."

"Thank you," Sadie says with a smile, stroking the back of my head. It feels too good. I want to fuck her again, but I know our time is up.

"Everything alright now?"

"Everything is alright," she answers. "Let's go."

I always wondered if what I felt for Sadie was really love, or just misplaced affection while I was going through some hard shit. Watching her now, being with her and knowing she's even more than I could have imagined, I know what it is.

It's really love. Always has been, always will be, and I won't regret for a second when it demolishes my heart. I won't regret that I'll never belong to anyone else because I'll always belong to the girl next door.

22

Sadie

I'm off my game but for once it's not because I'm tired or sad, or worn to the bone, but because I can't stop thinking about being with Logan in his apartment. The amount of times a day I'm staring into space thinking about some aspect of our time together is astronomical.

Father forgive me for I have sinned, and I'm going to do again.

Then again, I'm not asking for forgiveness if I'm not really repenting. Despite how busy we both are I'm trying to figure out how we can be alone again. Other than a few stolen kisses, it's been days.

Soccer tryouts are this week and I can tell I'm playing different. It's my final season and I can't afford to compromise my scholarship. Then again, I'm not playing badly, but with a different intensity than I have before. Usually I'm a verbal, cocky player, but the last two days of tryouts I've been more quiet and focused.

I'm inside my own head too much.

Having free time in study hall is not helping the issue. I'm staring at my calculus homework and the numbers are blurring together.

"They don't even make sense," a voice hisses behind me. "Teacher's Pet and Logan Kurowski? I didn't even realize they knew each other."

I casually glance over my shoulder. Three girls in my year are huddled together talking. I don't know them, my class is huge, this is one of the biggest high schools in the state, and I don't even think I know their names. I'm not sure if they know me either, or they became aware of my existence because I'm dating Logan.

Dating.

Actually dating.

It's bizarre.

I'm not sure what's happening to me but I think I like it.

"Maybe he's got a thing for virgins," one of them giggles.

"Deflower the prude just to say that he did," another snorts. "More likely than he actually wants her."

"She dresses like a boy and kisses ass to the teachers, I can't imagine they have any fun together." More giggling. "Plus she hangs out with that…you know…so maybe it's a cover."

My blood boils but I say nothing. They didn't use any directly derogatory terms and Darcy was very clear with me that she didn't want me to fight people for her. That to her, high school people weren't worth the time to educate or eviscerate, and leaving it alone is her choice. It's how she's choosing to protect herself and her relationship. I hate it, but it's her life and her identity, so I'll respect what she wants.

"Maybe he's using her. Trading sex for homework."

One of them snorts again, she really should go to a doctor about that. "I'll do his homework in return for sex."

I tune them out because emotions start to pull me down and I'm not strong enough right now to fight them off. Still not sleeping, spending all my awake time floating off into Logan sex fantasies, and emotionally raw from everything that happened on my birthday. I'm beyond burnt.

I'm angry that people treat Darcy like she's diseased.

I'm afraid of my house, and I'm so tired of being afraid. I'm tired of holding in my fury and disgust around the people I'm forced to live with. One of these days I'm going to lose it and I don't know what kind of consequences the meltdown will have.

I'm tired of being seen as less than a person. By my mom, Cole, the girls at that other table. I want to break out of my body, transform into something else. Something fearsome and powerful. Something with unbreakable skin and an unbruisable heart.

It's time to use goody two shoes privilege.

I slam my textbook closed and stand to pack up my stuff. I hear the girls behind me gasp and fall silent, and I turn to meet each of their eyes. My face is blank because they don't deserve to see my reaction to anything they said, but I want them to know I heard them say it. We stay in this staring contest way past uncomfortable and into painful. That's when I take my leave.

The study hall monitor looks up from her desk, then back down when she sees that it's me. I don't even need a pass, she just assumes I have somewhere legitimate to be. Kissing ass really does get you places.

Since it's the last period of the day, I head toward the locker room to change for the last day of tryouts. I might as well try and work out some of these emotions on the field. The storage room is already open so I grab the bag of balls and the drill cones to start setting up the course for warm ups.

The best thing about it is that I don't have to think. Setting the cones, prepping for warm ups, is a habit. My mind can go totally blank as I go through the familiar motions of a practice.

There's peace for me out on the field. Boiled down to the basest version of myself. Movement, strategy, observe and respond. Blend into my teammates until I'm not a me, I'm a we. Despite the fact that I'm considered a talented individual player, I'm nothing without my team.

"Hey kid," Coach Minski calls as he comes out onto the field. When he's not coaching, he's an algebra teacher. "Thanks for setting up."

"No problem."

"You know you're on the team, right?" He stops with his hands on his hips. Minski is still built like a soccer player, long and fluid, but he's got a beard that goes almost down to his mid-chest. He's already wearing an Edgar's Bluff hat to cover his balding head. His wife wants him to stop wearing ball caps and wear the ones she knits for him instead, but he says the hat is lucky. Given our record the last few years, I side with superstition.

"Yeah. Just needed to do something."

"Braverman, get over here." I walk over and stand in front of him, looking around him instead of at him. "You good?"

"Yeah."

He frowns at me in the silence, but lets it go.

After a moment of waiting to see if he says anything else, I step back and keep setting up. Other teammates and prospective players come out onto the field, some stepping in to help right away and others grouping together to stretch and talk. When the warm ups are set, I start.

I don't wait for coach's instructions, and after a few runs, the other girls fall into place and start doing it too. After awhile, coach sounds his whistle and we're divided into teams. The last day of tryouts is a scrimmage, testing the skills we've practiced the last few days.

Darcy is on my team, the second striker for me like she always is. With all the final snow melting, the field is a muddy mess. Our cleats are packed and dirty fast, the grass slipping beneath me, sometimes to my advantage. Today, I'm brutal.

Moving, passing, barely breathing as I work my area of the field and decimate the other goalie. I score twice before we've finished the shortened half of our scrimmage.

Darcy approaches me when we take a break.

"Sadie," she starts.

I shake my head. "Nope." My water is cold in my throat, my sweat is cooling on my body, and before she can press me, I move back onto the field to start. The second half goes in a blur, but my body feels good. My joints feel smooth, my steps sure, and I'm disappearing into the place where I belong the most. I love it.

When coach whistles that the game is over, we all stop where we are.

"Roster will be posted Friday. Hit the showers."

I appreciate that he isn't going to be overly wordy, trying to be motivational about not making the team. He knows people that want it bad enough will come back next year.

"Braverman," he calls my name and I stop where I am, making him come to me. It's away from the larger group and I just have a feeling that whatever he wants to say to me I don't want him saying in front of everyone else. Darcy stops and tilts her head at me, but I wave her off.

Honestly, if I end up walking home today I won't mind it at all. I'm still restless and unhappy.

"You're different this year. I feel like you're taking it more seriously. Prepping for what college play will be like."

"Oh?" I don't know what else to say. Minski has never criticized my play before, or shared that he thought I didn't take things seriously. I've been a leader on the team all four years, varsity for three of them, and junior team captain last year. I'm not sure how much more seriously I could be taking it.

"Don't get me wrong, it's been fun the last few years to watch you run your mouth on the field, but this quiet intensity," he points at me, shaking the finger in the air, "that's the mood of a legend. Go hard and go for it this season, got it?"

"Yep." I'm still insulted. And shocked. This is the person that wrote me recommendation letters for college, for my scholarships, who was questioned about me when I was recruited by the Madison coaches. Insecurity and an edge of panic race through me, wondering what he said about me and if any of it could be interpreted negatively. What I don't know can hurt me, and suddenly I'm feeling like I trusted someone I shouldn't have. Another person in my life who hasn't been honest with me.

I always go hard. I don't have any other mode. How can he think anything else? How can Minski not see I've gone as hard, maybe even harder, the last three years?

I can never win.

Nothing is ever right.

Nothing is ever good enough.

The locker room is empty when I get inside, and I don't bother to shower or change. I grab my stuff and head out the door. Everything feels heavy as I start walking in the direction of my house.

It takes a few moments to register that someone is calling my name.

"Sadiebaby!" That gets through.

I turn to find Logan leaning against the beater he drives around town, arms crossed over his chest, one ankle crossed over the other. His jeans fit perfect, his jacket is tight on his broad shoulders, and the air is cold enough that I can see his breath. The intensity of his gaze overpowers everything else I'm feeling and gives me a shiver that isn't about cold. My nipples tighten and everything clenches.

"Get in the car." He jerks his head and then pushes himself up. Logan gets in the driver's seat and waits, watching me. I'm not moving, my brain trying to catch up with reality. I take a deep breath and step wearily forward.

I throw my stuff in the backseat and then slide in front next to him.

"Alright?" he asks as he shifts into gear and slides onto the road.

"No."

"What do you need?"

Nothing comes to mind, nothing comes out of my mouth. I'm stunned. Frozen. Paralyzed. I look over at him, blank and lost.

Logan reaches out and cups my head, pulling me toward him. I don't realize what he's doing until I tip over. His thigh pillows my head and he strokes my hair, driving toward our houses, not our homes. The feeling of his fingers through my hair, scratching along my scalp, the brush of the rough callouses on the sensitive skin behind my ear and over my pulse, it's so utterly relaxing.

It's exactly what I need.

I'm not ready to talk about anything. I don't know that I'd even have the words yet. Articulating my feelings would be impossible right now.

I feel the car turn beneath me and then come to a stop. I sit up and look at him.

"Better?" he asks softly, still stroking my face and running his fingers through my hair. I lean into his hand and close my eyes.

"Yeah." We lean toward each other and kiss softly.

"I'm here, if you need me."

"Thanks." I mean it, and kiss him one more time before getting out. I grab my backpack and gym bag from the backseat and head up the porch steps to go in the front door. I'm too tired to drag myself around the back.

What I don't anticipate is mom waiting for me in the living room.

Cole is sitting at the dining room table behind her, his homework spread around him. He's taken over the spot where I usually study with James, and I notice that my brother isn't there. James probably does his homework in his room now, since I'll be doing mine after dinner now because of soccer. It bothers me that my brother has ceded space to Cole.

"What were you thinking?" mom hisses, pulling my attention to her.

I feel like my eyes are barely staying open but my heart is racing in my chest. I'm down and up at the same time.

"About what?"

"Kissing that boy in our driveway, for everyone to see." She steps forward and grabs the strap of my gym bag, ripping it down my arm and yanking it to the floor. The material pulls at my skin and hurts. "You look like a complete slut. It's bad enough you play such a messy sport, but letting everyone know you're seeing Logan Kurowski...have some dignity, Sadie."

I'm not sure what comes over me, but my filter is gone. "It's not like I sucked his dick in the driveway."

The sentence is barely out of my mouth before her hand snatches out and the slap reverberates across my cheek.

"You do not speak like that in my house." Her chest is heaving and the hope that she has a heart attack comes over me. That she finally goes apoplectic.

"Go take a shower, you smell like a pig." Mom turns on her heel and stomps back to the kitchen. I'll have to pass by her to get downstairs.

My cheek hurts, my body aches, I can feel the sweat residue on my body, the dried mud cracking on my skin. I want to shower in water so hot my skin burns and melts off.

I pick up my bag and start walking.

"Hey," Cole stops me, his voice barely a whisper. "I...I didn't know it was like that."

"I told you." I stare straight at the door into the kitchen, not looking at him or even truly acknowledging him.

"I didn't believe you."

Now I turn to look at him. "Of course not. No one ever believes me. Just your luck."

Cole pales and gulps, and at least I know I got one over on him this time. I leave him to his thoughts, and hopefully his fears.

23

Logan

Sadie is breaking in a way I've never seen before, but she keeps letting me into her darkest moments. It's like she knows I've already been in the dark with her all along. The ghost by her side until she was able to see me. God, nothing bolsters my fucking ego like the way Sadie Braverman trusts me. The kind of surrender that makes my dick hard.

I park the beater and head into the house, throwing things around as I get in, whipping off my shirt and throwing it down the stairs for the laundry later. Most of my work shirts and undershirts are dirty, so I'm due for a heavy wash load. The stains never really go away but they get clean enough.

Not to mention the constant stains on my hands. I look like the gearhead I am at all times. No regrets about that.

I open the fridge to figure out what I can pull together for dinner before I dip into the cash from my mother to order something.

"Logan."

"Fucking hell!" I jump and smash the back of my head on the top of the fridge as I stand up quickly. My mother is standing in the kitchen doorway.

I rub the back of my head, trying to soothe the throbbing pain in my skull. Then again, it might be from having to interact with her and not from the blow to the head.

She stands there, impassive to my pain, not even cursorily asking if I'm okay. Even though I often compare her to a ghost it's a lot more like a robot sometimes. Like she doesn't understand pain because she's decided that it doesn't exist anymore.

So I play her game, I don't say anything, I wait her out. We stare at each other in awkward silence. She wants me to ask her what's going on, and I want her to just fucking say it. To initiate.

She clears her throat. "I'm leaving on a trip for work. 10 days." Ah, so she's telling me because it's longer than her usual. At least she knows I'd notice she's missing. I wonder if she could say the same - if I moved out without a word like Tori wants me to, would she even notice? How long before she would go into my room and see my stuff was gone?

What would she do? Leave me be, reach out and ask me why...be relieved?

My stomach roils with nausea.

I don't say anything to her pronouncement.

"There's cash for groceries and takeout. Don't forget to take the garbage down on Sunday night, please." Like I'm not the one who does it already. Like I don't take care of and maintain this house as if it's my own because she doesn't do shit.

I don't say anything.

I want to know what she'll do.

My mother nods at me, and turns to head into the dark of the house. I hear her go upstairs and I'm surprised she's sleeping in her bedroom for once. Must be that night of the week - or she's that desperate to avoid me.

My own mother didn't ask me how I'm doing. How school or work are going. The end of the year is coming, graduation is coming, and she has still never asked me about my post-graduation plans. I cannot recall the last time she took an interest in anything in my life. The last time she asked me a question even. She assumes she knows what I need (money) and never inquires any further.

Fuck her.

Maybe Tori is right.

I should leave.

Loneliness whirls in my chest like a black hole, and I feel as if it's about to destroy everything around me.

The only thing I want right now is Sadie. I've been helping her get out from under the weight of her problems, and I want to know now if I'm not alone. If she's as in this with me as I am with her. If I reach out, will she be there?

I text Sadie.

Logan: I don't want to be here.

She answers immediately.

Sadie: Me either.

I love that she uses punctuation in her texts. It tells me so much about her mood. The period isn't a good sign.

Logan: Let's get out of here.

Sadie: Meet you at the car.

We both exit our houses at the same time, turning and meeting each other's eyes across our backyards. Sadie's hair is wet like she just got out of the shower, hanging around her face in long waves. There's a fire in her eyes that tells me she's gotten past her weariness and found her ferocity.

I wait for her to come to me, and even though it's unexpected, I go with it when she grabs a fistful of my t-shirt and drags my mouth down to hers. Sadie's tongue slides past my lips and I inhale, the taste of her and the scent of her shampoo taking over everything. It's a filthy, not for public consumption kind of kiss and we're doing it in my driveway in the early evening. Anyone could see.

It makes me crazy but I keep my hands to myself, letting her use me the way she needs to in this moment. Sadie could take and take from me until I'm nothing and I'd still be grateful for the ride.

"I need you," I growl against her mouth when she finally lets me breathe. I roll my hips forward, pressing into hers. Sadie gives me a naughty smile that I never could have imagined, and walks around me to the car. It's not the direction I thought this would go, but I'm not going to deny her.

After a deep breath to get some of the blood from my dick to my brain so I can drive, I join her in the car.

What I expect even less than that kiss is when Sadie leans over the seat like she did earlier, except this time she goes for the fly of my jeans. Once again, I don't question it as Sadie frees my dick and starts sucking. I'm not silent by any means, the air is cold and her mouth is warm, it feels incredible. I couldn't be quiet if I tried.

The silky feeling of her tongue and the inside of her mouth is heaven as she glides over me, slow and steady. Looking down to see her head bobbing, her lips stretched around me, makes me want to push her down and cum in her throat. But I'm more curious to see what she's going to do than I am desperate to cum. I'll get there tonight. Right now I'm Sadie's carnival and she can go on every ride and play every game.

"Little devil," I hiss when she drags her teeth along me. Not enough to hurt but it gives intense pressure. Sadie huffs a laugh and her warm breath is another intense sensation. It's tempting to keep driving instead of heading to my destination, but I'd rather see what she'll do when we have more space.

I park the car in the now empty lot behind Anderson's, but I don't say a word to Sadie. Now that I'm not focusing on keeping us alive, I can watch her suck my cock. Sadie's eyes are closed, her lips shiny with saliva, and peeks of her tongue drive me crazy as she licks me in between glides of her mouth.

"Let's go in the shop," I hiss out, holding onto my control.

Sadie pops up and looks at me with raised eyebrows. "Really?"

"I've thought about fucking you there a thousand times. Instead of fantasies, I want memories. I want my dick to get hard while I'm changing oil in a car because I see a place where I had your pussy around me." My words are dirty, but I gently stroke her cheek.

I feel the heat of her blush beneath my fingers, and she nods.

I put myself back in my pants and pull her out with me on my side of the car. The keys jangle loudly in the quiet parking lot. It's not even that late, still faintly light out, but the shop and the area around it are a ghost town.

Once I have the door open, I yank Sadie back to me and seal my mouth over hers, invading with my tongue. She moans into my mouth, and I wrap my hands around her tight ass. I don't even need to open my eyes to move us through the shop. I know it with my eyes closed, by feel, scent, and memory.

My hand lets go of one cheek to turn on the main overhead lights.

In between the bays is an open area with a couch. I've spent far too many breaks thinking about Sadie there. Absolutely pornographic things sure, but sweet shit too. Thinking about how it would feel to lay with her on the couch, snuggle her against me, her head on my chest. What it would be like to watch her wake up, her eyelids drifting open, sleep clearing from her gaze, the expression she would get when she realized she was sleeping with me.

That's the cute stuff, the things I'd never admit to thinking.

Right now we're going to act out one of my favorite fantasies.

When we reach the couch I turn us and fall backward, her body straddling mine, her warm cunt pressed against me. We kiss ferociously, hands tearing at each other, teeth digging in. Sadie scratches

150

along my scalp hard enough to make me groan at the edge of pain that shoots through my body.

"You want to make me hurt, Sadie?" I say and then bite into her bottom lip. "Take it all out on me, baby."

Sadie whimpers and paws at me, ripping down my jacket and fighting to get my shirt off. I do it for her, and then let my hands drop to slide into her track pants.

She's not wearing anything under them.

"You little slut," I pull back and look at her, sliding my hand between her pussy lips. She's soaking wet, warm and slick. I use that slickness to help my finger glide along her clit, soft and teasing, not enough to get her anything other than worked up.

"That's my little sinner," I purr, "you did this because you wanted it to be easy for you to get fucked, didn't you?"

"Yes," Sadie nods and grinds herself onto my hand, trying to get more pressure.

"Tell me what you imagined."

She gulps, and I wait her out. I press a little harder onto her clit and she gives a sharp gasp. "I thought about you bending me over, yanking down my pants, and fucking me. I want you to take me."

"I'll take you. Right into hell with me, making your soul black with the depraved things I'll make you beg for me to do."

"Please."

Nothing so gorgeous and decadent has ever come out of her mouth before than that desperate request.

I stand up and let her legs drop, then switch our positions. I step behind her and place my hand between her shoulder blades. It takes barely any pressure for her to bend over and grab the back of the couch.

"This is what you wanted?" I ask, not taking off her pants. My hands are running up and down her back, over her ass, over her pussy through them, but I'm not giving her what she wants.

"Yes."

"Then tell me what to do next, Sadie."

"Take my pants off."

I do as she says, sliding them so, so slowly over her, letting the material rub along her skin. We have hours, I can take as long as I want playing with her. Drawing all her dirty desires out of her.

Her pants slide down her legs to pool around her feet, and I'm amused when she steps out of them and kicks them away.

"Keep talking, baby."

"Get on your knees," she whispers. The grin on my face is purely feral. She's getting into this now. I do as she says, kneeling behind her like a penitent, grabbing her ass cheeks and spreading that pretty pink pussy open before me. Sadie is absolutely dripping with need.

"Make me cum on your face," she whispers again. By the time I'm done, I'll have her screaming her directions. None of this timid whispering.

I dive at her, pressing my tongue into her while one of my hands slides around so my thumb can play with her clit. I lick her from entrance to asshole, teasing her ass and making her moan low and harsh. That's for another time unless she asks, so I go back to working my tongue through her sweet flavor.

"Grind on me, baby," I direct her. Sadie pushes back, grinding her face into me, letting me get my tongue deeper inside her. I can feel the muscles in her thighs twitching as she gets close, her body shaking as she nears the edge.

"I'm cumming," she half-screams, half-cries, and then she buries her face in her upper arm to muffle her moans as she orgasms on my face.

"Fuck me, fuck me now, please fuck me."

"Like this?" I stand up and reach into my jeans for the condom I remembered to put in my pocket before leaving the house.

"Yes."

"Keep talking," I prompt again.

"Please. I need you. I need to feel you."

How can I resist that?

"Fuck me like I'm your slut," she says quiet but serious, and I nearly cum in my fucking boxers. Sadie Braverman dirty talking and begging for my dick still feels impossible to me.

I put the condom on and move close behind her, teasing the head through her pussy over and over. Sadie whines and pushes toward me, but when I don't give in to her she reaches her arm back to grab mine, and looks at me over her shoulder. Sadie is breathless and disheveled and she's never been prettier.

"Fuck me, Logan."

That's what I was waiting for. I press inside her, gentle but consistent, and get to watch her face as I do. Sadie's mouth drops open and she moans. Her eyes meet mine and then flutter closed. She turns back to brace herself, and I start to move.

I want to exhaust her. I want her to be so blissed out that she can't think, can't stress, all she can do is feel pleasure. My hips snap, thrusting in and out of her tight, perfect heat. The skin of my hips slaps against her ass, echoing through the cavernous garage, coming back at us over and over. It's a symphony of me fucking the perfect girl next door, and letting out her filthy side.

As much as I want to cum, I also don't want to stop.

"Logan," she whimpers, and tightens around me. Sadie is close.

"Let go, Sadie. Fall with me. Give me your soul, baby."

Sadie screams.

I don't know why that shit gets to her but I'll never stop saying it if that's the case. I do feel like I'm dirtying her up. Like she's slumming it with me. I like that there's a dark part of her that connects with all the darkness in me.

On impulse, I smack her ass, and she squeezes me so hard with her cunt I think I'm going to pass out. The rhythm of her tightening and releasing as she cums almost puts me over the edge, not to mention the sound of her screams bouncing off the walls.

"More," she huffs, breathless.

I laugh, and slide out of her.

Then Sadie looks at me over her shoulder, a pout on her sweet mouth, and lets out a noise that could be nothing other than a whine. Sadie is literally whining for my dick.

I move so I'm sitting on the couch again and pull her down on top of me.

We both moan when I slide home again, fucking deep into her.

"Show me you're my slut, Sadiebaby. Make me cum."

I lean back and put my hands behind my head like I'm waiting for the show.

Sadie looks at me for a moment, her head tilted, her wild damp hair falling around her body. She places her hands on my chest, and hesitantly starts to move. The last time when she was on top of me it was mutual, it was emotional and ravenous, this is much more deliberate. Planned but no less passionate.

I watch her hips shift back and forth. It feels good, but it's not what she really wants.

"Let go, Sadie." I reach up and slide my thumb into her mouth. Immediately, she sucks, and it's a jolt straight to my cock. "Baby, trust your body. Move."

Sadie's eyes lock with mine, still sucking my thumb, and I wait. The movement of her pussy on me changes, more of a glide, and I glance down to watch as her hips roll and drag her pussy along my cock, in and out. Her clit grinds against my hips, and I clench my teeth to hold on.

I want her to cum like this, and I want her to beg for me to give her mine.

My thumb drops out of her mouth and my hand glides down to her neck, her pulse fluttering beneath my touch.

"Slutty Sadie," I whisper to her, and when she looks at me her eyes are so dilated I can't see the color anymore. Her hips move wildly, and I hold her in place so she can't look away. "Sing for me, little sinner," I command.

Sadie's mouth drops open and she doesn't look away from me as another orgasm rocks through her body. Her voice echoes in the garage, a high crescendo that I'll hear in my head forever. She's shaking, her thighs are squeezing my hips, her nails digging into my chest hard enough to leave marks. Fuck, I almost hope she draws blood.

"Please," she asks, her body still moving erratically.

"Please what?" I grit out, waiting for her.

"Cum...for me." It's asked so sweetly, her body on the brink of being worn out. I yank her to me so her forehead is pressed to mine, her eyes the only thing I can see. I fight to keep mine open as pleasure shoots up my spine and down my legs, my cock throbbing as I cum inside Sadie.

"That's my bad girl," I whisper, and kiss her softly. "I own you." What I really mean is that she owns me. What little soul I have is all fucking hers.

24

Sadie

My heart is in so much trouble. I want to ask Logan to run away with me. Grab what we can, fuck my future, and just not be here anymore. I want to be somewhere with just him and me and whatever we decide to do with our time.

There was always a spark inside me for Logan, but now it's an inferno.

I'm falling for him.

I had all my plans laid out in front of me and I want to throw all of them out for him. This was a change that I never could have planned for because I had no interest in being in a relationship again. Allowing myself to trust and be invested in another person gave them the power to hurt me. The thing about Logan is that I already trusted him before a lot of the damage was done. He's exempt to my walls because he was already inside them.

We barely have our clothes back on when the same door we came in opens and slams shut. Linc can see us from where he's standing and we definitely don't look like we were sitting innocently chatting on the couch.

"Everyone's bits covered?" he asks before stepping further in.

"Shut up, yeah," Logan shouts back.

I move, feeling awkward and bashful, so I'm curled up next to where Logan is sprawled in the center of the couch. Linc ambles over and takes a seat on Logan's other side, and I can't articulate how I feel knowing that just minutes ago I was having sex on this couch.

"Needed to get away?" he asks Logan.

I'm still recovering from what just happened, and more tired than I expected. Logan has his arm around me and I lean my head on his shoulder, closing my eyes. I'll just listen to them talk, maybe catch a nap in a place where I feel safe.

"She actually spoke to me today." Logan's voice is full of a new bitterness, not the usual fuck-life-as-a-teenager bitter, but a true resentful wound. "Leaving for 10 days, here's some cash." Logan scoffs and automatically my hands squeeze around his arm as if to offer comfort. I'm surprised when Logan turns and kisses the top of my head in response.

"How much we talking?" Linc teases, trying to lift his friend's mood.

"Fuck off. She didn't even ask about school. Work. Acknowledge that I have a fucking life I live without any interaction from her. I'm less than a pet. I'm barely a goldfish to her."

I knew that Logan's mom didn't really have rules or boundaries for him, but I didn't know it was that bad at his house. Or even if I had, this is the first he's letting me learn how much it hurts him. It would hurt his dad so much to see their relationship this non-existent. Brian loved being a parent, and his mom wasn't like this when he was alive.

Then again, death breaks people in ways we never see coming. Grief is something felt in isolation but its impact can spread like blight. I'm suddenly angry with my parents for putting such a divide between us and the Kurowskis. It's not the first time I wonder what happened that caused it in the first place. It was more than Brian's death. It has to be.

"Want to stay at ours tonight? You know you can," Linc says. "Or crash at the apartment."

"I don't know that going from one empty place to another is the right move," Logan sighs, and moves his arm so that it's wrapped around me more tightly.

"I'll stay with you," I offer, quiet but determined. It would land me in the biggest pile of shit I've ever faced with my mom, but Logan has been there for me and I want to do the same for him. Time after time lately he's come through when I'm about to fall apart, in ways I never expected from him, and I know that I can be what he needs, too. This is all unexpected but it isn't one sided.

"Or sneak you into the basement," I tease.

Logan laughs. "The offer is appreciated, but I'm used to the haunted house."

I flinch and I know he feels it. He and Linc exchange a look.

"I'm okay, Sadie, I promise."

"I don't believe you."

"Me neither," Linc chimes in.

Logan glowers. "I'm okay enough. Counting down the days, but I have to see this through. I have to finish it so I don't look back and wonder..." he trails off. "Wonder if he'd be disappointed in me." Brian. "He'd want me to finish out what I owe her."

"If there's one thing I know, we only owe our parents what they give us. You get nothing, you give nothing." I swallow thickly. "They give everything, you give it back. He wouldn't be disappointed in you for taking care of yourself, Logan, and I can say that better than anyone."

It surprises me we haven't really talked about his dad until now. It's an open wound for both of us, and I clearly have negative associations with parents, but I cannot imagine how it feels for Logan. Especially knowing the way his mom treats him now. I want to fix it. I want him to do what will release this weight from his shoulders.

"Some part of me feels like staying is taking care of her, too."

"Finally, you admit it." Linc throws up his hands. "I guess you just needed your girl to make you soft enough to say it out loud."

"Nothing soft about him," I snark, and Linc laughs loud and claps his hands.

"You little sluts, fucking in the shop."

"Watch your mouth, Anderson," Logan snarls but there's no heat behind it. Linc grins at him, not sorry in the least, but apparently absurdly happy.

"No regrets, then," I offer, not letting the subject change. "If staying means you'll be able to move on without looking back, okay, stay, but...there has to be a way to make it better."

"Like what?"

"Turn on the fucking lights," Linc starts. "Sleep in your bed."

"Where are you sleeping?" I sit up straight. Only one of us needs to be getting crap sleep, and I already have dibs on that. And a better reason. I have to keep myself safe.

"Dad's office."

"Logan..."

"Logan..." Linc mimics me, pulling a pout. "Listen to your girl."

"I'm coming over on Saturday and we're going to clean your house. We're going to open the windows and let in light and air. Okay?"

Logan looks at me with an expression I can't decipher, something like wonder mixed with fear.

"Okay, baby." He leans forward and kisses me.

"Happy as I am to see you happy, this is gross, bye." Linc slaps his thighs and stands up. "I'll finish my work tomorrow."

"Nah," Logan says. "We should get out of here. Leave you to it." We both stand up and Logan tells me he needs to get some stuff, and he'll be right back. Leaving me and Linc alone for the first time ever.

Linc is looking at me, pure amusement on his face.

"He told me you asked him to be your boyfriend as a cover."

I panic and stutter over the start of at least five different sentences before Linc holds up his hands to calm me.

"If I thought for a second this was bullshit, I wouldn't be nice right now. You care about him. I can see it."

"I do."

"He's been hurt more than I think you know, more than he even realizes. I hope you end up being something that heals him, Sadie."

My heart lurches in my chest, pain and panic at war. It hurts me to think about hurting him and yet I can't help but fear it's inevitable.

"Me too," I answer, unable to meet Linc's eyes.

"He knows you're leaving. But leave him better than you found him, yeah?"

"Yeah." Tears are welling in my eyes, and I turn away when I hear Logan coming back. I don't want him to see me and get the wrong idea that Linc made me cry. Or get mad at Linc for being a good friend.

They say their goodbyes and I follow Logan out of the garage and into his car. I lean against him as we drive back to our houses. It's nearly impossible to force myself to get out of the car and go inside my personal haunted house. Somehow, knowing that he's feeling the same makes it a little bit easier.

"Thank you," I whisper after he kisses all my air away. "I'm here if you need me, too."

"I know," he smiles down at me, more relaxed than I've seen him in a few days. "Everything alright?"

"Everything is alright, now. Goodnight." I walk backward, unable to look away from him. Logan went from being a safe place to being my saving grace. It's like we were dancing around reality for a long time, and it was nothing more than putting the pieces together for it to be just right. I have never fit with anyone the way I have with Logan, and I didn't let myself see it.

Even when we were kids, he was the only person that never expected anything of me. I've never had to perform for him. I was perfect in my silence, my quiet, my concentration on a puzzle or project. Even for the last few years, he never questioned me sitting in his garage, doing nothing but watching him or staring off into space letting my mind work and run. He never once told me to go, or asked why the hell I sat in his garage freezing my butt off half the time. I was free to come and go.

Freedom has always been a gift he gave me.

I keep up my backward walk, glancing a few times in my periphery to make sure I'm not about to fall on my ass.

Logan stands with his hands in his pockets, grinning at me. I stop and wait when I reach the door. Logan nods, like he's giving me a confirmation that he's okay.

I go inside, but wish I was staying with him.

25

Sadie

I'm high on a morning with Logan. Like I'd promised, we cleaned his house. The windows were open, the spring light came in, the air lifted all around us. It was oddly transcendent. This moment where we were above the things bringing us down, finding peace and joy out of something sad and dark.

It's been years since I was in the Kurowski house, and it looked exactly the same. Abandoned in some ways, but lived in in others. It was like deja vu except it made me unbearably sad at first. They never got rid of any of Brian's things. There's still a note next to the phone to return a call to the cable company in his handwriting. His shoes were still in the back closet.

I didn't bring it up, and I won't, not unless Logan wants to talk about it.

So we both pointedly ignored the signs of their stunted grieving and dusted, washed, vacuumed, laughed, and kissed. He never tried to take it further, and it was an innocent intimacy that I've never experienced before.

The sense of safety I have with him is a blessing.

He keeps saying he's my demon, my devil, but I have to use both hands to count how many times he's been my salvation.

The happiness of being with him, the relaxation that I allow myself in his presence, works against me when I get back home.

The walls are down and I forgot to build them back up.

I'm in my room, singing along to music, picking out what I'm going to wear for the "adventure" Logan promised to take me on this afternoon. It's the last free Saturday I'll have for awhile now that soccer season has started, and for once I don't have any other obligations. Mom hasn't even tried to force me to go to anything. It made me too hopeful.

I step back, shaking my butt a little bit, and slam into a hard body.

Arms wrap around me, warm, heavy, suffocating. I'm mashed into Cole's chest, my own compressed by the tightness of his hold on me. It feels like more than two arms are holding me, and he doesn't loosen up at all when I try to pull away. My footing slips and I stagger against him.

"Hey angel," he murmurs in my ear and I shiver with revulsion. "You're in a good mood."

"Let me go, Cole." It comes out weaker than it should. I was vulnerable, he took his moment, and now I'm spiraling into memories that I've worked hard to get over. The places on my body that he's bruised throb with the echoes of pain. Nausea curls in my stomach. There's no way he doesn't feel the racing of my heart from how hard it's beating in my chest.

"Or what?"

"I will fucking scream." It's still quiet, but the threatening hiss is there.

Cole raises one of his arms so his forearm is resting across my throat. He isn't restricting my breathing but the threat is clear.

"I wouldn't recommend it."

"This isn't the wedding. Or your empty house. It's my house. People

163

are here."

"People who will believe me when I say you overreacted when I tried to make peace."

I swallow thickly because he's right, but I also don't care. He's holding so tight I feel my throat brush against his arm as I swallow. Physically I am no match for him, so I do the only thing that I can.

I scream.

"GET OFF ME!"

Cole lets me go. Finally I fought back and finally it worked. I whirl on him, a little bit scared of his thunderous expression and brace myself when he starts to raise his hand. Cole freezes when he sees the way I flinch and cower, raising my hands to block my face.

In the past, his hits were always surprises. This time I know it's coming and prepared myself, and it seems to shock him. Like the reality that he's hit me, and that my body automatically responds to the threat of it, is brand fucking new.

"What's going on?"

I can only imagine the way Dave interprets the tableau in front of him. Cole frowning, hand raised, me with both arms up to shield my face.

It's important that I control this situation, so I react before Cole can. I drop my arms and stand up straight.

"He scared me."

"It was just a prank," Cole lies.

"Very funny. Please get out of my room." I wave Cole toward the door and he goes without looking back or looking at Dave. He knows I just gave him an out and kept our secrets. Even if they wouldn't believe me in the end, it would make life difficult for him in the meantime. It's easier to put off a battle than to lose the war.

"He's just trying to reconnect with you, Sadie." Dave starts. I turn away from him and start organizing the few items I've unpacked in this space. It's not much, but it's enough that I can avoid him. Fidgeting with school books, putting away my pens and pencils, sliding my calculator into the cover, putting it all in my backpack.

He waits for me to say something, but I won't.

"You're family now. Despite the breakup, you'll be in each other's lives. Cole is trying to clear the air."

I snort with derision before I can catch it.

"Sadie," Dave reprimands. "You have to let go of these negative feelings."

"No thanks," I say lightly, grabbing my clothes off the bed. I turn to look at him. "I'd like to change. As you can see, I don't have a door."

Dave steps back, immediately awkward. "Yes, well, your sacrifice is appreciated."

"Cool." I step past him and into the bathroom, shutting the door with slightly more force than needed. I don't hear him leave, so I pointedly lock the door. After another few seconds, I heard him shuffle through the living room and up the stairs.

Thank everything I'll be with Logan and his friends soon. Somewhere that I can be more myself than I've ever been in this house.

Logan is waiting on his motorcycle at the end of my driveway. A perverse part of me hopes mom sees as I take the second helmet he offers and put it on before I climb on back. My thighs cradle his body, and I wrap my arms around him, snuggling in for the ride.

He shoots off with a whoop and it's like his whole body is grinning at my answering laugh. The one he can feel against his back.

As he drives through town, and other bikes join us. I recognize his friends, but there's a few people that I'm not entirely sure who they are. It doesn't matter. Right now, I'm one of them. Speeding along until buildings fall away and there's only trees on either side of us, a blur of green and brown.

There's a park ahead with a small lake mostly for fishing, and they turn into the lot. I take off my helmet and shake out my hair. Logan slides his off and glances over his shoulder.

"Best backpack ever." He leans back into me and I wrap my arms around him. It's a parody of what was done to me barely a half hour ago, with none of the malicious intent. My body stiffens for a moment and then I force it to release. The others are getting off their bikes and situating themselves.

A girl with short red hair and a fiery expression walks over to us with her hands on her hips.

"You two are disgusting. Congratulations."

"You must be Tori," I guess.

She gives me a bit of a smile. "I must be. Nice to meet you, Sadie." Tori gives me a sharp salute before turning around to get her actual backpack from her bike.

"Alright troops, let's roll," she shouts.

Everyone follows Tori as she heads into the woods.

"Where are we going?" I ask again as Logan twines his hand through mine.

"Sup, kid," Linc sidles up next to us. Thor and Ethan are here too. Ethan lights a cigarette and stares off into the distance like he's too good for everyone, and Thor won't meet my eye. I think he's scared of me now.

"You sounded a little loud," Logan starts, and he and Linc start getting into a conversation about recent changes he made on his bike. I understand most of it in theory, but I doubt I'd have the skills that they do in practice. It's different to hear about it or read about it than it is to actually do it. To know what to change and how to change it to achieve what they want to happen.

It's a good thing I'm more interested in structural engineering and the physics of combustion rather than the mechanical aspects.

While they talk, I enjoy the woods. It smells fresh and wet, surrounded by the soaring trunks of red pines before hitting a sky full of branches and needles. We could do this all day and I'd think it was a day well-spent. No one but us out in these woods, walking the needle-covered path, stumbling occasionally on a mushed pine cone.

The trees are thinning out, more ferns and bushes, and then we emerge into a dense grassy field.

Behind the convent.

The closed, condemned, convent.

The Sisters of St. Joseph has been shut down for 15 years. It's a huge building, over a hundred years old, that had a residential and hospice area. Not to mention a massive chapel that was deconsecrated shortly after closure when the first rowdy teens broke in. It didn't stop them from breaking it but it made it less profane.

The building and land was sold to a developer but there hasn't been much movement on that. It's just this piece of Edgar's Bluff history, hanging out in the middle of the woods, feeling scary and sacred at the same time.

"What are we doing here?" I whisper. The Catholic can be taken out of the girl, but it still makes me nervous to misbehave in church spaces. It makes me anxious to be disrespectful, and I start to spiral thinking about what might happen if we're caught.

"Nothing too bad, I promise," Logan smiles at me. "We go in, we play games, we go home. We don't break shit or do anything bad, promise. It's just a space."

I stare up at the looming red brick building, and find that the more I look at it the more inviting it becomes. Despite it's size, there's something oddly cozy about the space. The gardens are overgrown, the walls are covered in unmanaged vines, but it also looks like it's smiling. Human brains are built to see faces, to anthropomorphize objects, and if the convent residence building was a face, I feel like it would be amused to see us.

It makes me less nervous to go inside with them to see that none of the windows are broken. There's no graffiti. There's barely even garbage. Logan and his friends have clearly staked this as their territory in some way and no one has messed with it as a result.

When I follow them through a back door - the board blocking it easily pulled away - we are in a kitchen space. It's stripped of appliances, but still obviously made for cooking. A giant metal prep table stretches along the room, and everyone surrounds it like this is their normal thing. Two people pull electric camping lamps out of their bags and set them up.

Tori stands at the head of the table, waiting for a little light.

"Capture the flag?" she offers.

There's general nodding and murmured consensus, and a guy I don't know steps up next to Tori. She frowns at him, but something in the expression makes me think it's a show.

"What, Seth?"

"I'm the other captain. Me versus you."

Tori cocks her head and gives him a grin. "What do I get when my team kicks your ass?"

Seth doesn't say anything, just smiles at her. Tori actually looks flustered for a second before she rolls her eyes and agrees.

They pick teams, and I'm relieved that right after Tori picks Logan, she picks me. We can stick together then. Not that I couldn't hold my own in the game, but I am afraid to get lost inside the building. It might be floors of squares in the main building, but the boundaries of the game are this building, and any of the connecting buildings. That includes the hospice space, the administrative wing, and the chapel.

Logan can teach me all the best places, and then maybe next time...if there is a next time...I can find my own way.

Tori walks up to Logan and hands him a red bandanna tied to a stick.

"Go hide it."

She doesn't say anything to me, assuming that I'll go with Logan. I want to be offended but I'm not. Tori doesn't waste words when she already knows the outcomes.

"Come on, Sadiebaby. Let me show you my secrets."

I follow Logan through dark hallways, making turns that I can't remember until we find a staircase leading up. The residence is built into a slight hill, so where we were was technically the basement. Once we're on the first floor, it's brighter, full of tall windows obscured by the ivy outside.

While the building is clean despite being empty for so long, it's the emptiness that's disconcerting. So much space without a purpose. That's what makes it feel scary. Like the building is desperate to be filled and it wants to keep us here. To house us and fulfill it's purpose. I shiver with an unexpected chill as I imagine the hallways becoming an endless labyrinth, the building changing itself so it can keep us forever.

Then again, if I'm stuck in here with Logan I might be willing to accept that as my fate.

"You good?" he whispers, turning back to check on me.

"Good. Just...creeped."

He laughs but it's hushed. He doesn't want the other team to hear where we're going. Even that laugh bounces off the empty walls in a way I didn't expect.

"I've been here plenty of times and it still hits me too. Come on," he indicates our direction with his head. We walk straight back from the stairs and take a right, going down a smaller staircase toward two large, ornate, wooden doors.

The chapel.

I hesitate when he holds open the door for me.

"God isn't watching, Sadie. It was deconsecrated."

"I know."

"So?" he prompts. In this moment, I realize that I'm not afraid. It's that I feel like I'm supposed to be. That entering a space like a chapel fills me with dread, a dread so old and ingrained that it's automatic. To feel like I'm walking into a place where I'll be shut down, blamed, that will excuse what's been done. That will make me feel shame instead of safety.

There are plenty of times in my life where the ritual of mass was a relief. That the rhythm of songs, responses, and prayers felt safe. I knew the rituals, I could fall into them without thinking. It was an easy performance. It was an easy way to get mom to leave me alone when I would be chosen to carry the gifts before Communion, or be asked to do a reading on any of the celebrations for youth.

Except when I wasn't chosen, and that was always my fault. Another failure in mom's tally that I would have to scramble to make up for with some other success.

I didn't miss aging out of those expectations.

Walking into this chapel, secular space or not, feels like I'm facing something inside myself. Can I step inside this space and not feel a sense of impending doom? Will I be able to acknowledge my instinctive fear, and then move past it?

Logan doesn't know any of this is going through my head, but he watches me carefully. He waits without pressure. Being there like he always seems to be, knowing me without me having to explain anything.

I walk past him into the chapel.

All of the religious adornment is gone other than the intricate stained-glass windows. The pews are stacked to one side. The altar remains, the shadow of the removed adornment still visible on the front of the marble. All around are empty alcoves where sacred statues used to reside.

It still smells like church in here, the scent of incense probably sunk into the surfaces after a hundred years of services and worship.

Logan steps up and puts his hand on my lower back, leaning in to whisper in my ear.

"Let me show you the best hiding place." His breath on my ear and my neck makes me shiver for different reasons. He pushes me forward and we walk through the chapel, up the few steps to the altar. I follow him around it, and see before he tells me where we're going.

The tabernacle is built into the wall of the chapel. Logan opens the door with a little click, and places the flag inside.

"This feels weird," I laugh as he closes it. "Naughty."

"It can get naughtier." Logan lifts an eyebrow and steps back, then pushes himself up until he's sitting on the altar. I gasp in exaggerated shock.

"Heathen!" I step toward him and stand between his legs. His knees are around my chest, just below my armpits. From this view I can see that he's already hard, and it makes me feel dirty in the best way. Like giving the church the finger.

Not God. That's not the same as the Church.

God is something else. Something wilder, at least to me.

I could care less about the church, and seeing how it's hurt me, and even more how it abandoned Logan's family when they needed their community the most, makes me want to punish the self-righteous snobs who pretend at being saints.

I'd rather be a sinner.

It's time I surprise Logan. Without looking away from his smirking face, I move my hands to his belt. The smirk drops when I roughly pull the leather through the buckle, and when I undo the button and fly.

"Sadie..." he says, strained and hushed. I tease my hand over his erection over his boxers, still not looking away. The pained pleasure on his face is so intoxicating. It makes butterflies riot in my stomach.

I pull his boxers down enough to release his length into my hand, and I tease him. Like he teases me every time he touches me. A soft stroke that sets him on edge, that makes him desperate for more. I want him to be weak in my hands the way I always am for him. Logan's cheeks blossom pink as he stares at me, getting more worked up with each controlled flick of my wrist.

"Do you want to see heaven?" I ask sweetly, before bending down to take him into my mouth. Logan groans, no holding back, and it echoes in the chapel. I move my hand and my mouth in tandem, working all of him at once.

He tastes so good - clean and salty - and a hint of the smell of his skin, his sweat, the thing that draws me to him and makes my mouth water. I move a little faster and listen as his breathing increases, I can feel his stomach brush my head with each rushed breath.

"Baby," he huffs, and his hand slides into my hair, tugging slightly like he wants to pull me off of him. Like he wants us to stop before he gives me what I'm working for.

I don't stop. I press my tongue against his shaft, more pressure with each stroke of my mouth and my hand on the vein along the bottom. The feeling of him pulling and gripping my hair adds to it all for me.

"Fuck," he shouts, and I slide his cock as deep into my mouth as I can. He flinches and moans as I swallow around each pulse of cum. I stroke my hand up with my mouth, taking every last drop with me.

Logan looks dazed, one hand holding him up, the other still in my hair as I stand up.

I grin at him. "How was heaven?"

He roughly pulls me closer by the hair, my head leaning back and exposing my neck to him. I bite my lip when his other hand wraps around my throat, stroking the sensitive skin.

"I'm still there. You're heaven, Sadie."

Logan holds me like that and kisses me, undoing me, until we hear voices outside the chapel. Time to get back in the game.

26

Sadie

It's dark by the time we get back to our neighborhood. The rest of the day was spent running through empty halls, laughing until I couldn't breathe, and riding around with Logan and his friends - his real family - and seeing the town we both grew up in from a completely different perspective.

I don't think I've ever felt this happy in my life.

This free.

We leave his bike at Anderson's and Linc gives us a ride to our houses. He leaves us at the corner because it felt safe to tell him I didn't want my mom to see that we were back. That I was afraid of what would happen if she saw who I had been out with. Linc instinctively understood it wasn't embarrassment or shame - I wasn't trying to hide that I was with Logan - but that I was genuinely concerned about what would happen to me.

Outside of Darcy and Logan, no one has ever just...believed me. They always think I'm exaggerating or being dramatic. We all want to think that the kinds of horrors that end up in the news or in court can't be happening in the house next door. Lincoln knows what Logan's been through, and I don't know how much Logan has told him about me, but either way I appreciated his care in the moment.

Logan and I meander down the street, fingers entwined.

Tension is coiling in my stomach. The good kind.

When I glance at him, the heat I feel within myself is reflected back at me.

We don't talk about the fact that we both turn into his driveway. We don't say a word when he types in the code to open his garage.

We still don't speak but start communicating in a different way when I step into the shelter of the garage. I pull him to me, kissing him with all of the joy and passion that's built up inside me today. We're pulling at each other's clothes, taking off just enough to touch where we want.

My hands are underneath his shirt and sliding along his skin, his heat melting into me.

I cry out into his mouth when he tweaks my nipples, making my back arch and my breasts press into his waiting hands. I look down and watch as his hands trail over my body until they get to my jeans.

The callouses on his hands graze my skin as he pushes my shirt up and then works to undo and pull my jeans and underwear down. It's cold out now but Logan is keeping me warm. I don't even feel the chill when my legs are exposed.

I don't feel the cold metal beneath me when Logan lifts me and sets me on the hood of the Firebird.

"Never thought I'd have you here…like this…" he murmurs into my neck. I feel the graze of his teeth on my neck, his rough hands on my thighs, and I pull him between them. Getting him as close as I can without him being inside me yet.

"Why not?"

"You're you," he says. I slide my hand into his pants and wrap my hand around him, stroking slow and firm. "I've thought about fucking you like this so many times I'm not even sure this is real."

"I'm real. I'll prove it." Logan's jeans slide easily over his hips, and I give his cute ass a pinch when I get him free. One of these days I'm going to finally see him naked in the light and I will crystalize and preserve that memory so that I'll have it forever.

Logan grabs a condom out of his pocket before they drop too far, and I appreciate his preparedness. We both watch as I put it on, but I have to see his face when I bring him in close and position him where he can press inside me.

The wonder and pleasure in his expression undoes me. Like he truly means it that he can't believe he has me. I wrap my hand around his nape for leverage and with the other I brace myself on the hood, hoping that I don't dent it, and move against him. I'm not going to be passive with him - he moves, I move, giving back everything that I'm getting.

Something about the way we are together removes any inhibitions I might have. That I can give and take without worrying that I'm doing something wrong, or needing too much. I can just be.

"Every time you were out here with me, hiding with me," Logan says through clenched teeth, his hands digging into my skin as he holds me where he wants me, "I would dream about it. About going over to you and touching you like I wanted, make you scream like I wanted. You have no idea how many times you were staring off in your thoughts and my dick was hard for you."

A blush of heat runs over my entire body.

"Cum for me, Sadie, prove it's real." Logan kisses me, licking into my mouth, and I gasp as I get closer, everything inside of me coiling and building to release. "My imagination was weak about exactly how fucking good you sound. Give it to me."

He presses me close and shifts his hips just right. My orgasm starts slow, sliding up from my core and into my stomach until it's pressing out all the air in my lungs. Pleasure moves along my skin like lightning and I cry out, working hard to keep my eyes open so he can see exactly how good I feel. I don't muffle a sound, letting it go, letting him hear what does to me.

"Fuck, Sadie," he moans. Logan starts to move faster, harsher, and I know he's close. "I love you." Logan slams his mouth to mine and kisses me, groaning into my mouth with desperation as he cums.

Even after his hips still, he keeps kissing me, breathing in harshly as if he could inhale me. We kiss and kiss with him softening inside me, with my own pleasure drying on my inner thighs. I don't want to stop, but I know we'll have to soon. Leaving Logan always feels like too soon.

When we stop, we stare at each other.

I don't acknowledge that he said he loved me. It was an excited utterance. A heat of the moment, overwhelmed by sensations kind of statement. Logan searches my expression but doesn't bring it up either. I don't know what he sees, but he doesn't look upset.

Instead, he kisses my forehead.

"Stay right here."

I gasp when he slides out of me, feeling woefully empty now. I stay where I am, legs spread open and pussy dripping, as he disposes of the condom and pulls up his pants. He walks to the back of the garage and I can't see what he's doing, but he comes back with a box of tissue.

"It's the best I've got out here." I go to grab it from him but he pulls it back, taking one and gently cleaning my own cum off my skin. "Next time, I'll lick it off. I clean up my own messes." Logan winks at me and I melt, I actually swoon, and it would feel silly if it was anyone else.

But Logan Kurowski is worth swooning over, more than I ever could have imagined.

He even dresses me. It's so gentle and sweet that I want to take our clothes off and start all over again.

When I'm dressed, I get caught up kissing him again. It seems crazy to me that six weeks ago he was a distant fantasy, someone that I could trust to let me retreat and hide when I needed, but nothing more. Now he's real, and he's still my safe place, only now he knows it.

"Alright?" he asks, walking me to the back door.

"Perfect. Thank you for today. I won't get to do anything like that for awhile."

He kisses the tip of my nose and holds the storm door open for me to go inside.

We watch each other through the window after I close the main door and lock it. I stay there as he walks away.

"Have a good night, Sadie?"

I jump at the sound of Cole's voice. He's standing at the top of the small set of stairs leading from the back landing to the kitchen, arms crossed, staring down at me with disgust and judgment.

"I had a great night, Cole." He never used my name as much as he does now that we're broken up. It's like he's constantly saying it in the hope that I'll hear it echoing in my head. The sarcasm when I say his name can't be missed.

"You like slutting yourself out like that?"

He looks even more offended when I laugh.

"What are you talking about?"

"I saw you." Cole has the audacity to look wounded. As if me being with Logan has hurt him. As if he has the right to be hurt by it.

"You mean you watched us. Did you listen, too?" I turn and face him, not feeling the least bit cowed that I have to look up to meet his eyes. This is my monster, and it's time I started fighting him. "Bet that was new...I never sounded like that with you."

Cole's mouth drops open.

"So yeah, I guess I did enjoy 'slutting myself out' if it means that happens." I laugh again, stunned at how true it is. I can't say that the sex I had with Cole that I consented to was bad, I even came a few times, but it was...stunted. I was always holding back, always self-conscious, and my pleasure was incidental compared to it being what Cole thought it should be. Doing what he wanted and pleasing him was more important than it being mutual.

Logan and I have a conversation with our bodies. Even when the focus is one of us, it's still about both of us. I feel good when he feels good, and vice versa, and it's even better when what we're doing is good for both of us at the same time.

With Cole, I never got pleasure from the physical side, but from him confirming that I did what he wanted how he wanted it. That my performance had been acceptable.

It strikes me that most women I know probably share that experience, and it's sad.

"You might be my cousin," I start, and hold in my smirk when he flinches at the reminder that we're family now, "but my relationships and my decisions are none of your business. Goodnight, Cole."

With more confidence than I've had in this house since they moved in, I go downstairs and get ready for bed.

27

Logan

It's been too many years of grieving for me to still have days when I wake up and forget for a moment that my dad is dead. It's been too many years of quiet indifference from my mother for to me to wake up and feel like I did when he was alive. Yet it still happens. It probably always will.

On the anniversary of the day he died, I always know the second I come to consciousness what day it is. It's as if something inside me shifts because it was the day everything in my life was pulled out from under me. The day that all of the pieces that made up my life were rearranged and mashed together in a way that didn't make sense anymore.

I'm awake, and it's today. Pain curls inside my stomach, but that's not even the right word. It's as if my body is at war with itself, pulling back to the age I was when it happened while still existing as I am today.

I will never stop asking myself if we should have noticed something was wrong, but even in hindsight I can't see it. The school counselor told me enough about the common warning signs of suicide and I can't see a trace of them in his actions the days and even weeks before we lost him.

It's the one day a year my mother gives a shit. She called me out of school today. Not that she told me, but I heard her leaving a message for the school secretary.

I didn't say anything to her before I left the house and headed to Anderson's.

It's at least an hour before anyone else shows up and I'm already elbows deep in grease, replacing the fuel tank on an older truck. It's rusted out and made a huge mess, and I'm being extra thorough because the tedium is a distraction.

"Logan." Walker says my name carefully.

"Yeah?" I act as if I don't know what he wants.

"You good?"

How should I fucking know? Good hasn't meant anything to me in years.

"Get your ass out of that truck and talk to me." I've always appreciated that he's blunt. He calls me out, even if it feels like a slap in the face. Like the asshole I am, I stay under the truck doing nothing for a long moment, steeling myself for the conversation I'm about to have. Walker and his wife Maggie love me like I'm one of their own, I know that, but they also love me like I'm not. They don't let me pretend like my life never happened, and that it hasn't changed who I am at my core.

I slide out and move to stand up, not looking at him.

He leans against the tailgate and I mirror his stance.

"Where's your head at today?"

"That I missed something."

"You didn't."

"Yeah. There's knowing and there's believing."

We stand in silence.

"I'm tired of it being a secret. I'm not ashamed of him."

"I know. You weren't old enough to be involved in those choices when they were made. What your mom did…what the congregation did to her and to you…it's fucked, Logan." Walker looks away from me and squints like he's trying to see something far off, and I know he's gearing up to say something he think might piss me off. "But you still go along with it."

I freeze. "What do you mean?"

He turns to look at me, still squinting. "When you were younger, before you had it sorted in your head, that was one thing. But you've been of your own mind for a few years now and you don't talk about it. You don't tell anyone. You don't call out what happened. Silence is a choice too, Logan."

I sigh, not angry, because he's right. The same thought has crossed my mind a few times. I also have my suspicions why I don't say more.

"I don't think Sadie knows."

"The neighbor girl you're dating?" Walker knows that's a simplistic way to identify Sadie. Linc has given me enough shit about her in front of his dad in the last few years that he suspected my feelings for her, not to mention that he knows the whole story about my dad and her parents, and everything that happened after. They probably have no idea who Walker Anderson is and I hope they'd be humiliated by the things he knows about them.

"She would've said something by now. She would've said something then."

"How do you know?"

"Things she's said now - not understanding about church, about why her parents stopped talking to us, and she doesn't play dumb. It's going to hurt her if I start talking."

"From what I've heard, I think she's going to be more upset that you were hurting yourself. Yeah, it's going to be painful, but it's the kind of pain that's worth it."

182

"Not today."

"Fair enough. Finish this and then get the fuck out. I don't want you messing anything up while your head is up your ass. You call Maggie if you need anything."

I nod and move back down to my slider to get under the truck and finish what I'm doing. It's another hour at least to keep me occupied before I'll go home and stare at a wall.

I don't remember the drive home after I finished the truck. I don't remember pulling into my driveway and turning my car off, or that I didn't move to get out of it.

I don't remember anything until there's a knock on my window that jolts me out of the daze I'm sitting in.

It's Chris. Sadie's dad. He's not usually home during the day and I wonder if he stays home on this day too. If despite every action indicating otherwise, it's hard for him too. Doesn't make me think any better of him, but it doesn't make my opinion worse either.

He steps back when I open the car door, and doesn't say a thing when I take out a cigarette and light it. I lean against the car and smoke, waiting for him to say something. He doesn't look like the man I remember anymore. My dad was tall and broad and Chris was tall and skinny, but now...I feel bigger than him. Maybe it's because I'm not looking at him with a kid's eyes anymore, maybe it's because I know he's weak and beaten down in that house as much as his kids are, but the man in front of me is less than he was.

It makes me afraid for Sadie. That if she stays there too long she'll become less than she is because eventually that bitch will break her.

"It's nice to see you and Sadie together again. After..." he stops and swallows thickly, putting his hands in his pockets with self-consciousness. "I'm sorry. None of us were in a good place after your dad died, and we made a lot of choices I wish we hadn't."

I stare at him and take a drag, then exhale right in his face.

To his credit, Chris doesn't react. He doesn't even wipe the smoke away.

"I'm sorry. I failed you. I failed him. I'm sorry, Logan. I know that doesn't mean...shit..." I almost smirk at his hesitance to swear. Like I'm still a kid and he has to watch his mouth in front of me. "But I wanted to say it. I wanted you to know that I made a mistake."

Still I give him nothing, even if I do appreciate that he's finally fucking said something. We haven't spoken more than a handful of words to each other in 7 years, and I can appreciate that when he decides to talk to me again, it's to offer an apology. One I've been owed a long time.

"I like you and Sadie together. I like how she's been lately."

It takes everything I have not to say anything, not to shout at him that there's more he could do, more he could've done, to make her life better. To take the balls he's using to apologize to me and stand up to his wife. To protect his kids from whatever the fuck made her such a monster to them. To see that Sadie is in pain and exhausted every day. That he should enjoy her now because she's going to run away from us all and never look back. That none of us deserve her anyway.

"Thanks for the vote of confidence," I say flatly.

We stare at each other again, and Chris breaks first. He nods, and walks away toward his house.

Memorial Cemetery is empty today. Headstones in every direction, trees, bushes, a few dotted mausoleums, and a huge columbarium on the far side for those who preferred cremation.

Brian Kurowski's body is buried here, a pretty stone in a red brick color. Just his name and birth and death dates. I know it's just a body here, not him, not the essence of who he was, but it still pisses me off that he's here when he should be in Guardian Angel Cemetery across

184

the street.

The place where his father is buried. His grandparents, aunts and uncles, everyone in his own bloodline going back nearly a hundred years. If I die in this town I want to be buried in Guardian Angel just to give those religious hypocrite fucks the finger. My last act of fury being is buried in their consecrated ground.

Father Magnus wouldn't even ask the archbishop for permission to bury my father in Guardian Angel, and without the support of your parish the archdiocese won't even entertain your request. Mom made it anyway, and we never got an answer. She had to make a choice, and he needed to be buried. So here we are.

Mom and I stand side by side, staring at the stone, together but we might as well be alone. We were the only people there when he was buried, no ceremony or service, no blessing that would've mattered to him and none of it mattered to us. We're the only people who ever come here.

I wish Sadie was with me. I'd feel instead of hold back. Mom doesn't deserve my emotions because it will become an invitation to share her own, and I don't want them. I don't want to care about how she's feeling, I don't want to consider her any more than I already do.

Maybe I'll come back with Sadie. It might be the best way to explain everything to her. All the things I don't want to say but I know I need to tell her. My dad's death is part of her history too. It won't be right until she knows the real story.

I walk back to mom's car without a word to her. Waiting until she's done.

I turn my phone on for the first time today and it buzzes with alerts for texts and a voicemail. Most of them are from Sadie - and with every one I read I know that I have to let her all the way in, and let her help me carry my darkest secret.

28

Sadie

Today seems like it's taking forever. I knew Logan was going to be out, but this day always starts…different. It's the one day a year that my mom is actually nice to my dad. However else they might act toward each other, at least she has enough humanity inside her to not be the usual monster today.

I spend my precious texts letting Logan know that I'm thinking about him. That whatever he needs today he only has to ask. I don't care what trouble I get in or how mad it makes anyone, if Logan needs me today then I'm going to be there.

For way too many years I've let him mourn Brian alone.

At practice after school I'm distracted. Darcy knows and has my back, but I nearly trip more than once while running drills, and I miss every goal I attempt during our brief end of practice scrimmage. The look on Coach's face says he's annoyed, and this isn't what he meant when he wanted me to be serious. Lost in my head is the wrong kind of serious.

Except I keep thinking about the last time I saw Brian.

I wasn't allowed to go to the funeral. I never got to say goodbye in any way that felt meaningful. I was told Brian was gone, and then

I was told to forget. No more time with the Kurowskis, my parents stopped acknowledging his mom or Logan when we saw them, and it was as if he didn't exist anymore. They stopped coming to church, and it was like they'd never been part of our lives.

As if all the weekends, holidays, vacations were erased from our history. Pictures disappeared. Their names were basically forbidden until I stopped trying to bring it up at all. I grieved alone. Dad shut down and refused to talk about Brian, mom would get angry if I brought it up, and James was too little to understand. There was no one to talk to when one of the biggest supports in my life was suddenly gone.

The last time I was with Brian was when my parents took James to a dentist appointment. He didn't do well at the dentist so they both went to keep him calm. Or maybe to keep him in line - dad would be too nice and mom too mean so they balanced each other out.

Brian and I were at their kitchen table working on a puzzle. It was a picture of birds with lots of bright colors. We wouldn't even get through half of it. I was talking about being bored in my science class and he reminded me that I had to get really good at what I knew before moving on to something new.

"You gotta be so good you do it without thinking, Sadiebaby. That it's all second nature. You have to know the rules forwards, backwards, inside out, upside down. Then you can break them."

Brian gave me a reassuring smile and then ruffled my hair, which he knew drove me crazy and would distract me from my frustration.

Three days later, mom told me he was dead.

And we never spoke about it again.

The house is quiet when I get home, which is weird because usually it's time to eat dinner as soon as I walk in the door.

"Hello? Anyone home?" I call out as I leave my backpack by the basement stairs and head toward the dining room.

"In here," dad answers. Things are even weirder. My stomach hollows with nerves.

He's sitting in the dining room, the table not set, no smells that indicate dinner was even going to happen. Dad is pale, a little sweaty, more broken down than usual even.

"Sit down, honey, I need to talk to you about something."

I sit, and the pit in my stomach deepens. Like something is pulling me into myself by the stomach. It's already been a mess all day because I've been worried about Logan, but now it's even worse. I want to throw up.

"Has Logan talked to you about Brian?"

It takes me a bit to answer. "Not really."

Dad nods and swallows thickly. "We lied to you." His voice is raspy and quiet, and it takes me a moment to process what he said.

"About what?" Foreboding dominates my body and I start shaking.

"We did it to protect you. To protect us. What happened...it was better if you didn't know."

"I don't understand."

"Brian...he struggled sometimes. You remember."

I nod.

"It was suicide, Sadie."

"No." It's my immediate reaction and I can't keep it in. Brian loved his family too much to do that. Except I know what dad is talking about. Times when Brian would retreat inside himself and not talk to anyone, when he'd get fixated on a project as a distraction, a couple times he got drunk and sad and sat in their backyard staring at the sky. Muttering to himself. Crying sometimes.

It takes a moment for me to parse through my racing thoughts.

"Why are you telling me this?" My voice cracks and it makes me angry. I want to be so angry at my dad right now. Parts of my body feel numb with shock.

"I wanted to tell you before Logan did...before he realized..."

"That you lied to me?"

Dad flinches, but I don't feel bad.

"He was your best friend, you knew him your whole life, and you just...lied. Lied and abandoned his family."

I stand up but before I can say more, there's a commotion behind me. Everyone else got home. Either I got home late or this took longer than they planned.

"The church -" dad starts, ignoring that this conversation is about to get interrupted.

"You stopped talking to them because of church?!" More pieces are starting to fall into place for me now.

"Of course, suicide is a sin," mom's voice snaps from behind me. "What else could we do?"

There's a new hatred for her boiling under my skin as I turn to look at her. Dave, Julia, Cole, and James are all arrayed behind her. Like some fucked up intervention and I'm the one that needs to be confronted.

"Whose suicide?" James asks.

Mom looks stricken for a second. "Brian."

"Oh." James looks down at the ground, not as impacted by this information but still realizing that it's a big deal. That it changes things.

"So we just...stopped talking to them? Punished them for Brian's choice?"

"Yes," mom answers like it's so simple. Like it was the choice that made the most sense instead of being unfathomably cruel. No wonder Logan's mom is such a mess. She lost her entire support system in one day.

"We all did what we could to keep it quiet, so they weren't entirely shut out and had a chance to move on, but they weren't welcome anymore. Father Magnus was quite firm on that."

I have to breathe through my nose or I think I'll throw up. Father Magnus left about a year after Brian died. He was beloved by the congregation of St. Stan's. Logan and I were both baptized by him, received our First Communion from him, he watched us grow up.

He did the most uncharitable thing I can imagine.

For a second, I'm so dizzy I can't see anything. I lean back against the table and put my face in my hands, trying to pull it together.

"I hope you go to hell for this," I murmur, then look up at first mom, then dad.

"Sadie!" Mom is scandalized.

"Do you know what it's been like for him in that house? Do you have any idea what he's been through?" I shake my head. "Look after orphans and widows - it's literally in the Bible. This is how you look after them?"

"You don't understand," mom starts but I shake my head.

"There is nothing you can say that will make me understand." I turn to my dad. "How could you? You make me sick." Dad drops his eyes and I know he makes himself sick too. Good.

"You will not speak to your parents that way, they deserve respect," Dave finally adds to the conversation and steps further into the room.

To my surprise, I see Cole whispering to James and they both walk past us all toward James's room. Whatever is going down here, James shouldn't be around for it. Half of it he doesn't understand, and the rest will only make his life worse.

"They deserve respect for this, really?" I turn on Dave. "So if you died and they lied about it, I should respect that?"

Dave's mouth drops open and I think for the first time ever I've rendered him speechless.

"You're hypocrites. Brian wouldn't have done this to you."

"Maybe not, but we aren't Brian." Mom says it like that's reasonable.

Like any of this was sane or reasonable.

I shake my head, my brain swirling, my eyes watering because now that it's settling in I want to scream and cry. It's like grieving his loss all over again because it's all different now. Everything that happened before and after is shown to me in a completely different light. Not just how I feel about Brian, but it's irrevocably changed how I view my parents. The church.

"I wish you were," I look up at my mom. "I wish you were dead."

All hell breaks loose around me. Mom, Dad, and Dave all yelling at me. I don't care. I stare at the wall as they shout, not registering anything that they say.

"You're grounded!" Mom gets in my face and I look down my nose at her.

"No." It's said with more nonchalance than I think I've ever been capable of. I won't listen to her anymore. I don't care. I don't care what happens because she deserves nothing from me.

"And you have to speak with Dave about your behavior. Logan is changing you, Sadie. You've done nothing but be a brat since you started talking to him."

"Yes, it's definitely because of Logan," I snort, tears falling down my cheeks without my control. "I'm not talking to Dave. You'll be lucky if I ever speak to you again."

Dad says my name, but I can't even look at him. I push off the table and walk to the kitchen, toward the back door. I'm leaving. I have to get out of here or I might end up saying things I really do regret.

I slide into my shoes and grab my coat.

"You walk out that door and you are grounded, young lady."

"Cool," I throw over my shoulder before stepping out and slamming the door behind me.

I walk fast and cut through yards to get away, to get somewhere they won't find me if they come looking.

Thankfully my phone was in my pocket. It rings and rings but Logan finally answers. He sounds calm, and I know it's selfish but I need him. And I need him to know that he's not alone with this anymore. I don't even know how I'm going to begin to apologize, but I have to start now.

"Where are you?"

"Where are you?" Logan answers. "You don't sound okay, Sadie."

"I'm not. Where are you?" I ask again.

"The shop."

"Okay." I hang up before he can say anything else or offer to come get me. If he's at the shop, he's with the Andersons. That's where he gets support and I'm not taking him away from that environment. This is going to be bad enough, I want him somewhere that feels safe.

The walk is cold but I don't feel it. I can't feel anything.

It gives me time to think and process my own emotions so that I'll hopefully be more rational and in control when I see Logan.

The first thing I accept is that this doesn't change how I feel about Brian. It doesn't change who he was in my life, or how much his loss hurts. I'm not angry at him even when I want to be because I think I know how he felt. How it feels to be so utterly hopeless, that no matter how many good things I can think of, life still feels like a trial I have to win. I don't know anything specific about Brian's depression, but I can't hold something he couldn't entirely control against him.

More than anything, I'm angry at my parents, and I'm angry at myself for believing them and going along with the way everything happened after Brian died. I was young but I wasn't that young, and I've never been stupid. I didn't question it because I didn't want to - I was already hurting and didn't want to interrogate their strange behavior.

We all failed Logan. Even more than me, my dad.

Brian would've been there for me if anything happened to my dad. It should shame my father to know that his best friend was a better man than him.

I should've kept in touch. Reached out. Even though Logan had always been quiet and surly, and likely would've pushed me away or rejected my support...that wouldn't have stopped me, and it shouldn't have. If there's one thing I pride myself on it's being annoying when I know I'm right, and I would've annoyed him into relying on me. Into letting me support him.

I left him alone.

It's the biggest regret I'll ever have.

Things Linc said to me last week make more sense now. About leaving him better than I found him even if I'm still going to leave him. Linc and the rest of them know the truth and I've been walking around like an oblivious asshole. Linc was trying to tell me, even the conversation they had about Logan's mom takes on a different cast now, and I didn't see it.

I will never forgive my parents for this. I am madder at them for what they did to Logan than I am for anything they ever did to me. When it comes to me, it's been resigned acceptance. I'll get out and get away and be okay, I'll move on. I will pray for karma to burn them every day for the rest of my life for what they did to Logan.

When I open the door to the shop I realize how cold I am, the heat makes my hands throb with pain after the chill.

Logan, Linc, the other Andersons, a few of their friends, are all sitting around the couch. Just talking. Logan is sitting next to an older woman who I am assuming is Mrs. Anderson. He's staring down, listening but not engaging, and I know he's there because they want to keep an eye on him and he wants them to feel like they're being allowed to take care of him.

The door shuts behind me and Logan looks up, attention drawn to the sound. It goes quiet but as soon as our eyes meet, I could care less about anyone else.

"Sadie," Logan says and stands up, moving toward me without a thought for anything else. I don't know what he sees in my face but his expression shifts to something like resignation. The guard he's dropped around me the last few weeks is back up and I don't know why. Does he really think I'd react like my parents? That I would reject him?

I can't let him think it for another second.

I run toward him and jump, knowing that he'll catch me. My arms wrap around his neck and my legs around his waist, and I squeeze him as tight as I can. As if I could bring him inside myself and let him see for himself exactly what I'm thinking and feeling.

I press my face to his neck, tears streaming again, sliding onto his skin.

"I'm sorry. I'm so sorry Logan. I didn't know. I should've known." I can't hold back a sob and I feel so ashamed. Logan's arms wrap around me tighter, and we stay like that, lost in our own world.

"It's okay, baby. You didn't know." He makes soft shushing noises, and keeps telling me it's okay. It's not okay. Not even a little.

I pull back and look down at him. "Please forgive me."

"No."

My face crumples and he leans forward to kiss me quick. "There's nothing to forgive, Sadie. Not you."

I nod. "I don't think I can forgive them for this." Logan lets me drop my legs and slide to the floor but he keeps me pressed against him, our faces close, this conversation only for us.

"Then don't."

"I told my parents they were going to hell and that I wished my mom was dead."

Logan curls his lips trying not to laugh. "I wish I could've seen that."

"They weren't happy. I think I'm grounded."

My eyes close when Logan presses his forehead to mine. "Worth it."

"I'm sorry." More tears spill out and he kisses them off my cheeks. "Let's go."

Without looking back, he takes my hand and we leave the garage.

29

Sadie

This is different than any time we've been together before. While it's intense, it's not urgent. We can't stop touching each other as Logan walks me through his house and up to his room.

When I was here last weekend it was the only place we didn't clean, the only place he wouldn't let us go. He said it was still too private, and I understood.

He turns on the lamp next to his bed and takes off his coat. It drops to the ground.

We move toward each other, reaching out and removing layer after layer from one another. Stripping away more than our clothes, but any barriers between us as well. We've never gotten to see each other naked before so clearly, so well lit.

Logan's body is stunning. Lean, muscular, skin that looks so soft I want to sink my teeth into it. He's got a few tattoos, one on his chest, two on his arm, and now I can see them more clearly. The one on his chest is impressive - it's an engine that's also morphed to look like an anatomical heart - a blending of the two.

He sees me looking and touches it, making me focus on his hands. Long, defined, his knuckles permanently scarred from working as much as from fighting.

"Ethan's work."

I make some sort of noise of assent but I'm still too busy enjoying him. Logan is doing the same with me and I don't feel self-conscious at all. There's no universe I can imagine in which Logan looks at me and feels the need to say something critical. Even if he thought it, I can't imagine him saying it out loud.

Logan takes my face in his hands and kisses me, walking me back until I land on his bed. His mouth leaves mine and starts traveling, across my jaw, down my neck, lower and lower. Every kiss and lick is measured and slow, as if he's savoring the taste and feel of me. I can't stop running my hands over his body, pressing him into the places that feel the best. Allowing him to map my pleasure points for future use.

His palms are rough on my thighs as he spreads them open, and before I can sit up and tell Logan he doesn't have to - his head is pressed against my core and his tongue is sliding along my clit. I cry out and fall back, letting my legs fall open further to give him more access.

I can feel every brush of his tongue, every press of his lips, and he gently slips a finger inside me and it's like I leave my body and I'm also more present in it at the same time. Everything he does feels incredible.

"You want more, Sadie?"

"Yes," I moan. I look down as Logan looks up at me, a soft smile on his face. He keeps watching as he slides another finger inside and presses against me. My eyes close and then he's sucking and licking again.

"Give it up for me, Sadie. Sing for me, little sinner." All the air leaves my lungs and a feeling overtakes me, an inferno of pleasure. Nothing is making me be quiet, and I let it all out. I scream his name, pressing hard against his mouth and his fingers. At some point he stops, but it takes me a second to get back to myself.

Logan is already kissing the inside of my thighs, over my stomach, between my breasts. He's leaning over me when I turn my head to meet his eyes.

"Want to taste your depravity?"

I nod, and Logan kisses me. I've never tasted myself before, and to know that he so clearly enjoyed it is intoxicating. He breaks our kiss but doesn't go far, reaching around without looking to his bedside table. I'm not sure what we're communicating as we look at each other, but it makes my heart stutter.

Logan gets a condom and puts it on. He wraps his arms around me, I do the same, and we're pressed tightly together as he slides inside me.

I lift my head to kiss him, and we don't stop. Our bodies move in perfect rhythm, close and away, my tongue sliding along his, the taste of him and the taste of me, the warmth of his body permeates all the way through me.

It might be the first time in years I've been truly warm.

I moan into his mouth as I start to cum again. He holds me even tighter and follows a few minutes later. We don't move, our chests pressing together as we try and catch our breath.

After taking turns in the bathroom, Logan pulls me back onto his bed and wraps himself around me. My body is curled up against his, overwhelmed by his size compared to mine. I feel unbelievably safe. Contained but in a way that feels secure rather than a trap.

"Are you ready to hear about it?" Logan asks quietly into my neck.

"If you want to talk about it."

"I do. I want to talk about it with you. It's different with you…"

I don't say anything, I wait for him to say what he wants to say.

"I've thought about it a thousand times and didn't see it. The only thing I've ever asked my mother about it was if there was any hint...she said no. He was good. It had been ages since he'd...gone dark."

"It's not your fault. Even if there had been a sign...it's not your fault."

"Yeah, I know."

"He took pills and walked into the woods. Left a note in my mom's car. Told her not to look, just to call." I feel him swallow. "She looked. I think it broke her."

"Even if she hadn't..." I shift so I can see his face. "Are you okay if we talk about this? We don't have to."

"No, we need to - it's different talking to you. You actually knew my dad, and knew him well. He loved you. It's the closest thing to feeling the same way I do."

My eyes well up with tears again, not only at the statement but also the sincerity when he says it.

"They really loved each other," I start, my voice hesitant and raspy.

"I remember." It makes the way his mom treats him so much worse. I snuggle into his shoulder, squeezing him tighter to offer what small comfort I can.

"Losing the love of your life that way...some things we don't recover from. It's not an excuse for how she is, but I can't imagine..." Logan doesn't say anything and when I look up to check on him, he has an expression on his face that I don't understand. "Sometimes losing love does more damage than hate."

"I wish I could hate her," he whispers. "It'd be so much easier if I did." Even though no one is around to hear us, this is a conversation made for whispers and low murmurs. For admitting dark secrets, and being accepted for them rather than judged.

"I hate my mom. I'm...I don't even know how I feel about my dad now." I explain to Logan what happened tonight before I came into the shop, that I was reeling from the revelation of it all and horrified by how everyone responded to something so tragic. Feeling ashamed of myself for believing the lie.

"I could've said something. I was old enough to challenge them. Mom wasn't going to, she was already checked out after the whole burial drama, I could have called them all out. It was easier to go along with it, at the time."

"What do you mean burial drama?"

Logan explains everything, and I sort of want to find Father Magnus at his new congregation in Illinois and punch him in the face. Or spit in his holy water. For the first time all night, Logan laughs.

"Calm down, killer. I've come to terms with it."

"I'm not going back to church. I can't. I won't be able to look at any of those people without going nuclear and trying to kill them with my mind."

Logan kisses my forehead. "If anyone could do it, it would be you."

I sigh and lean into him. "What can I do?"

"Nothing, for me. You keep giving your family hell and finding your way, and let me have your back. Have mine when I'm struggling. Just...be there."

"You were always there for me, even if you didn't know that's what you were doing."

"Same goes, Sadiebaby. You have no idea how much you gave me sitting in my garage in silence."

We kiss again, slow and soft.

"He loved you. You know that, right?"

"It took a few years to accept that one, but I know that. Without a doubt. It had nothing to do with loving me, or even loving mom. I think that's why I stick around. It'd be so much easier if I could blame her. But it's like a contract I have to finish. I have to see this through."

"Whatever you want to do." We stare at each other for a long time, memorizing this bittersweet moment. I'm sleeping in his bed. I'm staying the night. I have no intention of going home, damn the consequences. My brain needs a bit of time to recover and process it all before I face them, and that means sleep.

Logan pulls the blankets more tightly around me. "Go to sleep. It's a school night."

He might be the only person who tells me what to do and I want to listen.

30

Logan

It's not even embarrassing that I watch Sadie sleep for awhile. Feeling her breathe against me is reassuring. It's so certain. I've never felt more at peace in my life.

Even before dad died, I was never at peace. I was never truly relaxed. He was sick, we knew it, we never knew when things would change, and it meant there was always an edge of anxiety. I was always on alert to do what I could to make him feel better. When I was young I didn't understand what I was trying to stop, I just knew that I was.

I didn't understand dying, much less taking your own life.

But the fear of it hung over our house nonetheless.

I've never asked mom, or anyone, but I'm assuming there were attempts in the past. Something that happened that made her so vigilant.

Knowing I have Sadie to support me makes me want to ask those questions. Knowing that she would want the same answers makes me feel bolder. Instead of stuffing it all down inside, pretending like I've got it all handled, I can let it out.

Maybe that's what I've been waiting for with mom - for the bravery to demand answers from her. I needed Sadie to find it. To believe getting the answers was worth it.

Almost as if it wasn't entirely real until she knew the truth.

For all intents and purposes, she was a daughter to him too.

A wave of anger comes over me.

If he was here, he never would've let her mother get away with what she's been doing. Sadie has been so fucking alone in a way I couldn't even guess at, and part of the reason that happened was because he died. Because he couldn't fight through the darkness to stay. I forgive him for not knowing how to fight, I do, for not seeing another way.

I struggle to forgive him for all the potential things that were lost. How different my life would be, Sadie's life, mom's...even her parents would be in such a different place if he was still here. Dad might've had darkness inside him but he brought so much light to other people. It's like looking into the abyss made him wiser than most. His advise was always rock solid.

Whenever I asked for his help when I struggled at school, when I thought I was stupid, when other kids gave me shit for my bad grades...he was always the one who put it into perspective for me. Who taught me to only give a shit about the opinions of people worth listening to and trusting.

It made me selective and careful, and I feel like I've picked well when it comes to the people I let into my life.

The best choice I ever made was picking Sadie.

I take my phone out and send a text to her dad. That she's here and she's safe and that she better not be in trouble when she gets home or I will make some fucking trouble.

He replies that it's okay and he'll see her tomorrow.

Telling her the truth and talking about how I felt was more of a relief than I ever expected. I thought I'd feel like I was burdening her when we talked but it ends up I was lifting something off both of us. The horror of my life changing over one choice and the terrible ripples it caused were something I couldn't carry alone.

"I love you," I whisper to Sadie's cheek. She smiles slightly and turns deeper into me. Finally, I close my eyes.

31

Sadie

The fear of going home today was so strong that I vomited before last period, and after practice. It's not normal to be this scared of your parents.

I wore one of Logan's sweatshirts to school and I never felt more his girlfriend than walking around in an Anderson's Garage shirt that was nearly to my knees. It was the only thing that kept me feeling remotely safe. It smells like him. Which has the strange affect of making me feel turned on and cozy at the same time.

Darcy drives me home, and I start to hyperventilate sitting in her car. I can't move. I don't know what's going to happen. I've never behaved like I did yesterday, I've never defied them so drastically. I have no frame of reference for this level of punishment.

When I get home, mom and dad are both sitting at the table. Mom at the head, dad to her right. It's always strange to me to see how they orient themselves. I did a report on royalty and seating etiquette and it can't help but filter into my brain.

I sit down across from mom at the other head. This is a showdown, and I want to take a place of power.

It's so weird to me that every interaction with my mom is a battle.

I'm always at war with her, and I don't think there will ever be peace.

Looking at them both now after sleeping and then processing yesterday's revelation, I'm at best apathetic toward them when not actively angry. Before, I thought there might be a chance that I still have a relationship with my dad when I leave, but I'm not sure anymore. I'll do what it takes to get James through it and out of this house.

"I understand that you were upset yesterday," Mom starts. "And you may have said some things in the moment that you didn't mean."

I don't say anything. She's waiting for an apology that won't come.

Her lips tighten and she takes a breath, but dad reaches over and puts his hand over where hers are wrapped together on the table. Mom looks at him and her shoulders drop as she exhales. I don't know what they talked about while I was gone last night, but it's the most influence I've seen him have over her, ever.

"You're grounded for two weeks. School, soccer, nothing else."

"Okay."

We look at each other. They're waiting for me to say more but I've got nothing for them. When it comes to them, I am so emotionally spent and mentally empty that I can't even feel anger right now. They are no longer worth my energy and my effort.

At some point, when I'm somewhere safe and no longer constantly exhausted, I'll grieve. The parents they were, and the parents they weren't.

But since we're making demands...

"I'm not going to church anymore."

My parents both flinch. Dad has the dignity to look down at the table and nod.

"Sadie. How will that look?"

"I don't care."

"Father Paul isn't like - he had nothing to do with - " Mom doesn't know what to say, but I find it very interesting she knows why. She knows exactly what's led to this.

"Everyone else did. I don't want to be affiliated with that kind of cruelty. The only reason I'm tolerating you is because you're my mother."

Mom's head snaps back like I slapped her, and her cheeks pinken with shame. If only I had it in me to do to her what she's done to me, but I'll never sink to that level. She opens her mouth and then closes it.

"I'm 18. You can't make me."

"You live in my house!" She stands up, starting to get her usual fury back.

"I don't have to live in your house!" I shout back. "Don't start going down this road, mom, you won't like where it ends."

She swallows down whatever she's going to say, knowing that I'm right.

"I'm grounded, I understand." My voice is calm, a contrast to her shrill energy. It's the thing about me that makes her the most angry, maybe because she envies it. Mom can't keep her emotions down, whereas mine can stay buried deep. I'm calm in the face of ridiculousness while she can't stop herself from responding.

"Go to your room," she hisses.

I do.

I can hear them upstairs eating dinner. Not being allowed to join them is another punishment.

I should be doing homework or something productive, but I don't. Instead, I sit and I stare and I breathe, letting everything wash over me. Letting myself be in this place and this house, this purgatory until I can move forward with the future.

I'm so tired.

My heart is still pulsing with pain, bleeding for Brian and that he was shoved away, hidden, lied about, and it didn't even help anyone.

It only made Logan and his mom more isolated, gave them more pain. It's sickening.

The house goes quiet.

I sneak upstairs and out the back door, knowing exactly how to keep quiet.

Before Logan, I never had to sneak out of the house. I was just allowed to go, wander, assumed that I would come home. It didn't mean I wasn't prepared for when I had to sneak.

Logan is in the garage, working on the Firebird. He's smiling, so it's going well tonight. I lean against my house and watch him, enjoying seeing him when he doesn't know he's being observed. The more I watch, the more the tension slides out of me.

I am in so much trouble.

I don't want more things to tie me to Edgar's Bluff. I don't want reasons to come back. I don't want to feel bound to this place and if I fall for him, I will. If I really fall in love with Logan I won't be able to walk away. It will not leave either of us better than we were. It will only be pain, and eventually I'll resent him for keeping me here.

But right now I don't want to worry about that.

I run across our mucky yards, and Logan's smile gets bigger when he hears me coming and turns to look at me.

His arms open and I smash into them, burying my face in his chest.

"Take me for a ride?" It's muffled but he can hear me.

Logan laughs and it moves from his body into mine. "You like it, huh?"

I look up at him, letting my eyes smile. "Yeah."

He pulls me with him toward the other side of the garage where he keeps his bike. Without asking, he knows we're being incognito. He pushes it down the driveway and into the street before getting on and starting it up. I get my helmet on and climb on fast, wrapping around him is the most natural thing in the world now. It doesn't take any thought, an instinctive move.

We zoom off down the road, the chill dark sliding along my skin. The feel of Logan against me giving me everything that I need right now. The roads are empty in this small town, and it's as if we're the only two people in the world. There's no one left but us.

That's a world I'd be willing to live in. Logan and me against the elements.

It'd be easier than taking on either of our mothers.

32

Logan

Sadie is grounded, which means I only get to see her at school and if I can get out of the garage in time to drive her home from practice. Her mom watches me like a hawk - it would almost be funny. She gives more of a shit about me than my own mom, watching me out their kitchen window, stopping and staring when she's outside and I'm coming or going from my house.

I smile and wave and greet her every single time. She could never accuse me of being rude, that's for sure. Imagining how much it must infuriate her gives me so much joy.

That's what I'm thinking about in English class when there's a knock on the door.

Sadie's friend Darcy comes in holding a basket. It's St. Patrick's Day and the athletic teams do a big fundraiser every year. It goes to all the teams that aren't football to help them cover the costs of equipment and stuff.

"Favor deliveries!" Darcy smiles and gives me a wink that I don't understand. She hands off a few to people sitting around me, and then smirks when she stops in front of my desk.

Darcy tips over the basket she's carrying, dumping about fifty shamrock-shaped chocolates with little notes into my lap. I pick one up and see a sparkly red lip print and Sadie's name. Every single one has a kiss from her to me.

I laugh.

"Just wait, neighbor boy." On that amusing but ominous note, Darcy waves to the teacher and leaves.

I slide the favors into my backpack and try not to let my girlfriend being cute ruin my reputation by sitting here grinning like an idiot. If I let other people know that my girl can make me soft, it's going to make them think they can take me.

More deliveries are made in my next two classes, although the athletes doing the deliveries look more confused than amused. I've got a pretty massive stash of candy in my backpack by the time I head to lunch. When I put my bag on the table the shamrocks spill out, sliding in every direction.

"Holy shit," Thor says, and takes a handful. He looks at the notes, one after the other, and frowns when he sees they're all from Sadie. It doesn't stop him from eating them but he doesn't look quite as happy as he did at first.

"Sure, help yourself." I shake my head and go to the line to get food. Sadie has the lunch hour after mine, or I'd be saying fuck food and find a way to sneak off with her and make her cum so much she cries for being so adorable and embarrassing. She can embarrass me all she wants by making declarations like this, but I'll definitely punish her for it later. In all the best ways.

Thor and Linc are arguing when I get back to the table, and I know I was the topic of conversation when they both pull back when I sit down. Janet has moved away from where she was sitting with Thor to sit next to her brother. He must've really pissed them off.

I look at them both and Linc rolls his eyes.

"Something to say?" I turn to Thor. I keep eye contact, not blinking, eating my lunch without tasting it. I need him to know I can intimidate him and get shit done at the same time. Thor can't do the same. He takes a bite and swallows quickly, unable to keep consistent eye contact.

"Just think it's kind of weak," he shrugs, gesturing to the candy. "She's on your ass man. She's embarrassing herself."

I huff out a laugh with no humor, and sit up straighter. Thor pulls back, putting more distance than the table between us. Everyone else shifts away from him, fully aware of how stupid he is in this moment.

Before I can say anything, someone else speaks up.

"The only one being embarrassing right now is you," Ethan drawls, eating a french fry. "You fucking reek with envy. Leave."

Thor looks confused, looking around at the rest of us to see if we're going to say anything or come to his defense. No one does, and I have nothing further to add to what Ethan already said.

"You support your friends," Linc adds quietly. "Whatever your problem is with Sadie, get over it."

"Whatever." Thor grabs his backpack and gets up. I look over my shoulder as he walks away, leaving the cafeteria without eating.

"You gonna share?" Ethan asks, reaching over to take a shamrock. "Have at it."

The pattern of favor delivery continues the rest of the school day, rivers of chocolates being poured into my lap. Sadie kissed over 200 pieces of paper and signed her name with a heart on every single one. For me. Outside of the Andersons, I don't know the last time someone put in so much effort to do something nice for me.

Not nice in the basic decency survival kind of way, but something pointless, silly, joyful. Something that was done purely because it would make me happy. That's all Sadie wants from me, and it's all she wants me to give her.

I skip out of my last class of the day early so I can meet her by the locker room before she goes into practice.

Her teammates surround her as they walk down the hall and they all break out into giggles when they see me.

Sadie doesn't smile with her mouth, but I can see it in her eyes. She rations her smiles, as if only letting them out when something really deserves it. Boosts my ego to know how much she's given those smiles to me. Sadie's smiles come easy when we're together.

It's the best thing I can give her.

I approach her, ignoring her friends, not caring what they see.

I reach behind Sadie and wrap my hand around her ponytail, pulling her head back as I step close until we're chest to chest.

"Proud of yourself, hm?" She's doing the best she can not to laugh right now.

"Did you enjoy your treats?"

"I'd enjoy you more," I whisper against her mouth before kissing her fiercely. Her friends whoop and cheer, and Sadie smiles against my lips. A smile I devour, happily, and she lets me.

"Had to make sure everyone knows you're mine," she says, and something crosses her expression. Some hint of shame that I don't understand.

"Do I need to shout it? Wear your name on a shirt?"

"No," she shakes her head, laughing a little.

The hall is full of other athletes getting ready for their practices, heading towards the locker rooms. I recognize one of the baseball players.

"Hey, Schmid, did you know Sadie is my girlfriend?"

He stops and looks confused, looking to the other guys around him for confirmation that I spoke. "Uh, yeah?"

"Great."

Sadie's blushing scarlet. "Guys aren't the problem."

Now I move, pressing her into the wall. We've had an intense few weeks, so if something happened with another girl talking crap, there hasn't been a chance for her to tell me about it. Whatever they did or said really got into her head, though.

"Who said something to you?"

"It doesn't matter. They know now."

"They already did, baby." I kiss her nose. "But now I gotta make a fucking t-shirt. Just to prove a point."

Sadie laughs, but hides it in my chest. She's wound so tight she doesn't even want to share her laughter with other people. Doesn't want them to see her bigger emotions in case they use them against her.

"I'm going to be late."

"I'll give you a ride."

"No. I want to talk to Darcy. Need some girl time."

I pout, and it makes her smile again. "Fine." I pull her to me and kiss her fiercely one more time before heading out the back doors to meet Linc at his car.

My girl. All mine.

And she's finally embracing that I'm hers, too.

33

Sadie

It's the first soccer game of the season and we're starting out against our nearest rival, Burnfield. At soccer, we beat them consistently, but they like to talk a lot of crap because their football team has beat ours for the last three years. Football beats everything, so even if they are about to get their butts handed to them on the pitch, they'll walk away with a feeling of superiority.

In high school, it doesn't matter how good your other sports are, your whole reputation is made or broken by football.

How irritating.

Coach already gave us a Talk in the locker room, going over strategy, reminding those of us who returned about what we learned from video of last year. We're kitted up, got all our gear and tape and braces, I'm wearing my lucky shoelaces that I only put in my boots for games. The only thing that I let myself be superstitious about.

I keep them in my locker at school because I don't trust anyone at home not to mess with them. Cole knew about my lucky laces and I could see him holding them hostage. I could see mom suddenly deciding it was pagan to have a lucky item and burning them. She gets weird about things like that but not consistently - it's like she wants to punish me and invents a reason and religion is convenient.

As always, I'm the last to leave the locker room. I check that everyone is ready, that we have everything, and to take a last breath when no one is looking at me. In order to actually center myself I need to be unobserved.

Coach is waiting outside the door.

"I need to know that you're focused today."

"I'm focused."

"None of that cocky shit."

It takes all of my control not to roll my eyes. I'll do what I need to do, what feels right in the moment. This year I've been pretty quiet but sometimes I have to open my mouth and let it out. Coach should know that better than anyone - he never keeps his mouth shut either. It's never impacted my skills, my playing, or our team performance. It's exhausting to have to carry his expectations too.

I don't say anything. He says my name as I walk past him and down the hall toward the exit but I keep going. If he doesn't want me to talk then I won't say anything. Honestly, with all the time I'm spending with Logan, my sass is going to be taken to another level. He's taught me that you don't have to say a word to speak volumes. There's power in silence too.

I used to think my silence was weakness, was fear, and now I realize it can be protection and an attack, too.

The team is waiting for me, gathered around waiting for our final huddle. We've got our game faces on. There's no hooliganism until we're on the field.

I tighten my cleats and take the open spot in the circle, closing the huddle and blocking out everything and everyone else. Coach stands away, he knows this isn't for him. At least he gets the message when it matters.

We wrap our arms around each other, and I can feel the heat from their bodies. My teammates, my friends, my sisters. I can hear and feel them breathing, the intensity of our desire to play is a scent in the air.

"We know they're going to talk shit," I start, "but we also know they've never beat a single person on this team. We know it's all they've got because they can't put their money where their mouth is. They're all talk and we're all play. Right?"

"RIGHT!" They reply in unison, violence in their tone.

"Victory is ours!"

"RIGHT!" This time it's even louder.

"BOBCATS!" I shout.

"BOBCATS!" We all roar in unison.

My heart is racing and adrenaline is starting to work it's way through my system. We move onto the field for the start of the game, and I look toward the fence. We don't have bleachers or stands - that's more money than the school would be willing to spend no matter how good we are - so instead people bring their own chairs and take over the grassy strip between the fence around the field and the sidewalk.

James is right up to the fence, leaning on it. He'll stand the whole game, cheering and shouting even though he knows I won't understand a word. It's the commitment that counts. I do the same at his volleyball games - I stand on the side of the gym and shout for him. We have each other's backs, always.

Behind him, mom, dad, Dave, Julia, and even Cole sit in camp chairs. Cole looks really self-satisfied, as if being here will throw off my game. If anything, it'll make me remind him that I'm stronger than he thinks. That there's violence and power inside me and I'm not afraid anymore to use it against him.

The rumble of an engine stops me mid-step.

Logan, Linc, Ethan, Tori, and Janet are walking across the grass to the fence. They greet James and Logan moves to stand next to him while the others set up chairs to sit. Janet is carrying a cooler. It's adorable. It makes my heart flutter to see them all.

It takes a moment for me to understand what I'm seeing when I look at Logan, and then I can't help it - I laugh.

He's wearing a hoodie in Edgar's Bluff High School forest green, and put my name and number on the front with duct tape. Proudly on his chest it says "SADIE" and "9."

It's so sweet that I can't stop smiling.

"Give 'em hell, Sadiebaby!" Logan cups his hands and shouts at me. I blow him a kiss to let him know I heard him.

I laugh again when I see the disgruntled look on Cole's face as he glowers over at Logan and his friends. It makes my heart feel full to see them all here to support me. They could be doing literally anything else with their Thursday night, but instead they're here. For me.

Every day they show me a new reason why Logan is so loyal to them. Even if it's not about me, they'd be here for him. It makes me feel better that he's not alone, even if he's lonely sometimes. They won't let Logan fall.

Letting the good feelings course through me, I turn my focus to the game.

It's brutal.

Burnfield is working hard to show no mercy, so we give as good as we get...and then some. They're no match for us, although the strategic part of my brain gives them credit for upping their game. We have the edge though, our players just that little bit better.

That little bit angrier, too.

I play at maximum the whole game, and I can feel my teammates right there with me. We're aggressive, we catch calls, but I also beat the ball like I'm mad at it. I'm so focused on the game that everything else fades around me. My family, Cole, what the last week has been like, even the darkness and exhaustion that haunts me every day like an anchor around my neck - it's gone.

Even the good things, like knowing Logan and his friends are here. Even that fades in the wake of my focus.

We're almost out of time and I'm running, heading toward the opposing goal, in tandem with Layla. As if we're reading each other's minds, we both see the opening and she makes the lateral pass to me.

I can feel how perfect the shot is as soon as my foot connects, and I watch the ball soar to the upper left corner. Just out of the goalie's reach.

Darcy slams into me from behind, wrapping her arms around my stomach and lifting me into the air. There's two minutes left and we're up by two. Still, that's no reason to rest on our win as if it's guaranteed. Nothing is guaranteed.

I brush her off and we play until the final whistle blows.

The team crashes together, whooping and celebrating our win. My face hurts from smiling and I finally feel the tightness in my chest from the sustained cardio, but the win feels good. We get in line and slap hands with the other team, who don't even make eye contact but don't blow it off either. That's classy of them, given how much crap they talked.

When it's done, I run toward the fence.

Logan is walking onto the field, grinning at me. Unafraid to show how proud he is.

"That's my fucking girl!" he crows, and I jump into his embrace. We kiss but it's messy and unconnected because we're both smiling and laughing. My legs drop and he spins in a circle so they fly out. I'm sweaty and smelly and content. Content with him.

Logan kisses me again. "That was sexy."

"Sure," I laugh.

"Are you questioning me, Sadie?" his voice, smile, and brows all drop and a shiver goes down my back. "I'll prove it to you later." Logan nibbles the tip of my nose and then lets me go.

His friends wave at me, and they retreat back to their car.

I wave at my family instead of going over to them. James will recap everything for me later, and provide a critique, of course. He's watched me play his whole life - the only person who knows my game better than me is him.

Cole is standing with his hands in his pockets, Dave talking to him but he's not really listening as he watches me.

It strikes me then that despite dating for two of my high school seasons, not to mention club soccer games, this is the first time Cole has ever been to one of my games and seen me play. Even though football and soccer are different sport seasons, and club football isn't a thing so he had the time, he never showed up. Cole has never seen me play before.

Whereas Logan came today without me asking. It was a given for him that he would show up for me. He even wore my number.

My eyes water and I turn away to head toward the locker room.

The way I was blind to the way Cole treated me hurts, even if I never want to be near him ever again. I undervalued myself and that surprises me.

The contrast between Cole and Logan is a smack in the face. Even before he hurt me, Cole gave me less than the bare minimum. Logan continuously sets the new standard for me. He shows up, he listens, he lets me breathe, he has my back. My idea of the bare minimum has changed.

My idea of perfect isn't the same anymore either.

Fear swoops through my stomach and stops me in my tracks.

I'm really falling for Logan.

Part of me has always loved him - I've always cared about him, and will never deny that I found him attractive. Not just physically, but I always admired his skills and quiet competence. Logan gets shit done, and I've respected that. I loved him as an important, if complicated, figure in my life.

But being *in love* with Logan is something else entirely.

Something I can't afford.

It might already be too late. My biggest sin will be loving Logan and leaving him. I feel that down to my bones.

And there's nothing I can do to change it.

34

Sadie

The locker room is loud and boisterous, but I'm still up in my head about Logan. The plan has always been to run and that's been my light at the end of the tunnel. Literally the thought that kept me alive when I wanted to fall asleep and never wake up. Being with Logan has showed me how much I closed off when I should've been open. That's terrifying.

I'm the last to leave the locker room before a game, and I'm always the last to leave after one, so I take my time getting changed and cleaned up. The showers are all empty by the time I step under the spray.

The hot water washes away the dirty water and mud from the field, as well as most of the soreness from the game itself. If there's one thing I can say for high school locker room showers it's that the hot water lasts forever and the pressure is always good.

I gasp when the curtain of my stall is whipped aside. It only takes seconds to realize a naked Logan is stepping into the small, dim space with me.

"Later is now. I couldn't wait." He pulls me to him and my face automatically lifts so that my mouth can meet his. The kiss is soft but desperate, and our tongues press and glide in a way that immediately makes me wet and needy. Logan trails his hands over my shoulders, kneading into the muscles. I groan into his mouth and he gets lower, his powerful fingers undoing every knot and soothing every soreness.

He breaks the kiss and gently presses me against the cold tile wall. I can't take my eyes off him when he kneels before me, water cascading down his smooth skin.

Gently, he lifts one of my feet to rest on his thigh.

When he digs into the arch and starts massaging, my eyes close and a very unsexy sound escapes my mouth. It hurts and feels good at the same time. A painful relief I was craving.

After a bit, he works up to my ankle, then my calf. When he reaches my knee, he gently puts my foot down and repeats his ministrations on the other leg. It's decadent, and so tender and intimate that tears form behind my closed eyes. I give in to how I'm feeling, sinking in to being cared for in this way.

Logan takes care of me and that's terrifying when I've been so good at taking care of myself, and then doing what I can to take care of James, my friends, anyone who needs a rock to cling to - I've been there for them to hold on. Of all the people to step in and take the load off my shoulders, I never expected Logan. It's not like my friends haven't tried, but I refused to let them.

With Logan, I can't even put up a fight.

With the way his mom abandoned him, with the lack of care he had for so many years, it's a wonder to me that it didn't make him bitter. That it didn't make him suspicious of connection and care, or think that taking care of someone made him weak. I've been holding onto everything so tightly that I want to break apart.

"Let it out, baby," Logan murmurs as he puts my foot back on the floor. "You want to stop?"

I can't speak. I swallow the lump in my throat and shake my head no.

Logan smiles and leans in, pressing his lips to my thigh. I watch as his mouth and hands work teasingly slowly along my skin. He kisses everywhere except where I want him. All I can feel now is the needy pulse in my clit, and I whine.

Logan smiles against my belly, just above my pussy lips, and when he looks up to meet my eyes they're full of mischief.

We don't break eye contact as he spreads my legs open and puts one over his shoulder.

His breath is warm and I'm panting, waiting, needy.

Logan doesn't hesitate or tease now, he dives in.

My clit is under assault and my cry echoes through the locker room before I can muffle it. I don't think he would've come in here if anyone was still around, but you never know. I slap one hand over my mouth while the other braces against the wall, holding myself up.

Logan flicks at my clit in a way that has my hips jolting, and when he slides his fingers inside me it feels good but not enough. Still, I can't stop myself from grinding on him, pressing down and squeezing his fingers with my inner muscles as he sucks and licks at me.

"Logan," I breathe. He moans into my center, a grumbly vibration that heightens my arousal and gets me closer to the edge. At the way I react, he does it again, and I tip over into pleasurable oblivion. My hand drops my mouth and onto his head, nails digging into his scalp, pressing him into me as I ride his face for my orgasm.

The second he pulls away, I'm sliding my hands down to cup his chin and yank him up to me. We kiss and kiss, our bodies grinding together as the hot water slides over and around us but we're too close for it to slide between. We're surrounded by damp steam, and I reach out to shut off the shower.

"More," I whisper against his mouth, and turn around. Logan steps up behind me, bending his knees while I rise up on my toes so we line up. As his cock slides inside me, he wraps his arms around my torso, keeping me close to him. Logan rolls his hips, not so much moving in and out as he is grinding inside me, keeping our bodies close.

He buries his face in my wet neck, his warm tongue licking at stray drops as he fucks me as if we're about to die. As if something is going to keep us apart.

Because something is. Time marches forward, and we both know it. We both know this has an expiration date.

Nothing will ever feel like this again, and the knowledge of that is as painful as it is arousing.

We're moving as one and all I want is to feel him release. As his hips mover faster, I squeeze around him, heading toward an edge I'm almost afraid to fall over.

"Sing, sweet sinner," he whispers to me, a filthy rasp, as my second orgasm takes me over. I nearly go blind as pleasure races through my body, my hands and arms barely having the strength to hold me up. Logan groans into my neck as his movements stutter, and he presses deep as he fills me.

It's so, so risky. Somehow that makes it hotter, and I question again what's wrong with me.

We catch our breath and slowly untangle ourselves.

Logan turns the shower back on and pushes me under the spray. I watch his face as he runs his fingers through my hair, focused and thorough. He looks so soft and relaxed, the hard lines he keeps in front of everyone else are gone now.

I smile a little, and even without looking at me directly he sees it and smiles back. The soft smile on my face now didn't exist before him. I created a new expression just for him.

When Logan slides a hand between my legs I shudder from sensitivity, and he gentles his touch. Logan cleans himself from me, and it almost makes me sad.

"Get dressed." He kisses my nose. "Then I'll drive you home."
Before I can say anything, he slides out of the shower and away.

35

Logan

The only good part about Sadie being grounded is that I'm getting a lot of work done on the Firebird. At this rate, it will be done before graduation. I've got it scheduled for paint in two weeks. By then it will almost be running to my standards. It feels like a deadline, even though I can't explain why. All my free time is in my garage at home right now.

Even though she isn't here with me, we've spent so many hours together in silence in this space that I feel like Sadie is here. I feel connected to her, like finishing this is as much her project as mine at this point.

"So you got a Firebird."

I sigh beneath the hood and steel myself to not react. But I know Cole saw me still, so I make the choice to intentionally ignore him. When we were friends he knew I was into cars and I'd wanted to build one of my own after seeing it in a movie. The idea that I'd have the mechanical skills to do it made me feel on par with what my dad, and even Sadie, seemed capable of. Cole knew that I specifically wanted a Firebird.

I hate that he knows things about me now because parts of me are the same as I was in the past. The weird thing is that even though I would've called him my best friend then, it didn't surprise me or even hurt that he acted like I was invisible after what happened to dad. That his mom stopped answering my mom's calls. It was the line in the sand and I wasn't surprised that this was the side they picked.

Julia was a single parent with a demanding son - she needed the support of the Church. Transgressing their demands would have left them isolated. At the time, it felt inevitable and I didn't hold it against them.

The way he acts toward me now - I hold that against him. What I suspect he did to Sadie and how he didn't cherish every second she agreed to breathe in the same space as him - I want to rip him apart with my bare hands for that.

Cole steps further into the garage, stopping when he's almost next to me and looking inside the hood as if he has any idea what's going on in it.

"Nice."

I'm not sure why he's trying to kiss my ass right now but I'm not going to make it easy for him.

He rests his hands on the car, leaning closer to me. It's tempting to knock the bar out that's holding it up and let it slam down on his football scholarship fingers. See how Notre Dame likes him injured. But I don't.

"Sadie and I aren't done, you know," he starts, and my jaw clenches but I keep looking like I'm working. "She needs space, but whatever is going on with you is temporary."

Don't I know it. But I also know she'd rather chew her own arm off than get back together with him.

I snort. "Okay."

"We both know she's meant for bigger things than you."

I don't say anything, I just shake my head and step away to start cleaning up my tools. It's a temptation to smack him with one of them, but it's also why I put some distance between us. Cole is in serious need of an ass whooping to humble him, but I'm not the one who's going to give it to him.

Not unless Sadie asks me to because I would never say no to her.

"It doesn't matter what you do with her because I had her first," he sneers and crosses his arms over his chest, trying to make his chest and shoulders look bigger. "And whenever I wanted."

My gut turns to ice. I suspected, but I haven't asked her, and Cole basically admitted to me that he assaulted her.

"She can only keep me away for so long."

Sadie is trapped in her own house with her worst nightmare. With the monster that made her feel broken. With someone who ignored all her limits. No wonder she's so fucking exhausted. I wouldn't sleep if I was her either.

I have to get her the fuck out of there. Somehow.

Cole coming to me means he's feeling secure and he's feeling bold. It's only a matter of time until he hurts her again. Sadie needs to tell me what she wants and needs and I will make it happen; staying under the same roof as Cole is not an option. It's a guarantee at this point that he's going to do something, and I won't be able to protect her. She's too tired to be able to really protect herself right now.

He looks so satisfied with himself right now. As if revealing the kind of piece of shit he is should freak me out. Like I should be afraid of him because he preyed on his girlfriend who trusted and maybe even loved him. They were together for two years - how long did he do this? How long was she harmed by someone who should've protected her?

No wonder she's so mistrustful. No fucking wonder she seems constantly surprised when I show up for her. Sadie has every reason to keep me away, and I feel even more humbled that she's let me in.

That she lets me touch her.

I am so goddamn unworthy.

Then again, maybe not. Maybe I'm the only person worthy of her because I see her for everything that she is, I value and respect her, and I would do anything to make her happy. If she's happy, I'm happy. I would never feel the need to impose myself on her to feel powerful or in control.

I just need her, however she wants to give herself to me.

I am afraid of Cole now because I'm afraid of what he'll do to her. I'm afraid that if I can't stop him, he'll make the spark of hellfire inside my little sinner go out, and the world would never be the same after that.

The good news is that Cole is also afraid of me. He wouldn't be pulling any of this if he wasn't. I also know Cole - I know his weaknesses, and his ego is his biggest one.

"You're such a weak piece of shit, Edwards." Then I laugh. It's forced but it's loud and menacing, and that's what I need to be right now. I mirror his stance, crossing my arms, and stare him down.

"Sadie is meant for bigger things than both of us, and when she's done with me, I'm going to act like a gentleman and let her go. Instead of clinging like a pathetic loser because you know you'll never do better than her, and being with her was a reach in the first place."

I laugh again, quieter this time. "She settled for you because she didn't know then that she could've been with me."

"She's only with you to piss off her parents."

I put down the wrench in my hand and step closer to him. If we do end up fighting, it's safer for his face and my criminal record if only my fists are involved.

"Maybe. Or maybe she's with me so I can pleasure your memory right out of her. Sadie's going to spend the rest of her life thinking about me, and I'm going to make damn sure she never wastes another thought on you."

Cole's eyes narrow and his arm is his tell, twitching before he swings back to try and hit me. It's very clear that Cole has never been in a real fight in his life. Maybe a scuffle on the football field, but that's got pads and referees. This is my will against his, and mine is stronger.

He misses, but I don't. While he's trying to keep his balance, I go for his gut.

Cole bowls over and I easily wrap my arm around his neck, limiting his oxygen. He tries to fight, getting glancing blows onto my torso and legs, but there isn't much behind it. I knock his feet out from under him and he lands on his stomach.

It gives me great satisfaction to kneel on him, keeping him pressed to the cold ground, one hand pressing his head down into the grit.

"I bet you feel weak as shit right now. I could do anything I wanted to you, and there's nothing you could do to stop me. Break your arm. Suffocate you. Smash your head against the ground. Slit your fucking throat."

Cole tries to fight me and I put more of my weight onto the knee in his back.

"I want you to remember how this feels. I want you to be fucking haunted by the fact that I can make you feel like this. The fear that's making you nearly piss your pants right now? That's how you made her feel. So just know...I'm one good hit from putting you right back in this position and making you pay."

"Get the fuck off me!" Cole grinds out, still thrashing, still stuck beneath me.

"How's it feel, asshole?"

"HEY!" Someone shouts, and I immediately back off Cole. Dave and Chris are running across the yards to where Cole lays in the driveway. He's rolled over onto his back and is coughing pathetically. Other than some grit stuck in his skin, there's not a mark on him.

Dave helps him up and is talking to him in hushed tones.

"What's going on Logan?" Chris asks me, hands up like he's talking to a wild animal. I'm not the one he should be worried about, but if Sadie didn't tell her parents, neither will I. I doubt they'd be helpful anyway. They might even make things worse.

"Nothing." I drop back into my mask, not giving them a fucking thing. They can decide what this fight was about, or Cole can lie, but I'm not saying a damn word.

Chris stares me down and then looks from me to Cole.

"Cole, you shouldn't be over here."

"Excuse me?" Dave steps in. "Cole was the one on the ground."

"Cole was the one who came over here, onto my property," I snap.

"Why did you come over here, Cole?" Chris asks.

"Just wanted to catch up with an old friend."

I snort, and even Dave frowns like he knows that's bullshit. He looks from me to Cole, and seems resigned that he isn't going to get the truth of the matter from either of us. He turns to Cole and talks quietly.

"You're 18 now, and you don't want to risk your scholarship. You should stay away from," he pauses and looks over at me, "trouble."

Now that makes me grin. "In case it isn't clear, you aren't welcome here."

"Fuck off," Cole snarls and stomps away, realizing that everything about this little power maneuver he tried was a failure.

I stare after him, and Dave follows a moment later.

"Anything I need to know?" Chris asks, as if one good moment makes up for years of being non-existent.

"Nope." I turn my back on him and walk into the garage. My phone vibrates.

Sadie: i miss you <3

I have to find a way to save her. I know it means she's going to leave me, but I want her to be free. One of us deserves to move on, and I will always choose her.

36

Sadie

Logan's been acting weird for a few days but I haven't been able to focus on it, or sneak out and see him when he's been working in the garage. Advanced Placement testing was this week in addition to soccer practice and another game, and then I spent the weekend before tutoring other people for their AP tests.

Cole has been conspicuously grumpy as well, making snide remarks and shedding his usual kiss-ass persona. No one has said anything about it, because of course he can get away with being moody whereas I would get a smack in the face.

I feel good about my AP tests though, and the letter from the scholarship should be arriving any day now. Even if it's a rejection, I just want to know. I want to know which plan for my future I'm going to need to follow. Will I spend another four years scraping and working multiple jobs in between studying, or will I have a little breathing room?

I can't do the camp this summer without the scholarship.

Either way, I'm going, and I have a lot of support in Madison, and I have to keep telling myself that until I believe it. I'll have a team, coaches, trainers, even a sports psychologist that can maybe help me start looking at some of the things that have happened to me.

Even if I'll be mining the past, I am so looking forward to a clean slate in the future. For my chance to climb out of the shadows of mom's pressure and into the light. Because of Logan, I feel like I'm on much firmer ground to do that.

I wish I didn't have to leave him, too, but I think that I do.

I can hear him working in the garage, the engine of the Firebird is rumbling.

When I'm sure everyone is in bed if not asleep, I quietly go up the basement stairs. I'm barefoot so my steps are nearly silent. I'm practiced at moving silently through the house. This grounding is real because I was told no night walks, which was really them telling me that I can't go see Logan.

I wonder if they even knew that's where I was half the time. If they knew about the hours I sat quietly, yards away, and rebuilt myself.

The doorknob is almost turned all the way open when the landing light snaps on.

Mom is standing in the doorway to the kitchen, triumph on her face. Dad and Cole stand behind her.

That motherfucker turned me in.

"Dining room," mom hisses, and then turns, pushing dad and Cole out of her way.

I trudge up the stairs, and find the whole family, even James, are in their pajamas but awake and sitting at the table. Dave is once again at the head of the table, a look of sympathetic disappointment on his face. His hands are together in front of him like he's praying for me.

Cole sits next to his mom and Julia pats his arm, as if to reassure him that he did the right thing by telling on me.

Mom sits next to Dave, then dad, then James. I stand at the other end of the table and face my jury.

"Why were you sneaking out, Sadie?" Dave asks.

"I wanted to see Logan, he's in his garage."

"You're grounded," mom adds. "You know better."

I have nothing to say to that so I shrug. There's only so many more months that she can ground me. I'm not sure how much worse things can even get, and I'm so tired that I'm not sure I care anymore. There's no capacity in me to be afraid of punishments right now. She can hit me, ground me, say horrible things to me, make me live in the damn basement, but none of it matters.

I am getting away from her.

It's become clear to me lately that while she's strict with James, it's unlikely she'll be with him the way she was with me. He's a boy. He's protected by his gender, and in this instance I'm totally okay with male privilege because it's going to keep him safe until he can get to me.

The depths of her ignoring the obvious right and wrong because of the view of the Church has shifted everything I think about her.

It also makes me feel oddly satisfied that if hell is real, that's where she'll end up. Mom can be as pious as she wants but she'll never repent her true sins because she doesn't think she's doing anything wrong. Righteousness and pride are her downfall.

Mom's cheeks turn red and she starts to stand, but dad and Dave both stop her.

"A lot of new information has been thrown at you recently," Dave says. "You're on the brink of some major life changes, it's all intense. Acting out is normal, but that doesn't mean it's healthy."

More silence.

"Cole came to us because he's worried about you."

"Cole came to you because he's jealous," James murmurs sleepily, barely awake.

"That's not true!" Cole stands up. James glances at him and then rests his head on his arms, closing his eyes. Tired but unbothered. I love my brother so much right now.

"James, go back to bed," Dad says to him softly, rubbing his back. James gets up and taps the back of his hand against mine as he walks past me.

"Cole should go as well," Julia says, and stands to guide her son out of the room. Cole whispers harshly to her but I can see the grip she's got on his arm, and they walk toward the stairs.

It's me, my parents, and fucking Uncle Dave.

"I - we - decided," Mom starts, looking at dad out of the corner of her eye, "that if you will have a session with your uncle, I won't extend your grounding."

"Why?" I look between them, genuinely confused.

Mom looks like she swallowed a beehive, pain and distaste equally present on her face. "He's explained that your behavior is not surprising given the pressure you are under as such a high achiever." With every word I'd swear her voice goes higher. Her logical mind knows that he has a point, but the controlling monster that lives in her heart hates that. "You need a little help to sort out your emotions."

"And you want that to be with Dave?"

"Yes," she hisses.

"Let's go talk," Dave says and stands up.

"Now?" It's almost midnight. On a school night.

"No time like the present." He claps his hands and smiles, then holds one arm out like he needs to give me directions in my own house.

Whatever. I walk through the living room, out the front door, and sit on the porch swing. It's chilly but not uncomfortable. I close my eyes because I don't want to be here, and I can hear Logan still working on his car.

Dave sits down on one of the chairs near the swing, giving me some space.

"Are we having this talk as therapist and patient, or as uncle and niece?"

"Why not both?" Dave says pleasantly. I snap my eyes open and he's still giving me that weird look between sympathy and concern. It's so fake.

"Because if I'm your patient, you're bound by confidentiality, I'm an adult, and you would be breaking the law if you tell my mom anything I say to you. You can't be both my therapist and my uncle, it's a conflict of interest."

"What would you tell a therapist that you wouldn't want your mom to know?" He leans forward, resting his elbows on his knees, playing at casual.

"Don't even try, Dave. Right now you're talking to me as my uncle because I know you're going to tell her everything I say. You're already biased to her side, and I've been forced into this conversation which means it's not a genuine engagement with therapy. All of this is unethical."

"Thought about this a lot, have you?" He almost looks amused but mostly disgruntled. It's almost as if he really thought he was going to be the magic bullet that fixed me.

"Not the first time she's tried to get me to have a "session" with you." To emphasize what I think of that, I make sure to put air quotes around session. I believe that therapy is a good thing. I took AP Psych. So I know that taking care of our brains and mental health is important.

I also know who the therapist is, their approach, and their objectivity, completely matters. Dave isn't the therapist I would choose even if he wasn't my uncle.

"So here's what you can report back, Dave. I hate it here. I hate her, and I will never forgive her. I might even hate you."

Dave reels back, struck by the words, even though my tone is completely calm.

"I'm going to graduate, and I'm going to leave, and once James is out, I will never speak to her again. I will never be back in this house. I will remove myself from this "family" because the only thing I hate more than being related to *her*, is the fact that I'm now tied to *him* - because of you." My voice breaks and I take a deep breath to keep the tears in my eyes.

"You have no idea what it's like to be trapped with him." I'm saying more than I meant to, but I'm on a roll now and I can't stop. "And to have you all try to force him on me when he's done enough of that all on his own. You're all horrible, selfish beasts."

My lower lip is trembling and I look away from him. The silence lasts minutes, my words thrown down like bombs. I said too much. Way too much. I'm shaking with the power of it all, with both terror and relief at having let a little bit of it out.

Finally, I look at my uncle. This time, the look of concern on his face is genuine. He wasn't expecting any of that.

"You all think you're saints but I know what kind of sins you've committed," I say softly.

Dave takes a deep breath. "Sadie, do you currently have any thoughts of harming yourself?"

"No."

"Do you currently have any thoughts of harming anyone else?"

Uh, yeah, but not any that I would ever act on.

"No."

"Have you ever had thoughts of harming yourself?"

I turn to look at him and tilt my head as if to say, "what do you think?"

Have I ever wished I was dead? Have I ever wanted to literally bash my head against the wall just to make the thoughts and the panic stop?

"Have you ever harmed yourself?" he asks very quietly. This is Dave the therapist. For real, not the show. I'm still not telling him shit though.

Of course I have, but in subtle, strange ways. Ways that made me feel like I was in control when everything felt like it was slipping away, or I needed to be outside myself. Hot showers where I scrubbed my skin raw. Not allowing myself to eat. The long walks in the cold, allowing it to bite at me, causing pain that I could come back from. Pushing everyone away because the hurt of being alone was less than the hurt of being betrayed.

"I'm going to go back in the house, put on my coat and shoes, and go for a walk. You're going to tell her whatever you want, but I'm done. This is never happening again."

I slide off the porch swing and go into the house. Mom and dad are both still sitting at the dining table, waiting. They both look at me, then behind me where Dave follows. I walk through the kitchen and down the steps. I get on my shoes and my coat.

Logan isn't in the garage anymore, but I don't know if I would've gone to him even if he was. I need to breathe right now, and I need to be alone. I have to face all of this now. He'd be too much of a distraction.

So I walk my path, I wave and nod to my other night people. The other lonely wanderers like me, just trying to make it through the dark and sort ourselves out.

I breathe in the air that's finally getting warm, the scent of the first flowers on the wind. I will be okay. I am surviving.

When I get back to the house, there's a note taped to the back door.

My stomach swoops with the fear that I'll be told I can't come in, but the actual content is more surprising.

After this weekend, my grounding is over. Not only is it not being extended, it's being ended early. I don't know what Dave told them, but for now, I'll give him this little bit of gratitude. Mentally, anyway.

37

Sadie

Tuesdays are rough.

I'm already extra tired because Mondays actually put me in a good mood - it's another week closer to graduation. It's a fresh start, too, which I know is a nerdy way to feel but Mondays feel full of possibilities.

Except possibility means I go hard, full of energy that makes me say yes to things. Extra tutoring sessions? Why not. Helping youth group drive around town and pick up donations after soccer practice? Sure.

Part of it is done in the hope that I'll be tired enough to fall easily asleep, but that's not the case. By the time I got home Monday night I had an hour of homework, and Cole kept finding excuses to come downstairs. Once I was done and got ready for bed, I was so tense it wasn't going to happen for hours.

Tuesday was a dragging morning. I was yawning. I chugged the coffee Darcy brought me. I gave Logan a sleepy smile and leaned on him for a minute. Luckily we don't have a game tonight, just practice.

Which nearly takes me out, but when the day is done, I feel lighter. Darcy drives me home and lets me zone out.

"So...Logan."

"Yeah?" I turn my head toward her, still leaning on the seat.

"It's kinda serious, babe. What's your plan?"

My stomach tightens in fear. "The same as always. Graduate, leave."

Darcy looks over at me a few times, going back and forth between looking at the road and trying to get a good look at me. "What about him?"

"What about him?" I lie like I don't ask myself this same question in the dark of the night when I can't sleep. "We both know it's going to end."

"Does he?" Darcy asks, her hands gripping the steering wheel.

Logan and I have never discussed an end date except when I first asked him to pretend to be my boyfriend until May. In my head, real or not, that date was still in effect. For my own sanity. Especially now.

"Do you love him?" she asks softly, and I seize up. Darcy's face falls. "You do. I don't blame you, but shit."

"Yeah." I play with the strap of my gym bag. "Doesn't change anything."

"Maybe it can."

I don't say anything to that, and we finish the drive in silence. Darcy looks at me with pity as we say goodbye before I get out of her car to head into the house. I pity me, too, when it comes to Logan.

The car is gone from our garage so I'm not sure where my family went. Dave and Julia's cars aren't here either. Hopefully Cole is with them wherever they are and I can take a shower in peace, and spend a few moments of calm, quiet alone time.

My hopes are dashed when I notice that the lights are on upstairs. I keep my shoes on but put my bags down and take my coat off when I step inside the back door.

"Hello?" I call out, trying to see who is here and how scared I need to be.

I walk up the stairs and through the kitchen. Mom is sitting in the living room on the sofa facing me. On the coffee table in front of her are two large white envelopes. I can see the Madison seal on one, and the size of the envelope is good news. I'm trying to fight a smile as I walk into the room.

It's distracting enough that I don't register the angry look on mom's face.

I dash forward and grab the envelopes. I skip the one that I'm 99% sure welcomes me to the university, and look at the other. It's from the foundation that runs the scholarship.

After a few deep breaths, I open it, and read the letter out loud.

"We are pleased to name you this year's recipient of the Women in Sciences Grant." I scream and dance around the living room, the paper crumpling in my hands. The money is mine! I knew wanting to major in physics would pay off! This is going to change everything for me - the pieces of my dream are falling into place right in front of my eyes.

When I turn to my mom, expecting her to celebrate with me, the light bursting inside me immediately dims. She's beyond angry - she's furious.

"You didn't apply to anywhere other than Madison."

Gulp. "No, I didn't."

"When that," she says it with derision and looks at my acceptance letter, "arrived, I called the guidance counselor. No other letters have arrived and that was…suspicious. She said you never even took applications for anywhere else."

"I want to go to Madison."

"Anyone can go to Madison."

"That isn't true and you know it. Why are you so against it?"

She stands up and gets in my face, her finger pointing fiercely. "Because you'll go to that school and party and act like a slut and forget where you come from and what you owe us. You're already doing it since you've started spending time with that boy. Sneaking out, volunteering less, rejecting the Church. You're going to come home knocked up by some drunk heathen and ruin our lives."

"What?" The fact that is what she thinks is going to happen means she doesn't know me at all, and probably never has. I'm a nerd! I genuinely want to learn and be challenged, it's what makes me so excited about after high school. I'm truly stunned. I'm staring at her with my mouth agape, mind blank to reply.

This makes her even angrier, and I try to duck when she swings. Her fist connects with my ear, pain shooting into my head and down my neck. I'm on my knees on the ground holding my ringing ear when she strikes again.

The back of her hand flies across my face, pain bursting through my nose. It's wet immediately, and a few seconds later I feel a few drips of blood coming out of my nose.

I'm looking up at her when I hear the back door open and the sounds of many people coming into the house. When I look over my shoulder, dad and James are standing there with balloons and a cake. The cake is white with red frosting and says "Congratulations!"

She sent them away with the ruse of celebrating that I got in, but what she really wanted was to get me alone.

"What the fuck?" Dad says, shocking me. "What did you do?"

To my relief he's looking at mom, angrier than I've ever seen him. I can't imagine what this looks like - me on the floor, bleeding, her standing over me still red from rage.

James comes forward and pulls me away from her, putting himself in front of me. Dad and James form a barrier between me and her.

"I - we - " mom stumbles through her words.

"After everything Dave said, this is what you do?" Dad is gearing up to start a fight, but its too little too late. The time to fight was years ago, and it shouldn't have taken Dave to make him see that.

I take a few steps back before turning on my heel and running for the back door. I have to get away. I'm not safe. I have to hide.

Thoughts are racing through my head so fast I can't land on one, I can't focus. My heart is racing and my body is sweaty in weird places. The chill air of early evening soothes me as I walk, pace so fast that my muscles are screaming at me to slow down.

I can't slow down.

I can't stop.

I have to go.

Have to hide.

Go. Go. Go.

38

Logan

When I get in my car after work, I check my phone. Since I was with most of the people who would bother to call or text me, there was no need for it. Plus, there's a part of me that hopes my mom tries to reach me and freaks out when she can't. It's a big, pointless hope but one I have anyway.

There's about 20 missed calls and even some texts. Some of the calls are from numbers that aren't in my phone. None of them are from Sadie.

Panic crawls up my spine but I push it down.

We worked late tonight. It's almost 10pm. The calls started around 6pm.

Linc sees me standing half in, half out of my car as he comes out the door.

"What's up?"

"I don't know. I've got a bunch of missed calls..." I trail off and look at him. "Can you hang out a minute?" Linc walks over and leans against the car.

Most of the calls are from Chris, so I call him back first.

"Logan? Is Sadie with you?" My stomach drops to the floor.

"No. What's going on?"

"She left the house - her mom -" he sounds frazzled, and I can hear yelling in the background. Saying it was Sadie's mom is enough. I know. "It's been hours."

"Fuck. I'll look for her. But I can't promise that I'll bring her home."

Chris sighs. "I know. I just need to know she's safe. Please."

I hang up on him because I know that I'll say things that he doesn't need to hear, and that aren't his business. It's tempting to tear him to pieces, verbally and physically, for letting Sadie endure everything she has at the hands of his wife. But more of me knows that I have to find Sadie.

"Sadie's missing."

Linc stands up. "What do you need me to do?"

"Uh…" I rub my forehead, trying to think things through. "Drive around and check any place that makes sense. School, the church, the Bronze Cabin, whatever."

"Got it. I'll call you."

"Yeah." I move to get back in the car and he stops me.

"She's going to be okay. We'll find her. You can both stay at ours tonight."

I can't say anything because there's a lump in my throat. All I can do is nod.

It occurs to me that Sadie could be hiding at my house, but if that was the case she would've found a way to let me know. Darcy doesn't live far from the shop, in a fancy subdivision with high end new houses. I turn into it and look for her car because I'm not sure which house is hers.

My car lifts onto the curb as I park like an asshole and don't even turn off the car before I get out and run to the front door. I pound on it like a cop making a drug bust and it swings open a few moments later.

Darcy's bewildered mom looks at me. "Can I help you?"

"Is Sadie here?"

"Who are you?" She takes a step back, trying to mask fear in her expression.

"Logan?" Darcy comes up behind her mom. "What's going on?"

"Is Sadie here?" I repeat the question through clenched teeth.

"No - I haven't heard from her since I dropped her off after practice. She hasn't even been online."

"She got in some kind of fight with her mom and ran off."

"Crap." Darcy looks at her mom, and her mom puts an arm around her. "What do we do?"

"Where do you think she'd go? I have Linc checking places."

"Give me his number, I'll text him. You go home." I look confused and she elaborates. "If she comes back she'll be coming to find you."

I nod because that makes sense. Darcy gives me her phone and I put my number and Linc's in her contacts.

The rules of the road don't apply as I rush back to my house.

There's a police car sitting in the Braverman's driveway, and all of them are outside gathered around the officers. I pull my car into my own, and clock that my mom's car is here too. She's actually home.

When I look toward the house, the kitchen curtain drops, letting me know she doesn't want to be caught looking.

I start walking across the yard toward the assembled group when Jodi sees me. She charges over and shoves me in the chest. It's so unexpected that I actually stumble back two steps.

"Where is she?" Jodi shouts in my face.

"I don't know!"

"I don't believe you!"

"Whoa, step away from each other," the cop steps in and puts his arms out to force some space between us. I have to waste time explaining that I'm Sadie's boyfriend and that I don't know where she is, that

I've been at work for the last 6 hours, and Walker's number to verify that it's true. The cop still looks at me like I kidnapped Sadie, which I totally would, but not in this case.

"He has something to do with this, I know it! I know it!" Jodi is screaming now, causing a scene. I know what she's doing. She knows as well as I do that all the neighbors are watching and she wants it to worm into their brains that I did this. So they'll be on her side. Jodi's already half the reason I've been isolated since childhood, it doesn't surprise me at all she'd employee the same tactic now.

Thinking of that, the fury I have for her finally boils over. There's been a dam inside me holding back the betrayal I feel toward them both. I loved Chris and Jodi, they were family to me, and one horrific action made them turn their backs on me. I was a kid, and they left me in the cold to die.

"THIS IS BECAUSE OF YOU!" I roar and step to her, Chris and the cop immediately grabbing my arms. They can physically hold me back but they can't stop me from speaking. "What did you do to her, Jodi? Did you hit her again?"

Jodi pales but then puts on a front. "I've never -"

"LIAR! I've seen it. I've heard it. And if anyone else standing her would grow a fucking backbone they'd say it's the truth. She's been living in a fucking house of horrors between an abusive mom and a rapist ex - it's no wonder she broke."

It's like everything moves in slow motion then as I realize what else came out of my mouth, and everyone sees when my gaze moves to Cole. They all turn to him, watching as my accusation lands like a blow. Cole takes a step back, his mouth drops open and his hands raise as if in defense.

"What?" Chris croaks, staring at Cole like the rest of us.

I jerk my arm out of the grip of the officer because Chris has already let me go.

"I'm going to go find Sadie, and all of you," I make eye contact with every one of those fuckers except James. "Can rot in hell."

I take a few steps back before turning around and heading back to my car. While I feel bad revealing Sadie's secrets, even if she never told me the entire truth, if it means they finally get some kind of punishment for what they've done...I'll apologize to her, but I can't regret it.

While I'm driving, I call Linc. "I think she went to the convent."

"Why?" I hear Tori's voice behind him, saying they should take the bikes.

"It's a secret. She's trying to hide." Where we both said it felt like heaven. A place she feels like she can't be found and that only has good memories associated with it.

By the time I pull into the parking lot, Tori and Linc are both waiting for me.

We head off into the woods without saying anything, not running to conserve energy but walking quick enough that talking would be difficult.

When we get to the kitchen door, Tori looks to me for direction.

"Linc, check the second floor, Tori, the first. I'm going to the chapel. You got your phones?" They both nod. "If I find her, we might need to call an ambulance. Tori, you know where we are - you make the call if it comes to it."

"No problem. Let's find her."

We walk through the kitchen and out into the dark body of the building. I've been here at night plenty of times but it's never felt threatening before. It's cold, a typical early spring night, and Sadie has a tendency to under dress for the weather when she's emotional. I've found her too many times without even a coat lately.

The second I open the door to the chapel, I know she's here. Like I can feel her with another sense, or her presence amplifies them so I can find her.

"Sadie?" I call her name a few times, looking around in the dark and cursing that I didn't think to bring a flashlight.

I text Linc that she's in the chapel, even though I haven't found her.

I step carefully along the stone floor, each step echoing menacingly in the dark. The altar is barely visible from the light in the dusty stained-glass windows.

"Sadie?" My heart is racing because she's not responding, and I know without a doubt that Sadie would not only recognize my voice but speak to me if she was conscious. My girl would feel it was me the same way that I feel her.

There's a soft humming noise, and I move toward it, smashing my hip against the corner of the altar. There's a form in the corner - a body in a white shirt - and I internally flinch at the ghostly image.

I run to kneel in front of Sadie, pulling her toward me. She's cold as ice, and her head flops back onto my arm. Another soft grumble comes out of her, but nothing else. She doesn't move.

"Sadie...baby...please..." my voice shudders out of me. "I have you, little sinner. You're safe with me. I love you. I love you." I press her face into my chest, trying to give her my body heat.

I pick her up and head toward the door. Linc opens it and see us, blanching, and he pulls the door open the rest of the way.

"Tori thinks it would be faster if we took her ourselves."

"Okay." I shift Sadie in my arms, and we run through the halls. Tori joins us just outside the kitchen and holds the doors. Sadie is so small and so light that I have to keep looking down to make sure that she's real and she's breathing.

I have to comfort myself by squeezing her every few seconds, feeling the firmness of her skin, and pushing out a breath of my own every time she takes one.

We get through the woods and I slide into the back of my car. Tori goes to the driver's seat.

"I'll get you there. Just get her warm."

I do as she says, my heart in my throat, Sadie's health in Tori's hands until we get to the emergency room.

39

Sadie

Everything is white.

If it wasn't for the fact that everything hurts, I'd think that I died.

It aches all the way to my fingertips. I can feel my blood pulsing beneath my skin.

The ceiling comes into focus. White drop tiles with lots of dots, fluorescent lights that are turned off. Windows with beige blinds that are drawn shut. Definitely a hospital.

Thinking I'm alone, I groan and bring my hands to my face. There's an IV in one.

"Hey," a soft voice calls, and I drop my hands and try to sit up. "It's me, it's me."

I look toward the voice and let out a sigh of relief. It's James.

Of course I start to cry immediately.

He comes over and hugs me as best he can while I'm in a hospital bed, patting me wherever he can reach while I cry into his shoulder. When the tears stop and I can breathe normally again, James pulls away and sits down on the edge of the bed.

"What happened?" I ask.

"What do you remember?" he returns.

"I got into Madison and mom punched me."

James nods. "Those big envelopes came and everyone got excited - she told us to go to the store and get cake and stuff. Dave and them went to get pizza. A celebration. You clearly got the scholarship, too, so it was a big deal."

"I'm surprised she didn't open them."

He snorts. "Me too. So off we went."

"I ran. I just shut off my brain and ran and ran."

"Logan won't tell anyone where they found you."

"Logan found me?" I sit up at that.

James nods. "Him and Tori Anderson brought you into the ER. But since the cops know he didn't kidnap you or anything they aren't pressing too hard about it."

"The cops?!" I sit up and nearly tear out my IV. James pushes me back into the bed.

"You were missing for hours, dad finally convinced mom we had no other choice. Big show down between her and Logan in the backyard."

I don't say anything, just squeeze my eyes shut in horror and stress. The machine I'm hooked up to starts beeping and I take a deep breath to try and calm down.

"He said some things. About Cole."

I squeeze my eyes shut even harder. "I don't want to talk about it."

"Okay." James takes my hand. "But I believe you." We sit in the silence of that for a moment before he clears his throat like he's trying not to laugh and my eyes snap open. "Mom was asked to go to the station. He made it pretty clear how she behaves. Even though you're 18 now, it's still a crime."

"A misdemeanor now." I sigh. "Has she been here?"

James shakes his head. "Dad won't let her see you. She's at Dave and Julia's house."

"How long have I been out?"

"Two days. The rebuild is done and they agreed they can all live with the smoky smell for awhile."

"Wow." I look down and away, trying to fight the guilt that I've broken up my own family.

We're interrupted when a nurse walks in and looks surprised when I meet her eyes. She backs out of the room and a few seconds letter, a doctor enters. The nurse checks my vitals while he asks me questions about what year it is, who's president, all those things to make sure I don't have amnesia.

Amnesia sounds kind of nice.

"We'll have a psychologist come and talk to you later today, if you're feeling up for it?"

"Why?"

The doctor tilts his head. "You're too smart to play dumb, Sadie. Your uncle also expressed some concern and said you needed support."

Fucking Dave.

"As long as it's not him, I'll talk to them." The doctor nods, and then asks James to step out. He looks to me for confirmation, and then tells me he's going to get dad.

The doctor and nurse take a step back, like they're giving me space.

"It was reported by your father that you may have been sexually assaulted."

"I'm not talking about that."

He holds his hands up. "Okay. I understand. But I also want you to know that the psychologist is a confidential resource. With few exceptions, what you tell them is protected by doctor-patient confidentiality."

I can only nod.

"Is there anything we can do to make you more comfortable?"

"When can I leave?"

"Tomorrow. You were hypothermic. Mild, but it's still serious and it can cause mental confusion. We need to make sure you're out of the woods, so to speak. But you'll need to take it easy for at least a week."

I frown at him and internally disagree.

There's a knock on the door and we all turn to look as my dad steps inside. He looks different, but I can't put my finger on why. The doctor and the nurse say they'll be back later.

Dad stands next to the bed with his hands in his pockets and I can't meet his eyes.

"I'm so sorry, Sadie."

"Okay." I'm not ready to say anything other than that.

"We're getting a divorce."

I start at that and look up at him. That's a sin. That's a you-can't-take-communion-anymore sin.

"I don't want to see her."

"You're 18, you don't have to."

"What about James?"

"I'm taking care of it. I've got a good lawyer."

I nod.

"What can I do?" he asks, voice cracking.

"Nothing. But...." I finally look at him. "I don't think I can go home."

He nods and looks away, taking a few deep breaths and I know he's trying not to cry. "We'll figure it out."

Dad offers me his hand and I take it.

"Congratulations, by the way. Madison, the scholarship...you're amazing. I'm so proud of you."

"You don't think I'll become a party slut and ruin my life getting pregnant with some random guy?" It slips out before I can stop it. I think hypothermia wrecked my walls and now I can't keep my mouth shut.

Dad's jaw drops. "Is that what she said?"

I nod, and for some reason, I start laughing.

"That's not you," he shakes his head. "Fuck. I should've done this after Brian...I should've left, but I felt so alone. She just stepped in and took control and I went along with it. He was my best friend."

"I know, dad."

"She worried you were like him, you know. It's always been her explanation. That she's afraid if we don't push you and watch you, you'll..."

I swallow thickly because I don't know if she's wrong. I don't know that my mind is any less dark than Brian's. But I also know that the source of so much of my agony and my desire to hurt was caused by her. I'm not telling dad that though. The last thing I want is to make him worry more.

Dad lets go of my hand and moves to sit down on the chair next to the bed. He turns on the TV to some sitcom rerun, and we try to find companionable silence. There's nothing else to say in this moment. Nothing else that I would say to him.

I know that I should report Cole, but I also know...I'm not up for that. I've barely processed what happened. It will open up a wound and a war that I don't have the strength to fight. This is a small town and even if I'm leaving it - they'll just believe I'm a vicious ex-girlfriend trying to ruin his life.

They won't believe me, and I don't think I can handle that now.

I'll find another way to make him pay, and make sure he never hurts anyone the way he did me.

I want Logan, now, but I have a feeling I'll have to bide my time if I want to see him alone.

The only other thing I remember is hearing his voice in my head say that he loved me.

I remember hoping it was real.

40

Logan

It's a sign of how bad I'm doing that neither Maggie or Walker gave me shit about skipping school. My future is set, I really don't care about my grades all that much. I'm crashing in their basement even though Linc is trying to get me to move into the apartment. I'm not ready for this to be permanent yet.

But I know I can't be in my house. I can't be around the emptiness, and I don't trust myself being next to Sadie's family while she's still in the hospital. The desire to destroy them all still burns in my chest. The cops took Sadie's mom for questioning but at this point that's all I know.

I haven't reached out to anyone, but I get text updates from Chris. I don't respond but I appreciate that he's not cutting me out. Sadie isn't awake yet.

Maggie comes to see me first. I'm watching some trash on the TV, not paying attention, and she sits down beside me on the couch. Still, waiting me out, testing my mood. When I don't move away or ask her what she wants, she scoots a little closer.

We watch the show together for about 15 minutes before Walker comes downstairs too. He sits in the chair on my other side and leans forward to rest his elbows on his knees.

"It's been two days."

"Yeah."

I watch him and Maggie exchange a look.

"You know you're welcome here," she says and moves a little closer. "But where's your head at? What can we do?"

When Tori drove me here that night after we dropped Sadie off at the emergency room, I was a mess. All it took was a hug and I was spilling everything to them - everything that I knew about what was happening to Sadie but everything that was happening with me, too. I crumbled apart and I needed to do that. Even I fell into the trap of thinking I could deal with it all on my own.

After exhausting myself, I went to sleep.

That's what I've been doing on and off for the last 48 hours.

They let me sort myself out, but I knew that wasn't going to be on the table forever. It shouldn't be. I need a push to make some decisions. To figure out what's next.

"I don't really know," I admit. "I don't think I'll know anything until I talk to her."

Walker nods, and I see Maggie do the same out of the corner of my eye. She starts rubbing my back, soothing me. I've slipped up and called her mom a few times and neither of us ever mentions it.

"What do you want to tell her?" Walker asks.

"That I love her. That I don't think I can give her up."

"What do you mean?" Maggie asks, softly.

"She's going away to school. She hates this place and wants to get out of here and I don't blame her." I swallow thickly. "I'm going to follow her. When this started I thought...just now would be enough, but it won't be. I need her. I think she needs me too."

I turn to Walker more directly. "I'm sorry. I know I said I'd be at the shop-"

Walker waves his hand and cuts me off. "Don't be ridiculous. We just want you to be happy, Logan."

"It's true," Maggie adds. "You don't owe us anything although I know you feel like you do." I nod, not disagreeing with her. "All you owe us is to use the help we give you to be happy. Working at the shop was what you wanted - it's not indentured servitude."

"I can help you find a job, too, wherever you end up. I know plenty of people in Madison."

I nod again and look away, clenching my jaw so that I don't cry. It's not that I believe boys don't cry or any of that bullshit, but that I need to finish this conversation. I take a few deep breaths and they let me. They're the most patient people I know. Tori and Janet inherited that from them; Linc couldn't wait for anything.

"Thank you."

"You need to go home, though," Maggie says, squeezing my shoulder. "I think it's time to talk to your mom. I'll come with you, if you want."

I hate it, but she's right. "Yeah...I don't need you there when I talk to her, but I don't want to go to my house alone right now. I don't - if they're still there -" Anger simmers again and I shut my eyes. I can feel the look that Maggie and Walker exchange, I don't even need to see it. Like the silent communication between them is that obvious.

"We'll both come with you."

"Okay. Can we get it over with?"

"Of course." I stand and Walker stops me. "You're family, Logan. Even if you go with Sadie to Madison, even if you move to another country or go into outer space, you're our family. Sadie too, if she wants to be. You got that, right?"

"Yeah."

We both turn our heads when we hear Maggie sniffle and she's crying with a smile on her face. "My boys." She pulls me into a hug and there's no hesitation to hug her back. This is the family that chose me, and I don't hesitate to choose them in return.

41

Logan

We park in the street, and Walker and Maggie both walk up the driveway with me. Mom's car isn't there, so this might be a bust anyway. Still, I have to get some of my stuff and on the way here we decided that Walker is going to drive the Firebird to the shop so I can finish it. Piece by piece I'm going to move out, and that's a pretty big place to start.

Our arrival doesn't go unnoticed. The back door of the Braverman house slams and I brace myself for another go around with Jodi.

Except it's Chris.

He's jogging across the lawns over to us. Walker looks to me, checking if he should prepare for a fight too, but I shake my head. Still, Walker and Maggie stand behind me, one over each shoulder. I'm not alone, whatever is about to happen.

"Logan - are you okay?" Chris is out of breath and his eyes dart between the three of us.

"Is Sadie?"

"She woke up an hour ago. I came home to get some clothes for her."

"Good."

"Do you want to come see her? You can come back with me." He points over his shoulder to his car.

"No, I have some things to finish here. I'm staying with the Andersons for a bit."

Chris nods, looks between Walker and Maggie again, then takes a step closer as if they won't hear whatever it is he has to say.

"Jodi and her brother and his family aren't here. They left. I told them to leave." Chris clears his throat awkwardly. "I should've done it a long time ago."

"Yeah," I agree. "What about Sadie?"

"We've been talking about her staying with Darcy for awhile until the legal things are sorted out."

"Legal things?" Did Sadie report Cole? Her mom? I feel like I would've heard about that if she did. Then again, I've shut everything out while I deal with my own shit so I can be there for her.

Chris clears his throat again. "I'm filing for divorce."

I rear back like I've been hit it's that much of a surprise. The second worst thing in the eyes of the church is divorce. Chris will never be welcome back in their congregation if he's the one asking for it, and while they'll initially rally around Jodi, at the end of the day...she'll be a sinner too.

Before I can stop it, I smile. Then I laugh.

"Sorry, I'm sorry - it's not - I'm sorry." I take a few steps away and turn my back on all of them. When I think I've got it all together, I turn back. Chris is red in the face but he's embarrassed, not angry. He nods like he knows why I'm laughing but isn't willing to say it out loud.

Chris knows as well as I do that this is punishing Jodi on many levels. It's just in bad taste for him to laugh too.

"I want to say thank you for being there for her. For forgiving her for what we did."

"Nothing to forgive her for."

Chris swallows thickly. "She's really hurting, and this isn't going to fix everything. I know that. But I don't want you to think you need to stay away from her - or that I expect you to - I don't."

"Not that she needs your permission, but I appreciate that."

"She's being released in the morning. You're welcome whenever you want." Chris turns to walk away and then turns back. "If you need help, just ask. Okay?"

"He's got help, but thank you." Maggie steps up and wraps her hand around my elbow, a show of support for me and ownership for Chris to see. I am not alone.

"Right." Chris walks away and I watch, seeing the same dragging sadness in him that I sometimes see in Sadie. It worries me for them both, but Chris isn't my responsibility. Sadie is, if she wants to be.

42

Sadie

First thing the next morning the doctor clears me to go home. My body temperature is normal, no signs of any confusion or fatigue. I want to be out of here. It feels so invasive even though they ask permission every time they're going to check my vitals.

When we don't turn toward our house, I don't say anything.

James is in the back seat. He notices but doesn't say anything, so wherever I'm going, it doesn't seem too concerning to him. If they were shipping me off somewhere he would tell me.

"Where are we going?"

"You said you didn't want to go home so I asked Darcy's parents if you could stay for a bit."

Wow. Okay. "Thank you." I sound more surprised than I meant to, but I really am shocked that not only did he think of her but he actually reached out to her parents. Dad never had any obvious issues with Darcy but he went along with mom's views on her. His silence said enough.

"It's what you need." The answer is so simple it shocks me again. I shift in my seat and make eye contact with James. He shrugs and lifts his eyebrows. I don't think I've ever known this version of my dad but him without mom seems to be a much better parent.

Darcy is waiting on her front stoop when we pull into the driveway, arms crossed, face suspicious.

I get out of the car and walk straight for her. We hug, and I breathe for the first time in days.

"I got you," she tells me. I nod into her shoulder. "You want the girls to come over?"

"Yeah."

Darcy's mom and dad come out the front door as well and they're talking quietly with dad. He hands over my overnight bag, and I doubt he packed what I would've but beggars can't be choosers and I think I'd freak out if I went to the house.

I want to go home, but I need some space first.

James approaches and I step away from Darcy to give him a hug. "Dad promised he'd drive me over whenever we want to see each other."

"Okay. You good?" I check on him. "Mom tried to talk to you?"

James shakes his head. "Once and I said I didn't want to see her."

I lift one side of mouth in a half-smile. James steps back and there's now an awkward moment between me and dad. We've never been the most affectionate family and things are even weirder right now.

Dad lifts his hand in a wave and I do the same.

If he shows me that he's really changed, that he's really going to stand against mom and follow through on the divorce, maybe then we can start to rebuild our relationship.

I stand with Darcy as James and dad get in the car and leave.

Her mom steps up and pats my back. "We got the guest room ready if you want to lay down."

I turn to her and smile. "Spent too much time laying down. Let's watch movies."

"You got it," Darcy claps and pulls me into the house. "The girls are on the way."

Two movies later, covered in blankets, my friends piled around me, I start to talk.

It's not like they didn't already suspect what was going on - Darcy knew outright and I know she told Amelia some of it, but Layla and Chloe had no idea it was so bad. That my mom was more than just controlling and demanding.

Once I start telling stories I can't stop - hitting me with rulers and wooden spoons, slapping my face, throwing things at me. How nothing was ever good enough.

I don't even realize that tears are streaming down my cheeks until my eyes focus and I see that all of them are crying too.

"You're seriously the smartest person I know, how could your mom not know that?" Chloe sniffles.

"Because she's a bitch," Amelia snarls and then sniffles too. "Such a bitch."

"Such a bitch," I agree. "But it's going to be okay."

"Are you going to go to therapy?" Darcy asks softly. "I think you should."

I nod, unable to articulate right now my complicated feelings about it all. It's been a habit for so long not to talk about anything, to pretend it's not there, shove it down, act out the lie until the lie becomes the truth, that I don't know how to open up.

The psychologist at the hospital didn't get much out of me. I said enough that she doesn't have any concerns that I'm going to hurt myself, but she was pretty firm that small hurts count too. Just because I'm not physically harming myself and don't feel the urge to doesn't mean I'm fine. She told me trauma can impact my brain and my body in ways I can't expect or control unless I work through it.

So yeah, I'll probably go to therapy.

"Visitors!" Darcy's dad calls down the stairs. I hear the sounds of at least two footsteps, and my hopes rise that it's Logan. I've texted him a few times but haven't heard much back. It scares me, but I don't have the energy to do anything about it yet.

"Ladies," a semi-familiar voice greets us. I look over the back of the couch and see Linc, holding flowers, and much to my surprise - Ethan. He's frowning even more deeply than usual.

Linc steps forward and hands me the flowers, and Darcy tells the two of them to come around and have a seat on another part of the huge sectional. I go through the motions of telling them how I'm feeling, that I'm okay, and thank Linc for being part of my rescue.

Ethan even tells me he's glad I'm alright.

"Aw, he has a heart," Chloe teases.

"That's not all I've got for you." Ethan's face is still a glare but his voice was all innuendo. Chloe blushes and looks away.

"How is he?" I finally break and ask Linc.

"He's okay. He's been at my house. It was...a lot for him. I've never seen him so freaked out." Linc rubs his hands together. "I keep trying to get him to come see you but he says not yet."

"Is he mad at me?"

"He better not be," Darcy threatens.

Linc laughs. "No. He's just being careful. It's okay, Sadie. Promise."

"Surprisingly, he's the cautious one," Ethan teases. "But he's still your boy."

"Sure," I scoff and shake my head. I don't understand why he's keeping his distance and I have to admit that it hurts. All I want is to talk through that night with him, to talk through how I feel about him, and how being with him has changed everything that I want for my future.

When I yawn for the third time, Darcy steps in and kicks everyone out.

I walk up with them all and get drowned in hugs, even from Ethan. Linc hangs back to leave last.

"He's coming for you, I promise. Let life surprise you." He ruffles my hair with his massive hand and then walks away. The only person who might be able to assure me of that is him.

Darcy makes me go to bed and tucks me in. "It's going to be okay, Sadie. You're not alone." I've never been more aware of how many people care about me, but no matter how amazing they are, they aren't the person I want the most.

43

Logan

I feel her before I see her. The air changes when she's close to me.

"Hey," she says softly. I brace myself to see her and take a deep breath before turning away from my tools to look at her. The Firebird is gone, but I want to pack and organize my stuff. Most of my tools belonged to my dad, so I want to take them even if there's better things at the shop itself. They have sentimental value to me.

I'm afraid that when I turn around Sadie will be angry. Or resigned because it's time to end things. Since finding her and everything that happened, I've avoided her. I've been scared as hell and afraid of what it will mean to tell her that I love her and I don't want things to end. The terror of being rejected by someone that I love is paralyzing. It's happened to me too damn often and I don't know how I'll survive if it comes from her.

She has every right to be mad at me. Sadie has asked me to come see her, and I've said no. I've barely responded to her texts when she asks about how I'm doing - I don't want to tell her where my head is at and definitely not over a text. I haven't been there for her. My friends have gone to see her, and they don't understand why I won't, but I'm afraid to say any of it out loud.

I don't want to be anything that holds her down or holds her back. I want to be someone that lifts her up, but I don't know if she'll let me. Sadie might think I'm giving up on my dreams, but she's my dream. The only dream worth fighting for. The kind of thing that's worth it because it will be work, but work worth doing.

"Logan," she says and there's so much pain that I turn around immediately. The look in Sadie's eyes is fear. That I'm the one that's going to reject her.

"Hey, baby." I open my arms, and Sadie runs at me.

The second her body slams into mine, I know we're both safe. I know it's going to be okay.

"What the fuck is wrong with you?" she sobs into my chest, and I feel even worse that she's crying.

"I'm in love with you and realized I didn't want to let you go," I whisper into the top of her head. Sadie stills. "I was afraid."

She looks up at me, eyes fierce, tears dripping down her cheeks. "Come on."

Sadie steps away from my but hooks her arm through mine and basically drags me down the driveway. It's late, but it's a warmer night than we've had in awhile. The hint of late spring that makes you feel like summer isn't too far away.

Despite everything the last few months, Sadie has never asked me to come with her on one of her walks.

We don't say anything as we go, and nerves build inside me. Sadie is making a point, and I need to stay patient so I don't miss it.

She waves to an old man sitting on a recliner in his garage. He waves back.

"Nice night," he says loudly.

"Yes it is," she says back, and keeps walking. When we get a little further away, she starts to talk to me. "That's Mr. Bailey. He's an insomniac, has been his whole life but he also worked the night shift and doesn't know how to change since he retired. He watches TV in his garage to keep himself occupied but doesn't want to wake up his wife. They've been married since 1969. She has really bad arthritis now and needs her rest."

"How do you know all that?"

"He asked if I was okay. A couple years ago. Worried about a tiny teen girl wandering around at night." All this time I thought she was out alone, but she was being taken care of in a way only these strangers knew how. "He recognized a fellow night owl."

We keep going and then she stops and turns toward a dense, red brick house. The curtains twitch in the large front window. Sadie points to me, then gives a thumbs up. A hand shoots out with a matching thumbs up. We resume our walk.

"Arnie Tucker, Vietnam vet, a little paranoid. We've never actually spoken, but he knows everything that goes on on his street. Needed him to know that I'm not in danger when I'm with you."

Sadie links her hand with mine now, and I sink into this feeling. This is her secret escape. Her other safe place, even safer than when she's with me. And she's letting me see it, all of it. Letting me in when she could keep me out.

"That's Miss Serena," she gestures to a white house with green trim and a large wrap around porch.

"The dentist?"

"Yeah. She has dementia."

An old woman with her white hair pulled back in a severe bun paces on the porch, arms crossed over a knit cardigan. She's muttering to herself, angry and worried. A younger woman on the porch lifts a hand to us, and Sadie waves back.

"It's not a good night," Sadie says sadly. "She forgets that her husband died. She's pacing because she's waiting for him to come home."

"That's...tragic." There's no other word for it.

"Yes and no. Miss Serena has forgotten almost everything about her life except him, and her love for him. Imagine a love that big and brain-altering that it's the only thing you remember when everything else has been lost."

We wander slower now, absorbing being together and the night air. There isn't so much light pollution here so there's still plenty of stars in the sky when we look up. An infinite universe, supposedly, and I'd still pick being here right now with Sadie.

There's someone else walking down the street. Older guy, gruff and sad, and he stops when he sees us.

"You good, kid?" His voice is raspy like he doesn't speak much.

"I'm good." Sadie replies. The man looks between the two of us, narrowing his eyes at me as if analyzing if I'm safe. He nods, looking between us.

"Have a good night." We walk past each other, ships in the night again.

"That guy?" I whisper in question.

"I don't know. He showed up about a year ago. He's sad. I think he lost someone."

"It feels like that." We turn and start heading back toward our houses. "I'm glad you weren't alone out here."

"Me too."

Tension fills the silence, and I know Sadie is building up to say something.

"I thought I knew what it meant to be in love, and I thought it meant opening yourself up to being hurt by someone. That's what I knew." She swallows and looks down at our feet as we walk. "That's still true, but it's also trusting that the person who could hurt you the worst - won't. I realized that love is trusting someone to protect your vulnerable parts, and you do. I hope I do the same for you."

"You do, Sadiebaby. In ways I didn't even know I needed."

One side of her mouth kicks up. "I don't want this to end, even if it's going to be hard work to keep it together."

She stops and turns to me. "I've always loved you, but this…this was falling in love with you. Wildly, sinfully, unabashedly in love. I love you, Logan."

Heat races through my body, and I'm struck by a wave of happiness so strong it's like a blow. My vision wavers as I let her words sink in. I take Sadie's face in my hands.

"I love you. I'm in love with you. I've been in love with you since the first night you sat in my garage and watched me work and I realized I didn't feel alone when I was with you. I didn't feel empty. You fill me up, Sadie, and I'll do whatever is necessary for us to keep trying. To keep fighting. I love you."

We're kissing and smiling and it should be awkward but it's not.

"Everything alright?" I ask when I break the kiss.

Sadie gives me a blinding smile, clinging to my arms. "Everything is finally, truly alright."

44

Epilogue: Sadie

"Sadie Braverman."

There's an absolutely obnoxious amount of loud whooping as I cross the stage and collect my diploma holder from Principal Stein courtesy of Logan's friends and mine. I wave at them and then follow the line to return to my seat.

Even though I'm technically valedictorian, I'm very lucky that our school elects its graduation speakers instead of letting academic success determine that anyone in their own class would want to listen to them speak.

I got to sit in the audience like everyone else and enjoy the celebration of the conclusion of high school.

When Logan's name is called, I stand up and tuck my fingers between my lips to whistle. Tori taught me how just for this moment.

The whistle pierces through the noise and he turns his head to look at me in shock. I just grin back. Since therapy and escaping my mom, it's been a lot easier to smile. It's easier to believe now that my emotions won't be used against me, and I'm not at fault for having feelings. I've come a long way.

Logan blows me a kiss from the stage. He still spends most of his time glowering and intimidating people, but also has no hesitation to show me that I'm loved, and who cares who is watching.

I sit back down and we barely break eye contact as he saunters off the stage and down the aisle back to his seat.

Things are better. Supposedly mom is here somewhere, but she's not sitting with dad and the Andersons. Logan's mom is here, too, but I've been too afraid to look just in case she's not. Just in case she takes this one last chance to devastate him.

After everything that happened with me, he wasn't ready to confront her.

He's moving out this weekend. He told her in a note. All she did was write at the bottom. "Okay. Let me know if you need anything."

Logan decided that he didn't owe her an explanation, and that he wasn't sure she would ever be in a place to recognize, let alone want to repair, the damage to their relationship. Him hoping that a confrontation would change things would only lead to more hurt. So he's walking away.

We decided to try long distance for now. I don't want him to give up what he has with the Andersons and the learning he'll get to do in their shop. I'll be busy with soccer and school anyway. We've waited this long to realize our feelings and be together - with much bigger barriers in our way. It's not going to be easy, but it's going to be worth it.

I look behind me and past him to where our families are sitting.

Dad is like a whole different person. There's things I still haven't forgiven and it will be a long time before Logan is ever truly at ease with him, but he's trying. Given everything that happened, James only has to have supervised visits with mom, and only once a month.

There's so much less worry inside me than there used to be.

I didn't even know how much of it I was carrying around until it was gone.

The future is bright, and things are alright.

45

Epilogue: Logan

Four Years Later

I've just watched Sadie graduate for the second time, with the highest honors, getting her bachelors of science in Physics. She's decided to stay in Madison all the way through her Ph.D. so this town will be home for the foreseeable future.

After graduation we had dinner - me, her dad, James and his girlfriend Farrah, and Darcy and Amelia joined us as well. They're moving to Oregon in a few weeks and wanted to say goodbye. It was nice to be all together and watch everyone celebrate my girl, but damn I am glad it's just me and her in her apartment now.

We've been apart most of the time for the last four years, and now all the pieces are in place for that to change.

Sadie is in the bathroom washing her face and brushing her teeth. I've changed into nothing but a pair of basketball shorts. It's her favorite "sexy" outfit that I wear. I'm sitting nervously on the end of the bed waiting for her.

When she comes out, bare faced, hair wet and wild down her back, the nerves dissipate. Sadie walks to stand between my legs, resting her hands on my shoulders.

"What's up?" She reads me too damn well.

I hold up a blue leather box in front of her and her eyes blow wide. Before she can start spinning out, I open it.

It's a key. The key to her apartment.

"Sadiebaby, will you let me move in with you?"

"What?" she says through a smile.

"Yesterday I got in early and did an interview with a shop. He called me this morning that I can start whenever I want."

"Here? In Madison?"

"Yeah."

Sadie's screeches and attacks me, slamming her body into mine so we collapse back on her bed. She's laughing and kicking her feet.

"Of course you can move in with me." Sadie adjusts so she's leaning over me, and starts running her hand across my scalp. I still keep it short, and the sensation of her touching me so gently still makes shivers run through my body. We've been together over four years now and there are things about being with her that I've never gotten used to, and I never will. Every touch from her feels like a miracle, and I don't want that to change.

I might have started out calling her my little sinner, thinking I was bring her into the dark, but in the end we pulled each other out of the pit and found solid ground.

I still make her sing for me though.

Which sounds like a good idea right about now. I run my hands down Sadie's body until I get to the bottom of the big t-shirt she's wearing, and start sliding it up. I already know there's nothing underneath it, I can feel the heat of her against my leg.

Sadie slides over so she's on top of me, and I watch with amusement as she reaches between us to slide down my shorts. I'm already hard and ready for her - I was the second she walked out of the bathroom looking so soft and vulnerable for me.

She tries to tease me by pressing the tip against her opening but not letting me go further. When I feel things line up just right, I thrust my hips up and the gasp of pleasure she gives me as I sink deep into her tight heat is so satisfying.

"Get that smirk off your face," she gasps, grinding her hips on me. She can't help it.

"Make me," I taunt, and grab her to move her the way she likes. One hand wrapped around her hip, the other wrapped around her neck, keeping her close as our bodies come together.

Sadie whimpers and I thrust from the bottom, moving more harshly. I watch as her body flushes, heat and desire burning higher within her.

She's so goddamn beautiful.

I can feel her tightening around me, and I'm barely holding on.

"Sadie," I say her name so she looks down at me, eyes drowsy with the edge of orgasm. "Sing for me, little sinner." Sadie's mouth drops open but I feel what it does to her, I feel her cunt tighten around me. I move her hips a little faster and feel the moment her thighs clamp hard around me before she cums.

"Logan!" Sadie moans my name and then I get lost in the chorus of cries and breathy sighs. Her pussy gets even wetter, slick and hot, and I move faster until the bolt of pleasure shoots through my body, all the way down to my toes. I keep my eyes open, seeing only her, as my orgasm crests and subsides.

Sadie crashes down on top of me. "You haven't called me that in a long time."

"It still turns you on."

"Yeah," she laughs, then sits up to look at me. "I love you, sin and all."

"I love you, Brainiac."

Sadie laughs, and everything is alright.

Playlist

Everything is Alright - Motion City Soundtrack

Le Disko - Shiny Toy Guns

You are the One - Shiny Toy Guns

Bruised - Jack's Mannequin

Ruthless - Something Corporate

The Pros and Cons of Breathing - Fall Out Boy

Same Ol' Road - Dredg

Magdalena - A Perfect Circle

No Name - Motograter

Ghost Town - Shiny Toy Guns

LGFUAD - Motion City Soundtrack

Acknowledgments

Husband. I wanted to give up and you wouldn't let me. I love you.

Todd, Kim, and Scott. Todd especially - my music taste is what it is because of you. I listened to Motion City Soundtrack because of you. I will never regret summers jamming out to the Snakes on a Plane Soundtrack or turning up the volume for the moment the bass drops in "Sweat the Battle Before the Battle Sweats You" by Cute is What We Aim For. Thank you to all three of you for every summer being stupid in the car and going where we wanted. I love you, friends. Also, Todd, thank you for letting me drive your car before I had my license.

Massive amounts of love to every friend that came out to me in high school, even when they wouldn't be out to the world. Your trust in me, especially the times when I was not expecting it to be given, made my heart bigger.

Annie, Viktoriah, Jenn M, Jenn S, and the readers who read even when I feel like an imposter. Thank you for your support, your love of books and reading, and always letting me spoil plots for you.

Sophie Lark and Nichole Greene. For answering stupid questions, for being reassuring, for being two women that I learn from and admire on so many levels.

Mom. For definitely not being like either of these moms. Every year of my life you only get cooler and more impressive.

My MIL and Aunt-in-law for being relentless promoters and supporters of my books. I promise that I appreciate it even though I blush and panic and can't talk about it.

Also by Ashley Mack

The Senses
The Sight of You
The Taste of You
The Sound of You
The Feel of You
The Scent of You

Companion Novellas
Look at Me
Savor Me
Silence Me

Heart Series
Take to Heart
Heart Set (2024)

Elmwood College Tales
Offerings
Preservation
Transfigured
Beguiled
Constraint
Obscured

About the Author

Ash lives in the Midwest with her husband, two girls, a dog, and a cat. She reads during every spare moment. She hopes that her characters go in new directions with terrifying, strong women who go feral for their men, and that sometimes the men are the damsels in distress who need saving. Connect on Instagram and Tiktok at @totalsassreads

www.ingramcontent.com/pod-product-compliance
Lightning Source LLC
Chambersburg PA
CBHW062132170626
46813CB00002B/661